Candlelit Square

Carrie Elks

PUBLICATIONS

For Meire

1

There are some things you should never communicate by text message. The end of a relationship, the death of a loved one, they all deserve the emotion that only a voice can give them, the space to breathe that only a conversation can lend. As I stare at the photograph of my boyfriend kissing another girl, I can't help but think that this is another thing to add to the list.

We've been together for eight years, on and off, since we were both fifteen-year-old school kids. He's been my first everything—first kiss, first love…

First heartbreak.

I unfold my legs from beneath me and stretch my body out on the bed, flinging my phone onto the cluttered table beside me. It's covered with books and magazines, half-used lipsticks, plus four empty coffee cups that I haven't bothered to take downstairs. There's a photograph of Luke, too. Leaning up against his BMW, hand shading his eyes. Tequila curls his lips, making them pink beneath the sun. The same lips that kiss me, whisper sweet words, tell me lies.

A sharp pain stabs in my chest as I think of the latest lie. Dinner with his family that turns out to be a party in Shoreditch. My thoughts wander to the phone again; to the blurred photograph of him kissing another girl. His strong hands grasp her hips as he stoops into her, the same way he has to lean down to kiss me. I think about confronting him and I wonder about deleting the text. An argument or a simple press of the button? At the end of the day it all comes down to the same thing. He believes he can swan back like nothing ever happened, and I'll forgive him and pretend that it didn't.

Just like I always do.

Maybe it was understandable when we were school kids. Trying on love like it was a new pair of jeans, struggling to see what fitted. Now I'm twenty three it's pitiful, yet it's a habit I can't seem to shake. I can sit here and say it won't happen again, but I'll end up forgiving him. I know it, Luke knows it, even my family knows it. My mum's way past thinking it's romantic. My brother Alex won't even let me mention Luke's name. And my big sister, Andie, only wants me to be happy.

I'm not happy. I haven't been for a while. Luke blames my college studies, keeps telling me to give them up, to go and work in a hair salon like my friend Sophie, or as a secretary, like Ellie. From the start he was against me going to university. He couldn't understand why I wanted to spend three years of my life in a classroom.

Going to college is something I've dreamed of since I was a teen. Since my year seven maths teacher told me I had a gift. And for once I ignored Luke's tantrums and the nagging feeling in the pit of my stomach and signed up for a degree in business studies.

He didn't speak to me for a month after that. Not until he came crawling back on my birthday, his lying fingers clutching a huge bouquet of flowers, his traitorous lips making promises we both knew he wouldn't keep. Though I refused to accept them, his persistence was astounding. He wore me down, one sweet gesture after another.

Luke *can* be sweet, he *can* be kind, and when he looks at me it's as if I'm the only girl in the room. He builds me up with love and passion, ready to break me down all over again.

It's like playing with Lego.

"Amy?" Mum calls from downstairs. Though our house is tiny, she still shouts loudly. A legacy from the noisy days of my youth when Alex would play music at the highest volume he could get away with, and Andie would scream at him to turn it down. Mum couldn't be heard without a voice like a foghorn, and unfortunately she's long since forgotten it has an off switch.

6

"Yeah?"

"Alex is here with Max and Lara. Come and say hello."

Smoothing my hair, I stand up and glance around my room. It still looks like a teenager lives here. Posters of groups are Blu-tacked to my pale pink walls, their corners curling away with age. Boy bands that have long since split up, actors who have grown old and complacent; it's a testament to my lost youth. It makes me feel wistful, remembering long hours spent in Luke's eighteen-year-old arms. Back then the future was laid out before us.

"Hey." I run down the stairs. Alex is kneeling in front of the radiator in the living room, his rusty blue toolbox by his side. His wife, Lara, is sitting on the sofa with their toddler playing on her lap.

"Maxie!" I reach out and tickle his chin. He makes a grab for my fingers with surprisingly strong hands. "Who's a gorgeous boy?"

Leaning down, I press a kiss to Lara's cheek. I love my sister-in-law so much. We first met when I was a fifteen-year-old brat, and she was lost in the misery of her mum's death. Somehow we hit it off.

"At home on a Saturday night?" she murmurs. "What's that all about?"

I shrug, trying to affect nonchalance. "I'm tired, and I start work on Monday. I thought I'd have an early night."

From the look on her face, Lara doesn't believe a word of it. She shifts Max about as he tries to scramble off her lap, reaching for Sam, our fluffy ginger cat who's dozing on the sofa.

"Leave him alone," she chastises mildly. "His tail isn't a toy."

Sam barely bats a whisker; he simply curls up and goes back to sleep. He's lazy, pampered and overfed—the last of my mum's babies. She's always happiest when surrounded by her kids, even if they're of the furry kind.

"Are you looking forward to it?"

I snap my eyes back to Lara. "What?"

"Starting work. Are you nervous?" She says it slowly. I've earned the reputation of being the family airhead. Always daydreaming, not in touch with reality. I blame the fact that I can never get a word in edgeways.

"A bit nervous," I admit, underplaying the way my stomach is churning. I've read the joining instructions about twenty times, and made the journey to work on at least five different occasions, just to make sure I know what I'm doing. I don't think those are the actions of someone with their head in the clouds. I could be wrong though.

"You'll be fine, they're going to love you. Like a breath of fresh air."

"Or a bad smell," I joke.

"Either way they'll never be able to get rid of you."

A loud clang catches our attention. Alex swears loudly, grabbing his toe where the wrench landed. When I glance at Lara she's trying not to laugh. I bite my lip to stop the giggles.

"Are you okay?" In spite of her best efforts there's humour in her voice.

"That fucking hurt."

"Alex!"

He rolls his eyes and mutters an apology before picking up the spanner and going back to his work. I don't bother asking him why he's messing about with the central heating in the middle of summer. Some things are better left a mystery.

"How's Luke?" Lara asks. Alex rolls his eyes again.

"He's fine." There's no way I'm going to fill them in on his latest stunt. Alex hates him enough as it is. I've seen my brother when he's angry—it's scary, and quite frankly dangerous. "Having dinner with his parents."

Mum walks in carrying a tray of mugs. Tea sloshes over the rims, pooling around the bases. When I take mine, pale brown liquid drips onto my jeans, staining them a dark, dark blue. "Oops, sorry." She flashes me a grin and I send her one right back. She may be crazy, but I love her to death.

"It's okay, they need a wash anyway." Greedily, I gulp down what remains of the tea, quenching a thirst I didn't realise I had.

"Have you decided what to wear on Monday?" Lara asks.

"I bought a dress from Next." I wrinkle my nose. "Grey, with a matching jacket."

"Sounds delightful."

"It's fine, it's just not... very me." I'm more pale creams and soft pinks. Tea dresses and floaty skirts. Not thick grey pinstripes and fitted jackets.

"You'll get used to it," she reassures me. "Before you know it you'll be a real city girl."

"Just like you were, babe." Alex smiles at his wife. There's a look in his eyes that says it all. Filled with adoration, he blinks slowly, lips still upturned. She blushes when she looks at him.

I'm not sure Luke's ever looked at me like that. His stares are normally full of heat. Buzzing with desire. Not adoring or sweet.

Is it wrong to want it all?

"By the time you met me I was ready to quit," Lara reminds him. "Remember?"

His voice is soft. A caress. "I remember."

She slides her eyes back to mine. "A new start. It's exciting."

"It is," I agree. There's something thrilling about it. Knowing I get a blank slate, that I'm free to be who I want to be. Not airhead Amy or faithful Amy or all of the other roles I've managed to take on in the past twenty-three years. I count myself lucky that despite the foolish choices I've made, and the relationship I've managed to get myself entangled with, there's still a small part of my life I can say is a success. Maybe the only part.

We spend the rest of the evening talking, while Alex finally gives up on the radiator and holds his son until he falls asleep, head lolling on his daddy's ink-vibrant arm. Although I'm stuck at home while my boyfriend is out doing God knows what, I can't help but feel like it's the best Saturday night I've had in a long, long time.

* * *

Luke finally shows his face the following evening. His hair is neatly combed, his sandy locks longer on the top, brushed back with gel. The sides are clipped close to his scalp. He's very touchy-feely, his lips coated with candyfloss lies—sweet yet somehow nauseating. As usual we go to my room, avoiding the living room where Mum's watching a reality show.

"Is this new?" He reaches out, stroking the hem of my green and pink flowery dress with his rough fingertips, his knuckles brushing against the soft skin of my thighs. "It's pretty."

"And old. You've seen it before." I pull away, and the silky fabric slides from his grasp.

"Still pretty," he murmurs. I close my eyes, trying to ignore the way he makes my heart speed. My body's conditioned to respond to him, even if my mind is screaming otherwise.

"How was last night?" I ask.

Luke looks at me, his blue eyes unwavering. "Boring. I wish you'd been there."

"You didn't ask me," I remind him. His parents are like my second family. His dad is a Romford boy made good. He owns a car dealership in East London and earns good money. Luke's been working there since he left school at sixteen.

"I will next time." He smiles as though he's doing me a favour. "You look so hot in this dress." His arms still carry the colour from his recent holiday in Ibiza, covered with a smattering of fine, sun-bleached hairs. A pale border of skin follows his hairline, freshly revealed by his recent haircut.

His fingers are gentle as they circle around my ankle. His thumb brushes against my skin. Though a thrill shoots up my leg I ignore it.

"What's wrong?"

"Sarah Stearn texted me last night. She was at a party in Shoreditch."

His face reveals the slightest flicker of unease. But like the great car salesman he is, Luke smooths it over immediately. "Oh yeah?"

"Yeah. She said you were there."

He pauses for a moment. I can almost read the thoughts flashing through his mind. How much do I know? Can he get away with lying? How long will it take me to forgive him this time? He shifts a little, enough to reveal how turned on he is. Eyes dilated, breath warm. I'm disrupting his mojo.

"I popped over after dinner. Mum wanted an early night."

"You said you had to stay at home. That it was important."

"There was a change of plan." He's so glib, so easy. Lies trip off his tongue like blossoms from trees. They cover us both.

"Why didn't you call?"

"I was going to. But then Nick phoned and asked me to pick him up. I found him passed out in the toilet. Had to carry him out to my car."

Squeezing my eyes shut, I remember that fuzzy picture. It wasn't Nick he was holding. Definitely not Nick.

"Nick was out with Sophie last night." I know this for a fact. My best friend, Sophie, posted photographs all over Instagram. He took her to some swanky restaurant near the City, and the two of them ate dinner overlooking the Thames.

"It was later, after he took her home." Still unruffled, Luke leans back on my bed, folding his arms beneath his head. His legs are so long they reach the end of the mattress, making me feel tiny in comparison. It's the story of my life—being 5'3" means I'm forever craning my head upward, even when we're both horizontal.

I stare at him for a minute. Enough to take in his smooth skin, his pale lips, the way the pale-blond stubble is shadowing his jaw. I rub my own face as a lungful of air slowly escapes through my pursed lips.

For the first time I'm wondering if this is it.

Is this all I have to look forward to? The bitter lies of a boyfriend who can't even be bothered to cover up his tracks. Once upon a time he would have been on his knees, begging me to forgive him, making promises he'd never do it again.

Now he's got his eyes closed. His lips are curled up into a half-smirk. There's no need to apologise, no need to make up a story, because he knows I'll take him back anyway. I'm Pavlov's dog, dancing to the tune only Luke knows the notes to. Too scared to question him in case I end up alone.

This is no way to live.

But it's been so long, I've forgotten how to exist without him. It's stupid, I know, but every day of my adult life has been interlinked with Luke's. Even on the bad days—the ones when we argue, or when he's criticising me—he's still there. Whether he's a red devil or a white knight, he's been the lead character of my story for as long as I can remember.

Swallowing, I glance at his face again. Seeing him so unaffected by it all gives me a strange kind of confidence. Rolling my shoulders, I brace myself for a confrontation.

"Did you have sex with her?"

"What?" His eyes blink open. The next minute he's sitting up, grabbing at my hand. "You think I had sex with somebody else?"

Silently I hand him my phone. The photo is on the screen, showing his indiscretion in its full glory. He looks at it and rolls his lips beneath his teeth, bleaching them white as the blood drains away.

"It's not what it looks like, Amy."

The urge to laugh takes over. My chest tenses, my throat gurgles, and it's like I'm watching a Richard Curtis film. I can see myself the way he sees me. Gullible, easily led. I'm the girl who's always been here, the girl who's eaten up his lies while he's done exactly what he wanted.

Some people might say I deserve everything I've got.

"What is it then? If it's not what it looks like?"

"She's just a girl, one of my mum's friend's daughters."

"Which friend?"

For the first time, he looks panicked. His knee starts to bounce up and down. "An old friend, you don't know her. Somebody my mum met when she was at college."

"Your mum didn't go to college."

His mouth sets into a firm line. The corners of his eyes wrinkle as they narrow. "Why do you keep questioning me?"

"Because you're full of shit."

I might sound brave, but my heart is hammering in my chest, making the blood flow too quickly through my veins. Luke leans closer, enough for me to feel his breath against my skin, and my own oxygen disappears in a whoosh.

"Amy…" It comes out as a warning, not an attempt to placate. "You don't want to do this, babe. Just back off and let me explain, then I'll leave and you can get some sleep."

The word "okay" forms at the tip of my tongue, so strong I can almost hear it. I have to grit my teeth to keep it swallowed down. My bedroom—the familiar walls, the comforting pictures—suddenly seems more like a prison. Being with Luke is making me feel claustrophobic.

Closing my eyes, unprompted images flash before me. Luke and me with children, in a house in the suburbs. More promises, more lies. Raising toddlers on my own.

That's where I'm going to end up if I don't step away. Maybe not this year, maybe not next, but one day I'm going to be that woman who sits at home and waits for a husband that never comes home. Or worse, one that comes home full of glib lies and secrets.

That thought settles it. I'm not that girl, I refuse to be. I'm better than that.

Opening my eyes, I catch Luke's gaze, and stop myself recoiling at his icy glare.

"Go home, Luke. I've had enough."

2

Stepping off the train, I follow the crowds as they move along the platform, allowing the sea of commuters to push me forward. The four-person wide queue thins down to two as we reach the escalators, and I have to cling tightly onto the handrail to make sure I'm not jostled over.

At the top of the stairs I pass through the ticket barrier and onto the wide plaza leading to the tall, shiny buildings of Canary Wharf. Clutching my bag tightly to my chest, I walk towards One Canada Square, the building that houses Richards and Morgan, the Management Consultancy firm where I start my internship today.

I was offered the position three months ago, and accepted eagerly. My college tutor told me that nobody from the University of East London had ever been offered a place at Richards and Morgan before. I'd snapped it up, delighted by the high salary, as well as the fact it's a short journey from my home in Plaistow, but now I'm having second thoughts.

There's no way I belong somewhere like this. Not Amy Cartwright, the girl who can't get the London twang out of her voice no matter how hard she tries. I'm never going to fit in among the Oxford and Cambridge types who usually get the internships. I'm going to stand out like a sore thumb. An impoverished, common, badly-dressed thumb.

Somehow I make it to the revolving doors, pushing on the glass and shuffling my feet until I walk inside the impressive lobby. My new shoes click against the polished tiles as I take small steps—my progress constrained by the tightness of my new dress.

Everything about this building screams opulence. From the brown-marble walls of the security desk to the cream-and-brown pattern of the ceramic floor that criss-crosses the entire lobby. Even the people—women in smart dresses and even smarter hairdos, men in crisp blue shirts and expertly knotted ties—add to the feeling of luxuriousness the architects were determined to create.

Ignoring my rising panic, I walk over to the desk. A security guard looks up, his eyes lidded, his face bored.

"Which company?"

Richards and Morgan isn't the only firm that rents space here. The tower is over 28,000 square feet and holds more than thirty different companies with over 9000 employees. I remember all this from my interview—that awkward half day when I had to persuade somebody in a suit to take a chance on me.

"Richards and Morgan, my name's Amy Cartwright. It's my first day."

The guard shoots me a withering look, one that tells me he really doesn't want to make small-talk. Instead he types something into his laptop and prints out a badge, which he slides into a clear, plastic sleeve.

"Clip this to your dress. You should have it on display at all times when you're in the building. Richards and Morgan are on the tenth floor. Take the left set of elevators and press the tenth button. Your pass won't allow you above that floor. If you're found walking any other floors you'll be reported."

Every word is accompanied by a narrowed stare, and I feel like a naughty school kid.

"Okay."

"When you leave this evening you need to hand the pass back. Richards and Morgan should arrange for you to get a permanent pass today."

This time I just nod. The guy is doing nothing for my nerves except heightening them. Clipping the pass to the neckline of my dress, I pick up my bag and head for the elevators.

There's already a crowd at the lifts by the time I reach them. Two cars fill up before there's a space for me. Squeezing myself against the wall, I watch as people press the buttons for their floor, willing somebody to press number ten so I don't have to say a word.

Of course, they don't.

"Can you press floor ten?" I ask quietly. Nobody takes the slightest bit of notice. They're all staring ahead, their faces neutral, their eyes glazed.

The lift starts to move. First stop is two, where only one person gets out. There's still not enough room for me to reach them.

"Can you press floor ten please?"

Everyone ignores me.

By the time we make it to the eighth floor I'm unnerved. It's stupid, I know, because if the worst comes to the worst I can get the right floor on the way down. But the memory of the security guard telling me I can't get out on any floors except my own is playing on my mind.

"Can you press floor bloody ten!" I finally yell, my accent making me sound like a fishwife to the power-suited professionals. This time everybody turns to look at me. More than one person raises their eyebrows, and somebody laughs at the back of the lift. A tall redheaded man reaches forward and pressed the button, barely able to contain his smirk.

When the lift comes to a stop I have to fight my way out, aware that every single person in the car is staring at me. Squaring my shoulders, I grimace and step onto the tenth floor, thankful that nobody else is getting out, and that none of them are going to be my co-workers. My relief lasts all of two seconds, until the button-pusher follows behind me, and I feel my stomach contract painfully.

"Ten was already lit," he tells me, his words shaped by a Scottish burr. "I'd pressed it when I got in."

"So why did you press it again?" I snap.

This time his eyebrows rise up until they're almost touching his messy, thick hair. "Because you asked so bloody nicely."

* * *

An hour later I'm sat in a boardroom with the other interns attending our induction session. At the front of the room, next to what might just be the most boring PowerPoint presentation ever, is the HR Manager for Richards and Morgan, Diana Joseph. She's already made each of us stand up in turn and introduce ourselves. I've discovered I'm the only intern that doesn't go to either Oxford or Cambridge, and the only one that doesn't know the others.

"In a few minutes your placement managers will be coming in to introduce themselves, and then they'll take you to your desks to get you started. Your log-in details are in the folders in front of you, along with a list of online training that you'll need to do before the end of the week."

Diana brushes a lock of blonde hair out of her eyes. She looks around thirty-something, with the porcelain complexion of the upper-middle class. "There's one last thing I need you to do. As you know, Richards and Morgan is an American company, and we follow the rules they set down for us. One of those is that we expect all our employees to follow the highest standards of conduct, and I'd like you all to sign the policy that's in your folders and return it to me before you leave."

Pulling the three-page policy from my folder, I skim read. It covers dress code, politeness and emphasises that no office romances should take place. Glancing around the room—at the three rich boys who form part of the intern group—I have no hesitation in scribbling my name across the bottom.

Diana collects the papers and shuffles them into a neat pile. Then she opens the door and calls our managers in. They stand up to say hello, explaining what part of the firm they work in, and their main responsibilities. I listen avidly, wondering which one will end up being my boss, hoping against hope that it's Maria Giles, who heads up technology services.

When they've finished, Diana stands again. "Okay, so let's start with Miranda Vesey." The girl sitting opposite me stands up. "Your placement is in Corporate Tax and your manager will be Stephen Spiller."

One by one she calls the interns until I'm the last person left. That's when she realises there isn't a manager to assign me to. Her panic is almost comical, as she glances down at her sheet then back at me, her brows drawing together as she stares.

"There appears to be an error."

The need to laugh disappears, replaced by a quivering inside my chest. I wait for her to tell me that I shouldn't have been offered the internship, for her to ask me to leave the building. By the time she starts to speak I'm already planning what I'll tell my tutor.

"You were supposed to be assigned to Sandra Davies in Organisational Development, but she's taken early maternity leave. Stay here while I make a couple of calls." With that Diana all but runs out of the room, leaving me sitting here on my own.

Leaning back in my chair, I run a hand over my tied-up hair, checking it's still smooth. Then I look around the room, at the polished wood table and state-of-the-art screens on the wall, and wonder what the hell is going to happen to me today. I'm too nervous to keep still, too antsy to do nothing, so I end up pouring myself another lukewarm coffee from the dispenser on the sideboard and sip away until Diana comes back.

It takes her ten minutes, and when she sweeps back in the harassed look is still painted on her face. Inclining her head, she indicates for me to follow, and I stand up and gather my things.

"I've found you a placement in Technology Integration. They're a head down due to a recent resignation, so you'll be working temporarily as a Personal Assistant until they've sorted out a project for you. Am I right in thinking you have PA experience?"

She's marching along the corridor, and I have to run to keep up. "Yes, but I need to work on a project in order to get my degree."

Diana huffs. "I just said you'll be given a project, it will just take a few days, that's all."

Chastened, I nod. "Okay."

"Well, this isn't always the easiest department to work in. The techies tend to be a bit abrasive and rude, but I can promise you'll get some excellent experience during your time here."

Eventually we reach the end of the corridor, and she leads me into a block of offices. Each one is fronted with glass. Diana points at a desk. "This is where you'll sit. Mr Ferguson sits in there." She gestures to a door, which leads into the main office. "He's the head partner for the Technology Integration division, so he's a very busy man."

For the first time, Diana smiles at me, and it seems to contain an apology. Then she raps at the door with her knuckles, taking a step back and waiting for a reply.

"What?"

"Mr Ferguson?" Her voice wobbles as she pushes the frosted glass door. "I have your new PA, Amy Cartwright." Turning to me, she gestures with her hand, telling me to go in. "She's a new intern, full of enthusiasm and ready to go."

Standing in the doorway, I see Mr Ferguson for the first time. He's bent over three LCD screens, hammering his fingers on the impressive keyboard that seems to cover half his desk. Slowly, he raises his head, and I notice the thick, dark red hair that falls across his brow, and the piercing green eyes that seemed to bore into me earlier.

"I know you," he says, still staring. This time there's no hint of a smile to his lips, just a granite-set jaw that tells me he isn't very pleased to see me. "You're the lift-shouter."

Nodding, I step forward, trying to hide the tremble in my legs. "I'm Amy Cartwright." I offer him my hand, but he ignores it.

"I don't take on interns, Diana, you know that. Doesn't HR have any slots?" He sounds almost bored.

"Amy's skills lie in the technical side, Mr Ferguson, and we've not been able to recruit a PA for you yet. It's only temporary, until we fill the vacancy and then we can move Amy to her new job."

Mr Ferguson drops his head to the side, studying me. "How much experience do you have?"

"I was a PA for two years before I went back to university."

"What university are you from?"

"The University of East London."

I don't expect he even knows there is a university *in* East London.

"Where did you work before you went to university?"

"I was a legal PA at Barker Moorefield LLP." I flash him a pointed look because I know he must have heard of them.

"But you set your sights on the lofty heights of the University of East London. It sounds very Jude the Obscure," he drawls. "Tell me, Miss Cartwright, what made you give up a well paid job in law to go to some shitty university in Stratford?"

Okay, so he *has* heard of the University of East London. He must have if he knows where the campus is. Even so, his words make me want to climb over his desk and land a smack on his face. Pompous, arrogant dick.

It might be because I didn't get very much sleep last night, or it might be because I'm still so angry with Luke I can hardly see straight. It might even be because I'm sick and tired of being left out and treated like dirt and the one everybody has a dig at. Whatever it is, I feel my muscles start to tense as a bead of sweat rolls down the back of my neck.

I give him a sickly smile. "Oh, I don't know, Mr Ferguson. Perhaps it was the knowledge that this country is run by elitist arseholes who think that they're entitled to everything just because they were born into money."

The corner of his lip twitches. "I'm guessing they didn't teach you diplomacy during your time at college."

"They couldn't fit it in between the cockney slang and spray tan refresher classes," I reply. I'm about to add that it's good of the upper class to even allow us to leave our hovels when I hear Diana clearing her throat behind me.

"Okay then, I'll let you settle in, Amy. Perhaps you can let me know when you've finished the online training."

With that, she leaves, and I'm alone with Mr Ferguson. The same Mr Ferguson who has decided to studiously ignore me, staring at the screen in front of him and occasionally pressing his keyboard.

That's when I realise what an idiot I am. This man holds the key to my future, the ability to dictate whether or not I actually get a degree. And I decided to be rude to him the first moment he clapped eyes on me.

"I'll just… ah… go and set up at my desk then," I say, slowly backing out of the room. Mr Ferguson looks up at me again. This time his green eyes look softer, hazier. The hard expression on his face has gone.

"Okay."

"Would you like a coffee, Mr Ferguson?" I ask, deciding that the only way out of the hole I've dug for myself is some serious arse licking. It might be my imagination, but I think I see a hint of amusement flash across his face.

"Black, no sugar." He nods, looking back at his work. Then, without raising his eyes up again, he adds, "And my name's Callum, not Mr Ferguson. Otherwise I'll think you're talking to my father."

"Does he work here too?" I ask.

"No, he's been dead for nearly thirty years."

Oh, well done Amy.

With that, I pull my foot firmly out of my mouth and decide to make Mr Ferguson—Callum—the best damn cup of coffee he's ever tasted. Before he ends up kicking my butt right out of here.

3

I switch on the computer, watching it flicker into life as the screen casts a blue glow across the glossy, white surface of my new desk. While it boots up I find myself rearranging the pens in my drawer; blacks then reds, blues then greens. Every now and again my eyes glance up and I peer past the glass door that opens into Callum's office. He's busy working on something. Whatever it is draws his lips into a frown, and I can hear the slap of his fingers as he types furiously.

First days are always the worst. Full of trying to look busy and failing miserably. The minutes drag past as I set up my email account, and when I glance at my watch it's a shock to see it isn't even twelve o'clock.

I'm about to go through the contents of my desk drawers just for the hell of it when a message flashes on my screen.

Simpson, C: How's it going?

I have to wrack my brain to remember who Simpson, C is. Eventually I recall that one of my fellow interns is Charlie Simpson. From what I remember he was assigned to Corporate Tax.

Cartwright, A: It's going.

Simpson, C: Oh dear, as good as that?

I think about telling him about my morning, and the boss from hell, but decide I've already shot myself in the foot once. I don't need to make a habit out of it.

Cartwright, A: Just teething problems. I'm sure it will get better.

Simpson, C: A few of us are meeting for lunch. Top floor restaurant at 12:30. You coming?

This time when I look up, Callum's staring straight at me. The intensity of his gaze stills my fingers. There's something about him, a rugged hardness that makes me want to tear my eyes away, and I feel my bottom lip tremble. I try to swallow, but my throat is too dry.

I'm still looking at him as I touch type a response.

Cartwright, A: I'll see you there.

Callum's phone rings, pulling his gaze from mine. He snatches it up, growling his name into the phone. Letting out a lungful of air, I finish my conversation with Charlie—whose boss is apparently a big sweetheart—then get to work on the online induction course. By 12:30 p.m. I've learned how to avoid tripping over trailing wires, that if there's a fire I should vacate the building, and if somebody sends me a dodgy attachment I really shouldn't download it. I store these gems of knowledge away in my mind and lock the screen on my computer.

Rolling my chair back, I stand up and walk over to Callum's office. He's facing away from me, looking out of his large picture window, leaning on the desk as he talks into his phone. Curling my fingers around the doorjamb I wait for his conversation to finish, but he goes on and on, talking about projections and prototypes.

Eventually I clear my throat. Loud enough for the inner lining of my neck to protest at the rush of air that tears across it. Callum's head snaps around and he runs a hand through his hair, pulling it off his brow.

For an arsehole boss, he really does have pretty eyes.

He covers the mouthpiece of the phone with his free hand. "What is it?"

I refuse to let him intimidate me. "I'm going to lunch." I literally have to bite my lips shut to stop myself from asking if that's okay. If he can't be civil to me, I'm not sure I can be bothered to do the same.

"Yeah, sure. Do you know where you're going?"

"Yup. The top floor canteen."

"Okay then." He turns away and resumes his conversation, effectively dismissing me. I stand there like a muppet, mouthing words that he can't hear, and I have to remind myself why I'm here.

First I get my degree.

Then I get a good job.

Finally I get the hell away from Luke.

That's the Amy Cartwright masterplan. If it takes nine months of working for Mr Charisma, then I'll do it.

Even if it kills me. Or—more likely—even if I end up killing him.

* * *

Balancing a tuna baguette, chocolate milk and the world's biggest cookie on my tray, I set it down on the table, sliding into a chair next to Charlie Simpson. I'm the last one here—my arrival delayed by the scintillating chat I just had with Callum Ferguson—and everybody else has already fallen into an easy conversation. I listen silently as the rest of the interns exchange stories about their mornings, spinning tales of laptop-based disasters and coffee-related mayhem. The girl sitting opposite me, a slim blonde with a tan only money can buy, turns her pale eyes onto me.

"Do you have a sweet tooth?" she asks, glancing at my milk and cookie.

I feel my cheeks warm as the rest of them look at me. I realise I'm the only girl here who isn't eating a salad. Tall, blonde and tanned is sipping from a bottle of Evian, her tray devoid of any nourishment. I'm guessing she lives on air.

"Not particularly." I tear off a piece of cookie and pop it in my mouth. If I were at home I'd probably do something disgusting like open my mouth and taunt her with the image of chewed-up biscuit. But I'm not at home. Far from it.

"I wish I could eat like that." There's a sneer to her voice that grates my nerves. "But I'd rather not put on half a stone."

I don't take a dislike to people very easily. If you asked my family they'd say I'm too laid back and put up with too much shit—particularly from Luke. But I've instantly taken against Caro Hawes with her high-pitched nasal voice and her tan that's come from weeks on her daddy's yacht.

"It's not something I have to worry about," I reply, taking a long sip of my milk. "But I can see it would be a concern for you."

Next to me Charlie splutters into his Chai latte. Caro huffs something inaudible and deliberately starts to talk to the redhead beside her. Her long hair falls down the side of her face like a golden curtain, but from the way the other girl keeps looking over, it's obvious that they're discussing me. It comes as a relief when Charlie opens his mouth.

"So what have they got you doing?" He turns and gives me a genuine smile. As much as I already dislike Caro, I sense I have an ally in Charlie. He reminds me of a richer, better-turned-out version of my older brother, Alex. He's cheeky, but friendly enough to carry it off.

"Not much," I admit. "At the moment they've got me working as a PA in Technology Integration."

He raises his eyebrows. "A PA?"

"It's only for a couple of weeks. Then I'll be given a project."

He wrinkles his nose. "That's good. I can't imagine your university professor being impressed if you spend nine months booking hotels and ordering coffee."

"Me neither," I reply glumly. At the end of my internship I have to present the results of my project to the faculty, and it counts for forty per cent of my degree. It's no exaggeration to say that unless I perform amazingly well here, I could end up with a mediocre degree and pretty depressing job prospects.

Charlie bumps me with his elbow. "It will be fine. First day blues, eh?"

Though I flash him a smile, it takes some effort. "Yeah. Things can only get better."

"Who is that?" Caro's voice cuts across the table. "God, they know how to breed good looking men here." She stares over my shoulder, a smile playing at her lips, and actually starts to flick her hair as if she's in a shampoo advert. Curiosity gets the better of me and I turn, arching my neck, following her line of sight.

My stomach drops when I realise who she's smiling at. My new boss is standing in the line for coffee, leaning casually against the wall as he chats easily with the man next to him. Like Callum, his friend looks in his early thirties, wearing a suit that's well tailored and sleek, though his hair is black compared to Callum's burnt umber.

The man says something and Callum laughs. It isn't a polite laugh, either. It's a full-blown, head-back, belly laugh that is loud enough to carry across the room, and I swear half the female population is sighing, audibly.

"Hot," Caro says.

"Delicious," the girl next to her agrees.

I hate to admit it, but they're right. There's something so earthy and masculine about his low, throaty chuckle.

Then Callum looks over at me. He's still laughing, but his chest calms, his lips uncurling at the same time his eyes narrow. I feel a response that's starting to become familiar; a shiver that snakes its way down my back. Tentatively I offer him a smile, lifting my hand and curling my fingers in a feeble attempt at a wave.

He doesn't even respond. The line in front of him moves forward, and he pushes himself off the wall, leaning across to give the barista his order. Picking up my carton, I take a final sip, feeling the tell-tale rush of air through the straw when the last of the milk has gone. While Caro and her sidekick continue to ooh and ahh over my boss and his friend, I look down at the half of cookie that remains on the plate, wondering exactly what I've done wrong.

If things don't improve it's going to be a miserable nine months.

* * *

Callum is in client meetings all afternoon, and I spend the hours working my way through a huge pile of receipts that he shoved at me before he left. He clearly hasn't done his expenses for months, and I try not to fume at the fact that he expects me to sort them out. If I'm being honest it's nice to have something to do rather than plodding my way through more online training courses, but I'm not going to let him know.

It's amazing what you can discover from a few printed pieces of paper. Callum stays at expensive hotels, but he rarely spends more than £20 on dinner. He prefers sushi to steak, and like me he has a sweet tooth, indulging in midnight snacks of cookies and cakes.

He has an old car—an MGB according to the expenses system—that guzzles gas, and he prefers driving to taking the train when he goes on UK trips. He seems to spend a lot of time in Scotland, and from a few more receipts I deduce it's mostly in Edinburgh. But he must have a house or a friend he stays with there, because none of his hotel receipts are for Edinburgh, only dinner and sundries.

By 4:00 p.m. I've managed to reconcile his expenses and black Amex card, and send his receipts to accounts for processing. For the final hour and a half I turn my attention to the company intranet, looking at organisation charts and photographs, trying to work out who's who. I recognise Callum's friend from lunch straight away as Jonathan Cooper, Senior Partner in Financial Consulting.

I close my computer down at 5:29 p.m. Callum still hasn't come back, and I hesitate, unsure of the etiquette for leaving the office without asking the boss first. After our dodgy start, I don't want to make things any worse than they already are, but I have a yoga class booked for an hour's time, and I really don't want to miss it. I can already feel my back aching from sitting down all day. Unless I stretch it out, I know from experience I'll pay for it tomorrow.

Eventually I stop prevaricating and scribble a note for Callum, leaving it on his desk. It's 5:45 p.m. by the time I leave the building, and there's a huge crowd at the entrance to Canary Wharf underground station where everyone's trying to clamber on to the escalators. I join the throng, letting it swallow me whole as the tide of people surges forward.

Half an hour later I run into the sports hall and head for the changing rooms at the back of the building. I quickly shed my office clothes and tug on my yoga pants and a crop top, feeling my back twinge again as I pull it over my head.

When I was fourteen I was diagnosed with scoliosis. My spine had a curve in it that made me lopsided and a little off-balance. Though it isn't always obvious when I'm dressed, if you look carefully you can see that one of my hips is curvier than the other, and my left shoulder droops down.

I've come to terms with it now, but back when I was a teenager I was devastated, especially when I had to wear a plastic back brace for eighteen months. Looking back, I think I lost all my confidence then. Maybe that's part of the reason I've let Luke treat me like a doormat for so long.

"You made it!" My best friend, Ellie, grins up at me from her yoga mat. "I wasn't sure you would. How was your first day?"

I unroll my mat and place it beside hers. We've been coming to this class for the past six years. My specialist suggested yoga as a way to keep my back limber and fluid, and I've been doing it ever since.

"It was..." I screw up my face, trying to hit on the right adjective. "Interesting."

"Uh oh. Interesting good, or interesting bad?"

I get down on my mat and start stretching. My muscles are tense and resistant. "Well, on the plus side my boss is hot as hell."

Ellie turns onto her side, balancing on her forearm. "Ooh. Best not tell Luke."

"I wasn't intending to. Anyway, he might be good looking but he's also a miserable arsehole. And I might have shouted at him in the lift." My cheeks pink up at the memory.

Ellie tries to stifle a laugh. She fails miserably. "You did what?"

We spend the rest of the session analysing my day as we move from pose to pose. By the time we get to the cool down, the conversation is exhausted, and Ellie decides to change the subject.

"So what's going on with you and Luke?" she asks. "Sophie said something about a picture." Sophie is our other best friend. The three of us met on our first day at senior school. She's also engaged to Luke's best friend, which makes everything so much more awkward.

"It's over." The instructor dims the lights as we go into Savasana, lying on our backs with our arms and legs stretched out. The ache in my back has disappeared, and I let my eyes close as the instructor tells us to slowly inhale.

"What do you mean it's over?" Ellie whispers. "It can't be over. Not you and Luke. You're meant for each other."

That's the problem with childhood sweethearts. You grow up together and create a network of shared friends. When things go wrong it breaks everybody's hearts.

"I've had enough."

The woman next to me tuts and I shut up quickly. But Ellie won't let it go.

"But you'll work it out. You two always do. It's not as if you haven't split up before."

I breathe in deeply, feeling the air pull through my nostrils and down my throat. My chest inflates, but the sense of calm I'm seeking doesn't materialise. Instead I start to feel awkward and panicky.

"Not this time," I say. Inside I'm wondering if my words are true. If I'm strong enough to stand up for myself. It's not just Luke I'm rejecting but a whole way of life. Things will never be the same again.

That's what I want, isn't it? To get a degree, get a good job and get the hell out of here? I repeat my plan in my head like a reassuring mantra. It isn't working. Ellie is right, we've been here before. I've ended things only to take Luke back, over and over again. No wonder she can't believe it's finished. No wonder Luke won't believe me when I tell him we're through. History has taught us all that when it comes to Luke Sayer I'm a complete and total pushover.

My thoughts flicker to Callum Ferguson, and the way I stood up to him when he goaded me this morning. Despite his foreboding demeanour, and the fact he's my boss, somehow Callum made me feel brave enough to stand up for myself. It was a good feeling, not taking any shit from him. Empowering. Maybe if I can be that girl when I'm in the office, it might spill out into my relationships, too.

By the time we roll up our mats and guzzle our water, my equanimity is restored. This time when Ellie asks me if there's any chance for me and Luke, my voice is as firm as my resolve.

"There's not a cat's chance in hell I'll ever take him back."

4

By the time I make it home the sun is setting, casting the usually grey streets with a peach and orange glow. I'm listening to music through my ear buds, my bag slung loosely over my shoulder, and my mind a thousand miles away. Maybe that's why I don't notice the man at first. We're almost face to face by the time I realise he's by my front door, and I stop suddenly in front of him as his eyes look into mine.

I watch as his mouth takes on the shape of his words.

"I'm sorry, I can't hear you." I pull the headphones from my ears. The lead dangles down from my hoodie.

He says nothing, but carries on looking at me. The vividness of his eyes unnerves me. He looks old, maybe in his early fifties with dark skin pocked with acne scars. His nose twists to the left as if it's been broken and set badly. There's a white line that leads from his ear to his jaw, that looks suspiciously like a healed knife wound.

I feel the hairs on the back of my neck rise up.

"I'm looking for Tina Cartwright."

That gets my attention. This isn't any old weird guy hanging around outside our house. This is a weirdo with an agenda, and it has my mum's name written all over it.

"Are you?" I counter question for question, trying to think the situation through. "Why?"

I'd like to say this is the first time a strange guy's been looking for my mum, but that would be a bald-faced lie. One of my earliest memories is hiding behind the sofa with my mum while a bailiff was banging at the door, calling out her name. She had a bag of toffees in her hand and fed me them to me slowly in an attempt to keep my mouth shut.

My mum's never been good with money. Her credit score is shot to hell, too, which means that any loans she manages to get are dodgy to say the least. And Plaistow is full of loan sharks.

The man doesn't reply to my question. Instead he keeps his lips tightly closed, the effort bleaching them white. He tips his head to the side, still staring. I notice that one of his eyelids droops, as if the muscles there have given up. His scrutiny makes me uncomfortable, and I'm all too aware of the way my yoga pants cling to my hips, and that a sliver of skin is showing between the waistband and my crop top.

Then he says something that makes me freeze.

"Amethyst?"

Nobody calls me that. Even Mum gave up trying after I begged her to stop. The shock of this man knowing my name—my real name—is enough to make me reach out to steady myself on the brick built wall that lines our boundary. I open my mouth to ask him how he knows who I am but I'm too damn scared.

What if he wants to hurt me just to get his money back?

"That's... that's not my name," I finally manage to say. The effect of not eating anything for hours takes its toll as my head starts to swim.

"Are you okay?" The man's expression softens, and he tries to steady me. I shrink away.

"I'm fine... I just need to, to—"

This time he catches my elbow, just before I collapse on the floor. A sudden nausea tugs at me. He looks at me, concerned.

It's not the type of expression I expect to see on a loan shark. The ones I've seen—and over the years there's been a lot—tend to have two looks at most. Pissed off and extremely pissed off. He lifts me back to my feet, then steps back, and runs a hand through his scant, black hair.

"Tell your mum I came to see her, okay?"

"Who are you?" I'm aware this is the second time I've asked him. I'm not sure if I want to hear the answer, or if I need to. He's just one in a long line of men who've taken advantage of my mum's need for money, for pretty clothes, for things that she can't afford on a cashier's salary alone.

By the time he answers my question, he's already at the gate, pushing it, making the hinges creak. "Just tell her Digger says hi."

* * *

The first thing I do when I walk into the house is open the fridge door and pull out some orange juice. Twisting the lid off, I bring the spout up to my lips and swallow citrusy mouthfuls. My hand shakes as I hold the carton, in fact my whole body spasms, though I'm not sure if it's from low sugar, fear, or both. There's a shock of cold as the juice hits, then a few moments until I start to feel the shivers subside.

I can't get his face out of my mind. The way he stared at me with interest. It's hard to put my finger on the reason why he intimidated me so much, because there was no lust or sexual interest there. It was more that he looked at me as if I was a specimen, a creature he couldn't quite understand.

My shower takes longer than usual. I feel the need to scrub every inch of my skin, and let the hot spray work the kinks out of my muscles. Though the dull throb in the base of my spine has gone, I know from experience that it will be back in the morning. Grabbing a towel from the heater beside the shower door, I wrap it around my damp body, using another to make a turban around my dark hair. Then I go back to my room to slip on some pyjamas.

It's only then that I check my messages. Two missed calls and a text from Luke.

Call me.

Seeing his name makes me shiver all over again, and I slip under the duvet just to find a little warmth. The final message is from my brother, asking me about my first day. Though I suspect my sister-in-law goaded him into sending it, I'm still touched that he's even remembered.

I think about texting Alex back, but after the confrontation earlier I'm still feeling jittery, and the thought of hearing his friendly voice is too much of a temptation. I quickly dial his number and lean back on my pink velvet headboard, closing my eyes as the familiar ringtone echoes into my ear.

It only buzzes twice before Alex answers. "Hey, beautiful. What's up?"

I smile as soon as I hear his voice. My brother is six years older than me, and along with our elder sister, Andie, has always been overprotective. Although I bristled against it in my teens, now I find it sweet and comforting, like unwrapping a much needed bar of chocolate.

"Not much. Just got back from Yoga. How's things with you?"

"Splendid." He puts on a stupidly posh accent. "Max is teething, Lara's had a shit day at work and I've somehow managed to piss them both off."

"Just another day chez Cartwright," I tease. It's so lovely to talk to him. Only a few weeks ago he was living here with Mum and me, trying to work through some problems with his marriage. As much as I loved having him home with us, I'm thrilled he and Lara managed to patch up their differences. Lara is one of the nicest people I've ever met. She always has time for me and doesn't treat me like a little kid, which Alex and Andie always do.

"How's Max?" I ask, hearing my nephew squawking in the background. "No more chest problems?"

"No, thank God." Alex sounds genuinely relieved. After being hospitalized for bronchiolitis, my baby nephew has managed to make a full recovery. Which is good, because we don't want to go through that again. "He's right as rain. Got a good set of lungs on him, as you can probably hear."

I start to laugh. As deadpan as Alex sounds, I know he loves Max to the moon and back. "He's as full of it as his dad."

"Careful..."

"Anyway, I wanted to ask you something." I reach out and grab the bottle of water that's resting on my side table. "Is Mum having money troubles again?"

There's silence for a moment, and all I can hear is Alex's breathing, and the distant echo of Max's cries. Then my brother speaks, his voice uncharacteristically quiet. "What's she done this time?"

Hastily, I backtrack. "Nothing, at least not as far as I know. It's just there was some weird guy hanging around asking for her."

"A weird guy?" Alex echoes. "What kind of weirdo? Did you see him?"

"Yeah, he was standing on our doorstep when I got home from yoga. Asked me where she was."

Alex's voice deepens. "Did you tell him?"

"I'm not stupid," I reply, exasperated. "But the odd thing was, he knew my name."

"What the hell? Tell me what he said?" For the first time I detect a note of panic in my brother's voice. Alex doesn't rile easily. I don't like it.

"He asked me if Tina Cartwright lived here. Then he said my name."

"He might have heard someone else talking to you..."

I bite my lip before taking in a deep breath. "He knew my real name Alex."

"Fuck."

The only way to know my real name is to go through my official documents. Look in the electoral register, or at my birth certificate. Absolutely nothing online—especially not my Facebook account—is under the name Amethyst.

"What did you say to him?" Alex asks. Then I hear him mutter something. I'm hoping he's talking to Lara rather than to himself.

"I said I wasn't Amethyst. Then I asked him who he was."

"And?"

"He didn't really say. Just said something about digging something up."

"Digging something up?" I can almost hear Alex running his hand through his hair. He used to do that all the time when we were kids. "What does that mean?"

I frown. "No, I don't think he meant digging. He said his name was Digger."

Silence. This time I don't hear Alex breathe. His lack of response makes my heart start to hammer, as if there's something I should be afraid of.

"Alex?" I finally prompt.

"He said he was called Digger?"

"He told me to tell Mum he said 'hi'."

"Shit." This time his voice raises an octave. "Did you lock the door behind you?"

"Of course I did, I'm not stupid."

"Where's Mum?" he barks. I blink in alarm.

"She had a shift at the shop I think. She'll be home by eleven."

"What room are you in?"

"Alex," I say, "You're really starting to freak me out. What's going on?"

"Amy, just tell me where you are in the house."

"I'm in my bedroom."

"I want you to go to the window and look out at the street. Tell me if you see anybody there, okay?" His voice wobbles.

"Okay." I swing my legs around until they hit the carpet, and step out of bed. The autumn chill hits me. I walk half a dozen steps to my window and pull back the corner of my curtain. Though it's dark, the streetlights illuminate the concrete paving slabs. There's not a soul to be seen, not even the she-fox who seems to delight in wailing like a baby most nights.

"There's nobody there," I say.

"Okay, good. You definitely locked the door, right?"

"Yes," I reply, patiently. "I locked the door and I saw him walk away. He's gone, Al."

"For now," he replies, dully.

It's like a light flicking on in my brain. "Do you know this Digger guy?"

"I'm... I'm not sure. But if it's who I think it is, he's a nasty piece of work."

"Who do you think it is?" I persist.

"Look, Ames, I don't want to scare you unnecessarily, and I don't want to say anything until I've talked with Mum. But if this guy comes up to you again, you scream and run, okay? Then you call me and I'll be over like a shot. In fact, I should come over now."

"Don't be stupid, I'm in bed. There's nothing to see here." I say it lightly, as if I'm joking. "I'm pretty sure he won't bother me again, but if he does, I promise to let you know."

"And run," Alex repeats.

"And run," I confirm. "Or at least kick him in the arse."

"I'm not kidding, Amy. Don't do anything to antagonise him."

"I'm not stupid, Alex." Nor am I a baby, I remind him silently. Sometimes I think he and Andie forget I'm twenty-three years old.

"I know you're not, kid. But this guy—if he is who I think he is—he's not right in the head. And I don't want you to get hurt." His voice breaks on the last word, and in that split second I go from exasperated to emotional.

"I won't let him hurt me, I promise. I love you, big brother."

"I love you too, Ames." That's something great about Alex, he's never afraid to wear his heart on his sleeve. Where some men might shy away from their feelings, he positively embraces them. "And you take care of yourself, okay?"

"I will."

When I hang up, there's a smile on my face. Not because I feel safe, and definitely not because I feel happy. My lips curl up because I feel loved and taken care of, and that's good enough for now.

* * *

When I wake up the next morning my body feels as if it's been through ten rounds in a boxing ring. My back aches, my muscles throb and there's a shooting pain on the left side of my brain that makes me wince. Somehow I drag my sorry self out of bed and into the shower, leaning against the cold tiles as the water cascades down.

In the kitchen, Mum is sitting at our old oak table, a half-drunk mug of coffee in front of her and a cigarette balanced between her finger and thumb. The ashtray is filled with smoked-to-the-stub fag ends, as if she's been chaining them all night.

"I thought you'd given up." I take the milk from the fridge, splashing it across a bowl of muesli.

"I did." She takes another drag. Blue-grey smoke curls from between her lips. "I'm just having a few. I've not started again."

She's wearing her pink, tatty bathrobe, belted tightly around her waist. Her hair is falling out of a bun that probably looked neat last night. I'm not sure if she's been to bed, or if she's been sitting here all night, which is strange, because unlike me she's usually a good sleeper.

"It's not good for you." I scoop a spoonful of cereal into my mouth. "Remember what the doctor said?"

She presses the cigarette into the glass ashtray. The dying smoke dissipates into nothing. "How was your first day at work?" she asks. There's a brightness to her voice that sounds false.

"It was fine." For a minute I think about confiding in her, telling her how everything went wrong. But she can't understand why I feel the need to get a degree, and I don't want to hand her any ammunition. "When I got home there was a guy looking for you."

She doesn't meet my eyes. "I know, Alex called me at work."

My head snaps up. "He did? Why?"

Mum sighs. "Oh I don't know, Amy. Who knows what goes through your brother's head? But I'll tell you what I told him, there's nothing to worry about, he's just an old friend. I'll ask him not to bother you again."

"How much do you owe him? I've got some savings..." I can't believe I'm saying this, but she's my mum, and I'm not going to leave her to flounder.

She reaches out and grabs my hand. "I don't owe him anything." Another curl of bleached blonde hair escapes from her bun. "He's just somebody I used to know."

"He knew my name," I say. "My real name. And he looked a bit menacing."

"He won't come here again," she promises. "I won't let him. I'm sorry he scared you, sweetheart, but he won't do you any harm. You're safe here, you know that." For the first time she smiles. Her lips are dry, her teeth stained with nicotine, but it's still genuine. I have no reason to disbelieve her, but I'm still not wholly convinced.

I pick up my now-empty bowl and rinse it under the tap. The kitchen window is dappled with rain, obscuring the view of the street. "You'd tell me if you were in trouble, wouldn't you?" I ask. "Because I could help, or Alex and Andie could. You don't need to be seeing people like that. Not any more."

Mum laughs, and it quickly turns into a cough. I wince at the way her chest wheezes. This is precisely why she shouldn't be smoking.

"I don't need your help," she says when the paroxysms die down. "Sometimes I think you forget who the parent is around here."

I shake my head. "How could I forget you're my mum?" Leaning down I kiss the top of her head. "I've got to go to work now, I'll see you tonight, okay?"

She squeezes my hand. "Have a good day. And remember what I said, there's nothing to worry about."

Oh sure, I think, as I leave the house, nothing to worry about at all. Unless you count a boyfriend who should be an ex, a weird man hanging around the house, and a back that feels as though it's been beaten with a mallet.

With worries like that, it's almost a relief to be heading to work.

5

At 7:30 a.m. I walk into the office with two steaming Styrofoam cups of coffee. I bolster myself with the determination to make this a better day, to create a better impression. Maybe I can become indispensable to Mr Callum Ferguson.

My resolution lasts for less than two minutes. Long enough for me to hang my damp coat on the stand that rests in the corner and toe my handbag under my desk. That's when I carry Callum's coffee into his room, where of course he's already on the phone, and find a three-inch space on his cluttered desk to put it down.

Turning to me, Callum covers the mouthpiece with his hand. "What's that?"

"It's a monkey." My voice is as tart as a lemon.

He rolls his eyes. "I don't drink coffee before nine."

Stupid, ungrateful bastard of a boss. "You're welcome."

Three vertical furrows form between his brows as he stares at me. "Are we having the same conversation here?"

I sigh. There doesn't seem to be any way for the two of us to be civil with each other. Which is fine for him, because he's in charge, but for me it's a few steps away from queuing up at the unemployment office. Or at my tutor's door.

"I don't know. Is it the conversation where I buy my boss a coffee and he's grateful I've spent my hard-earned wages on him?" I want to take back my sarcastic words as soon as I say them, but it's too late. He hangs up on his call without saying goodbye. Someone, somewhere in the world, is talking down an empty telephone line. I know how they feel.

Callum rubs his eyes, and I can see the skin around them wrinkling. There are shadows beneath them, blue-black as bruises. "Thank you for buying me a coffee, Amy. It was kind of you to think of me."

He brings his gaze around and any sharp retort dies on my lips. He really does look tired. I feel regret for walking in and immediately having a go at him when he's obviously not sleeping well.

"You're welcome." I say again, but this time my voice is small. Picking up his cup, I turn to leave his office. "I'll get rid of this."

"You may as well leave it." He reaches across the desk and covers my hand with his. His palm is warm and big and completely envelopes mine. I stare for a minute—at the taut tendons and the pale skin—and wonder what it would feel like if he just slid his fingers between mine. "A bit of caffeine would do me good, anyway. I didn't sleep well last night."

No kidding, I want to say, but I swallow it down. He's made an effort to actually be civil to me; the least I can do is try to be the same. "Tomorrow I'll wait until nine to get our drinks."

He smiles and my stomach does that stupid lurch again. He's both annoying and horribly attractive. It's in the way his lips curl and his eyes crinkle as if he knows everything I'm thinking. "Thank you."

When I pull out my leather swivel seat, I'm feeling hopeful again. As if I might have a chance to make a difference before he decides to call up Diana in HR and have me shipped out.

I have no idea why I'm always so rude to Callum whenever I see him. My mouth opens up and insults fly out. I don't behave like this around anybody else—and I certainly shouldn't with my boss.

As soon as I log into the network, a message pops up on my screen.

Simpson, C: Good morning, camper. Half an hour down, another seven and a half to go. Is it lunch time yet?

I smile at his words. It's reassuring to know I'm not alone in the building, and that I've managed to make at least one friend.

Cartwright, A: And even better, there's only 31.5 hours until the weekend.

Simpson, C: Way to put a downer on things, Essex girl. Are you trying to kill my mojo?

I smirk.

Cartwright, A: Your mojo? Try having a boss who doesn't drink coffee before nine. Plus he's the most miserable git in the building. Then you can complain about your mojo.

Simpson, C: He can't be that bad. Caro says he's a fox.

Cartwright, A: A fox? As in eats out of the dustbin and shits in your front garden? Yeah, maybe...

"Have you got a moment or are you too busy talking to your boyfriend?" Callum's thick voice emanates from just behind my shoulder. Immediately I press control-alt-delete, but even as my fingers make the movements I know I'm too late. My face flushes red, and it takes all my courage to make me turn around to look at him.

"We were just having a joke," I reply, wanly.

"So I see." There isn't a hint of amusement there. I close my eyes, wishing I was somewhere else. I'm such an idiot.

"Can I help you with anything?" I ask, desperate to change the subject. "Coffee, expenses? I can book you a hotel?"

Callum shakes his head. "I'm off to a project meeting. I was going to suggest you join me but I can see you're too busy here. Perhaps you can make yourself useful by doing some filing." He inclines his head to a box on top of the cabinet on the far side of the room. It's overloaded with paper.

"Of course." I stand up right away, walking around him and over to the cabinet. In spite of my two-inch heels, he still manages to tower over me, and it makes me feel smaller than I already do. "I'm sorry, Callum."

He walks over to the door, then turns to look at me one more time. His expression is unreadable, in spite of my best attempts to work it out. "I'll be back after lunch. Try not to break anything."

After he leaves, I grab hold of the metal filing cabinet and bang my forehead against it three times, but even that fails to make me feel better.

* * *

"You really wrote that about him?" Ellie sounds aghast. I'm sitting at a café a few buildings down from the office, picking at a Brie and cranberry panini while I jam my phone to my ear.

"I know," I wail. "I'm so stupid. It's like I lose my common sense the minute I step in the lift. He must think I'm such an airhead. I'm going to have to do some serious grovelling this afternoon."

"Can I recommend you don't buy him a coffee?" she says, dryly.

I can't help it; I let out a bark of laughter. "Thanks for the help, oh wise one. Have you thought about joining the UN? First Canary Wharf, then world peace."

"Don't knock my advice," she says. "How many times have I smoothed things over between you and Luke?"

The laughter dies. "Yeah, well you won't need to do that anymore, will you?" I push the plate away from me, rejecting the half-nibbled sandwich. What little I've managed to eat feels like lead shot in my stomach. "God, this has been a horrible week. And it's only Tuesday."

"Three more days until the weekend," Ellie says. Her cheerful tone makes me want to throttle her. "What are your plans?"

"I have none. I'm a social misfit with no boyfriend and no friends."

"Charming."

"I didn't mean you." I backpedal furiously. "I was talking about work. I heard one of the girls talking about a night out and I'm pretty sure I'm not invited." Stupid Caro and her sycophantic sidekicks. "I expect it will be champagne all round."

Ellie's voice softens. "Let's have a girlie night out. I'll call Sophie and we can meet you in town. Who needs work friends when you have us?"

Her offer brings tears to my eyes.

"Sounds good," I reply, my voice gruff. "I can't think of anything better."

"I'd better go," Ellie says, trying to lighten the mood. "The housing committee meets at three and I haven't printed out the agendas yet." Ellie works as a secretary at the local council. She tells me her job is just as riveting as it sounds. "Think of me when you're standing in your penthouse office and sipping mocha choco lattes won't you?"

"Sure," I say, "Because that's exactly what it's like there. It's a dirty job but somebody has to do it."

"And you're so good at it." She pauses, and the teasing tone disappears. "Seriously, Amy, you are good at it. I'm proud of you, we all are. You're like a better looking Donald Trump, but without the comb over."

I blink to get that image out of my head. "Um... thanks, I guess. Though not everybody's proud of me." I walk out of the café and into the crisp air. My thoughts turn to Luke again. He left another message on my voicemail this morning while I was at work.

"Everybody who matters is," she says. I hear a scrape of her chair as she stands up. "I'll call you later, okay? And don't do anything more to piss your boss off. Be charming."

"Easier said than done." I laugh. "Speak soon."

By the time we ring off I'm back at Canada Square. The security guard ignores me as I walk in and join the small crowd waiting at the bank of elevators. When the lift arrives I press ten before I get pushed to the back; I've learned that it's so much easier than shouting. The floor is quiet when I get there; most people are either still at lunch or in their first meeting of the afternoon. Everybody is more stressed in the afternoon, a side effect of our colleagues in the States waking up.

When I get to my desk I shrug off my jacket and hang it on the stand, the heating providing more than enough warmth. Maybe it's the low drone of the air conditioning that stops me from noticing initially, but it takes me a few moments to realise Callum is in his office.

"Have you heard from Sorensons?" An unfamiliar voice echoes through the half-shut door. I can't see who's in there, but it's definitely a man. I tap my fingers on my desk, wondering if I should interrupt and tell Callum I'm back, or if I should just leave them to it.

"They're baulking at the price." That's Callum's deep burr. "I'm going to have to fly over next week."

"Stay for a few days, make a weekend of it. I hear Berlin is pretty lively at night."

A low laugh. "I don't think so."

"Why not? All work and no play..."

"Makes this company a lot of money." Callum's words thicken. "And anyway, you know why not."

"It's been nearly two years, Cal."

I'm unashamedly eavesdropping now. I don't even bother to try to look busy. Anything that could possibly give me an insight into Callum has to be a good thing.

"So what?"

I can hear one of them shuffle across his office. "Maybe it's time to move on."

"I have moved on." There's an edge to Callum's voice that sends a shiver to the base of my spine. "I'm not exactly living like a fucking monk, am I?"

"You're not exactly having a functional relationship either. Jane wouldn't have wanted this."

There's a loud bang. "Don't fucking tell me what Jane would have wanted," Callum shouts. "At least spare me the bullshit."

For the first time I feel awkward and exposed. When the mystery man speaks next his voice is so close to the door there's no way I can escape without being heard. So I sit as still as a rabbit in the headlights, too scared to turn on my computer in case they notice.

"How's the new PA? I hear she's a looker."

It's one thing to listen in to your boss's conversation, another to hear him talking about you. I'm about to cough loudly and slam a few books on my desk when Callum replies.

"She's... interesting."

My fingers freeze. What the hell does that mean?

"Interesting how?"

Callum is quiet for a moment, and I'm picturing him rubbing his chin. He seems to do that when he's in deep thought, something I've noticed when he doesn't realise I'm watching him.

"She's mouthy and opinionated and doesn't seem to know when to shut up. But when I asked HR to move her somewhere else they showed me her test scores."

I have to bite my lip to stop myself from breathing, because I'm scared he might hear me groan. I *knew* he was going to ask to move me, but I didn't think he'd do it so quickly. I'm torn between wanting to hit him and wanting to run away.

"Were they bad?"

"Her scores? No, they were amazing—almost perfect. Which is strange because she's from some shitty university in East London."

"You're sounding very elitist, Oxford boy." The other man chuckles. "So, she's a clever girl with a rough exterior. Interesting."

"And off limits," Callum growls. "Remember?"

"Hey, there's no rule against looking."

The door swings open and the man walks out—the same one I saw with Callum in the cafeteria yesterday. He looks around the same age as Callum, with dark, closely cropped hair. His skin is tanned, and his cheeks redden as soon as he sees me.

"Hello." He flashes me a smile. "We didn't hear you come back." He looks at me as if he's trying to work out how much I've overheard.

"I just walked in. Is everything okay? Can I get you a coffee?"

He shrugs. "I was just leaving, actually." Leaning forward, he takes my hand, shaking it vigorously. "Jonathan Cooper. I work with your boss."

"Amy Cartwright," I reply, smoothly. "It's nice to meet you."

Callum appears, leaning on the doorframe. "Have you been here long?" There's a hint of alarm in his expression.

"She just came in," Jonathan replies. "Isn't that right, Amy?" He turns his head so Callum can only see the back of him, and sends me a wink.

"That's right." I ignore his attempt at conspiring.

"Good, good." Callum rakes his fingers through his hair. "I'll leave you to it, then."

With that, Jonathan leaves and Callum closes the frosted glass door that leads to his office, leaving me alone in the outer vestibule. I can't help thinking about the way he called me 'interesting'. It's a word that could be an insult as easily as it could be a compliment, and I still can't quite decide which. But more importantly, I'm itching to know who the hell Jane is, and why the mere mention of her name was enough to make him angry.

As I log into the network and go through my emails, I realise I'm starting to find Callum Ferguson as intriguing as he's finding me.

6

"Don't be angry, okay?" Sophie takes my bag as I step into her flat, taking in the familiar silver-papered walls, lined with hundreds of fairy lights that blink on and off. "This wasn't my idea. All right so it was totally my idea, but I only did it because I love you."

I walk across the thick shag pile rug that covers the sanded wooden floors. Since she and Nick bought this flat in August last year, she's spent every penny on making it into a hairdresser's paradise. Ellie calls it the Kitsch Palace, which describes it very well.

"Why would I be angry?" I inhale the aroma of lamb curry. Sophie may have terrible taste in decor, but her culinary skills are second to none, which is why I jumped at the chance of dinner at hers when she texted the offer.

As soon as I'm in her kitchen I realise exactly why I should be angry. Sophie guessed correctly; I'm bloody furious. Luke is leaning against the counter, chatting with Nick, holding a frosted bottle of Peroni to his lips.

"What's he doing here?"

Luke turns to look at me, his dark-blue eyes soft and appraising. He looks impossibly handsome with his perfectly-cut blonde hair, and the expensive designer jeans hanging from his hips. I feel a mess in comparison; still wearing my work dress and a pair of flat shoes that almost make the work commute bearable. But now all they do is make me feel short and dumpy, next to the tall and elegant arsehole.

"Nick invited me." His voice is as gentle as his expression. "I can leave if you want."

I stand there for a minute, listening to the whirr of the extractor fan and the sizzle of the pot. The table is set with four plates and glasses, plus four sets of cutlery. Asking Luke to leave isn't going to turn this into a night to remember.

Nick pulls a bottle of wine from the fridge and pours me a glass, passing it to me with a sheepish expression. He mouths a "sorry", and I roll my eyes in exasperation.

"Stay," I sigh. "Otherwise Nick will be eating leftovers for weeks."

"You sure?" Luke blinks, his thick lashes sweeping down. I wonder if this is how reformed smokers feel. Wanting something even though you know it's poisonous.

"It doesn't mean anything," I say, taking a sip of wine. "Sophie's my friend and Nick's yours. It's not as if I can avoid you."

Luke takes a step closer, lowering his voice, and even though I hold my breath I can still smell his cologne. The one I bought for him.

"I don't want you to avoid me, Amy, I want you to talk to me. I miss you, babe."

This is a mistake. I knew it as soon as I set eyes on him. I wasn't prepared to see him and I'm certainly not ready for a full-on charm onslaught. I need to work myself up, starting with short, benign exposures.

"It's ready." Sophie slides her hand into a pair of oven mitts and pulls the cast iron pot out of the stove. Stepping carefully, she carries the steaming dish over to the kitchen table, where she places it on the waiting mat. "Can you bring the rice over, Nick?" She takes off the lid and vapour escapes, momentarily turning the air above the table opaque. "Sit, sit." She gestures at the two seats opposite. "Don't let it go cold."

Glancing at Luke, I pull out my chair, smoothing my dress across my thighs. I can feel his gaze follow my movements. He offers me the naan bread, holding the plate as I tear off a piece, then he tops up my glass.

It's strange, because this is all so familiar. The four of us have been sitting around tables for years. From tea with our parents to teenage pig-outs at McDonald's, we've grown up eating together.

Now it feels like the last supper.

Sophie makes small talk about her clients in the salon, telling us about an old lady who insisted she wanted a cut and blow job. I choke on a piece of lamb, and it takes Luke slamming me to dislodge it.

"You okay? You went pretty blue there for a minute." It hasn't escaped my notice that his hand is still on my back, rubbing small circles against my spine.

"Yeah, I just need Sophie to stop making me laugh."

"It's not the first time you've choked on a blow job," she quips, and Luke laughs. I try not to look at him, because if I do he'll know what I'm thinking about. And I really don't want to be thinking about *that*.

"It beats getting caught with your knickers down in the art room." I smile back at her, and this time it's Sophie's turn to blush. Then all four of us launch into full-blown school reminiscences, talking about hated teachers and smoking behind the bike sheds. There's a cadence to this tableau; a familiarity that can only come from years of experience. It's as comfortable as a favourite sweater and I can't help but wonder if I'm fighting against the inevitable.

"Do you remember that time we skipped school, Ames?" Luke says, turning to me. "You made me hide in your room while you did all your homework. It was worse than being in lessons."

"It was exam year," I protest. "I wanted to finish a couple of essays."

"That's not what you're meant to do when you bunk off, babe." His voice lowers. "I had to make my own fun."

I swallow, remembering the way he kissed my neck as I tried to write a book report on *Tess of the D'Urbervilles*. In the end the only way I could placate him was by reading out the dirty parts.

"From what I remember, you had a lot of fun." I roll my eyes.

"I did," he laughs. "Who knew Dickens could be so sexy?"

"It was Hardy," I correct him quietly.

"What?"

I clear my throat. "*Tess of the D'Urbervilles* was written by Thomas Hardy, not Charles Dickens."

Sophie collects our plates and carries them over to the sink. Turning her head, she shoots me a glance, and I know without asking exactly what she's trying to say. She wants me to be quiet. To stop showing Luke that I have a brain. She honestly believes boys prefer girls who play dumb.

Luke shrugs. "Dickens, Hardy, who gives a fuck? They're a load of dirty old men. If they were around today they'd probably be running porn sites."

I reach out and grab my wineglass, resolutely bringing it to my lips. Sometimes it's not even worth arguing back.

"Did you see *Top Gear* last night?" Nick asks, thankfully changing the subject. He and Luke share a love of cars; the faster the better as far as they're concerned.

"Nah, I missed it," Luke leans back on his chair, stretching his legs in front of him. As they launch into a discussion on the latest Bugatti, I gather up the dirty glasses and take them over to the sink.

"Alright?" Sophie asks, brightly. "You and Luke seem to be getting on well."

I rinse the glasses beneath the tap. "What?"

"You should give him another chance. He misses you, you know? He told Nick he wants you back."

I pull the dishwasher door open and load the plates into the rack. "I don't think so," I say, scrunching my nose up. "We're over, he knows that."

Sophie stops scrubbing the pot, pulling her soap-covered forearms from the suds. "But you don't have to be. Take him back, Amy. That girl meant nothing to him, he was just having a bit of fun."

I look at Sophie. She's very pretty, in that perfectly made-up, well-dressed way. Her hair is curled, tumbling over her shoulders, and her skin is just the right side of orange. She's a far cry from the tomboy I met at the age of eleven, when she used to play netball like a demon on speed. Nowadays she'd run screaming if you threw a ball at her, scared she might break a nail.

I guess I've changed, too. If you asked her, Sophie would probably say I was a desperately shy eleven-year-old, lurking in the corner with my black hair falling over my face. I was unremarkable, rubbish at sports, nondescript in looks. The only thing I had going for me was a love of numbers.

But now I'm less awkward, and definitely less shy. I'm also not going to put up with being treated like a doormat anymore.

I wonder if breaking up with Luke means losing Sophie, too. Will she think she has to choose between the two of us, as if it's all or nothing?

"I'm not interested." Even though the boys are talking, I keep my voice low. I realise I need to have this conversation with Luke as well, but there's no way I'm doing it in front of an audience.

"You're being stubborn. Okay, so he messed up, are you really going to throw everything away for that? You've been together for years, Amy. He knows you inside out, he loves you for God's sake."

"Not enough to be faithful." If I'm being truly honest, I can feel myself start to waiver. It isn't just Luke I'm splitting up with, but seven years of memories, and a predictable future. Not to mention a whole crowd of shared friends. "It's not the first time, either."

I say that last bit to remind myself. I can't afford to deviate. If Luke thinks he has the slightest chance, he'll keep pushing until he wins.

"Men stray sometimes. At least Luke loves you and looks after you. He doesn't beat you up, does he?"

This makes me laugh. "No, he's never touched me. But if that's all he's got going for him then he's not much of a catch is he? I mean there are millions of men out there who don't beat up women. I've heard some of them might even manage to keep their dicks zipped in their trousers, too."

Sophie huffs, shaking her head. "Well it's your problem. Don't come crying to me when you don't find anything better."

* * *

The rest of the evening is a quiet affair. After our kitchen sink drama, Sophie barely brings herself to talk to me, concentrating on the boys and hanging on their every word. She listens as Nick complains about his boss at the Ford factory in Dagenham, and when Luke describes a sale he made today I remain silent, sipping my wine and wondering if it would be rude to say I'm tired and ready to go home.

In the end it's Luke who breaks up the evening, reaching his arms above his head in a stretch and yawning loudly. When he brings his arms back down, he reaches one across the back of my chair, the tips of his fingers brushing against my neck.

"You want to share a cab home?" he asks. "I'm going past yours anyway."

My house is a ten-minute taxi ride from here. I calculate whether we'll be able to say everything that needs to be said in such a short time.

"Uh, yeah, sure. I'll pay half."

He shrugs. "Whatever."

The cab arrives and I hug Nick goodbye before pressing my lips against Sophie's rouged cheek. She smells of Chanel and curry, a weird combination that's somehow still quite pleasant. "Thanks for dinner," I say.

"You're welcome." Her reply is as stiff as her hair. "Thank you for coming."

Soon we're in the cab, driving through the night-time streets. We stop at a red light at the end of the road, and I turn to look at Luke. His face is lit up, the shadow of his chin sharp beneath the ambient glow. I can see where his morning shave is beginning to lose the battle against his evening stubble, and for some reason I reach out to touch it.

"Luke," I say.

He shakes his head. "You don't have to say it."

He's wrong; I do. Not for him—although I think he should hear it from me—but for myself. I need to sever the final cords that bind us.

"I'm sorry." This is harder than I thought. It's like rolling in fibreglass; my whole body hurts. "It's really over."

He turns in his seat, grabbing hold of my hand. His eyes are glassy. I feel my own start to water as my heart hammers against my chest.

"I don't want it to be," he whispers. "I was a dick, but I love you, I really do. You know that, don't you?"

The car pulls away, engine rumbling dully. From the corner of my eye I see the driver glancing at us in the rear-view mirror. How many life-changing moments has he seen in mirror image? First dates, long kisses, short goodbyes. The fading embers of a dying love.

"You cheated on me, again and again. That's not love Luke, that's not even *like*. That's..." I try to find the right word. "That's disdain."

"Give me another chance." He brings my hand to his lips; his breath hot against my skin. "I won't fuck it up this time."

The wavering of moments ago is gone, replaced by a certainty that feels cold as ice. He's lying. He might not know it, he might not mean it, but there are some things in life that are crystal clear. The sun will rise in the morning, the world will continue to turn, and Luke will keep looking at other women.

No, not just looking. Touching, kissing... fucking.

Gently, I pull my hand away. "I can't, I can't give you another chance. If I do, I'm cheating myself. I won't do that."

He recoils as if I've hit him, and lets go of my hand so fast it drops right into my lap.

"Don't flatter yourself," he says, his eyes narrow, his mouth mean.

"What?" The sudden transformation startles me.

"You're nothing special, babe. You're pretty, yeah, and your body's okay. But you can't wear a tight dress to save your life without looking like a deformed freak."

I open my mouth to reply, but nothing comes out. The merest hint of a breath escapes my lips.

"You think I want you because you're perfect?" He carries on. "You're nowhere close. But you're easy, you're dumb and you turn a blind eye." He laughs but it's anything but funny. "You're the ideal girlfriend."

"You were right. You are a dick." I'm not going to cry, not in front of him. I try to keep my voice even. "You're an ignorant, cheating arsehole with the biggest ego I've ever seen."

I lean forward and speak to the taxi driver. "Can you stop here please?"

He winks. "With pleasure, love." He presses his foot to the brake, slowly pulling up beside the pavement. "There you go sweetheart, no charge to you."

"Thanks." I give him a tight smile. Then I sit back and grab the handle, putting my weight on the door to open it. Before I leave, I glance at Luke for a final time, wondering why I ever thought he was being sincere. "And by the way, your ego's the only big thing about you."

"Fuck off."

"Gladly." I get out, slamming the door behind me. Adrenaline rushes through my body, making me jittery and high. I breathe in deeply, letting the fresh air overpower the nasty taste in my mouth.

The driver unwinds his window, leaning his arm on the door as he looks out. "Best of luck to you. You're better off out of it." Then he pulls away, leaving me open mouthed. The last thing I see before the cab disappears into the darkness is Luke's angry face half obscured by the glass.

* * *

At exactly 9:00 a.m. the next morning, I slide a venti Americano with steamed milk onto Callum's desk, then turn to walk out of his office.

"Amy?"

I look over my shoulder. He's staring at me through dark, auburn lashes. "Yes?"

"Are you okay?" He tilts his head to the side, still looking.

I realise he can see my red-rimmed eyes, and the shadows that bruise the delicate skin below. "I didn't sleep well," I tell him. It's an understatement. In spite of the adrenaline and bravado that fuelled my late-night argument, I still managed to sob deep into the night. Even now I feel achingly empty—as though I haven't eaten for weeks and weeks.

Slowly, he peels the lid from his coffee. Steam rises up like a smoke signal. "I know how that feels." Taking a sip, he brings his eyes to meet mine again. "I thought you could come to this afternoon's meeting. You might find it interesting."

His offer feels like an olive branch, and I eagerly grasp hold of it. "Really?" The last few days of filing have taken their toll. I don't want to see another metal cabinet ever again.

"Really." He nods his head slowly. "But I recommend you dose yourself up on caffeine first. Project meetings can be deadly, especially in the afternoon." He fakes a yawn then smiles, and it's infectious. In spite of my shitty evening and hideous night, there's the tiniest pinprick of light at the end of the tunnel. The fact my boss isn't scowling feels like a major achievement.

And I haven't insulted him once today.

I shake my coffee cup at him. "Triple espresso. These eyes won't be able to shut even if they try."

I'm still grinning as I check my emails; replying to some, deleting others. Then a message from Charlie pops up on my screen.

Simpson, C: How's my favourite filing lady doing?

Cartwright, A: Piss off.

Simpson, C: Ooh, tetchy. Anyway, entertain me; what excitements do you have today? Photocopying? Hotel booking...oh, maybe you'll be able to snag him a table in a restaurant.

Cartwright, A: Actually, funny boy, I'm going to meet with some potential clients.

It's a big deal, I could tell that just from Callum's expression. He's pitching to them, hoping to score a million-pound project. No wonder he's losing sleep.

Simpson, C: Bloody hell, how did you manage that? Wait...you didn't, did you?

Cartwright, A: Didn't what?

Simpson, C: You didn't... make him an offer he couldn't refuse?

Cartwright, A: For your information, my very nice boss invited me to a very important meeting because I'm a very good worker.

Simpson, C: Uh oh.

I sigh, still tapping at the keyboard.

Cartwright, A: What?

Simpson, C: It's happened.

Cartwright, A: Stop talking in riddles, it's annoying. You're annoying.

Simpson, C: I think you've got Stockholm syndrome.

This time I groan.

Cartwright, A: I'm going now. I have work to do.

Simpson, C: Wait! If he offers you the blue kool aid, don't drink it.

Cartwright, A: Goodbye, Charlie.

7

I'm nervous before I take a step inside the conference room. While Callum walks in, carrying his laptop in one hand, with a large, bound file beneath the other, I linger outside. Reaching out, I hold on to the oak doorframe, my fingers curling around the warm wood. Callum stands with his back to me, his broad torso bent over the large table as he goes through a pile of paper.

"Are you coming in?" Looking over his shoulder, he raises an eyebrow. "I won't bite."

It takes effort to release my grasp. Even more to make my tone light and airy. "Of course. What can I do to help?"

"Would you think I was a terrible boss if I asked you to check if the coffee is on its way?"

"When has that ever stopped you?" I tease. Then I double check myself, wondering if I've overstepped the mark again. But no, that wasn't too cheeky, was it?

We spend the next ten minutes arranging the room, putting materials on the table and starting the multimedia screens. When the coffee arrives, I direct the catering staff to the side table, and Callum shoots a grateful look at me.

"This is a big deal, right?" I ask. He's nervous. I can tell by the way he keeps raking his fingers through his hair, and adjusting his tie as if it's strangling him. Maybe if I knew him better, or if I was a little bit bolder, I'd help him even up the knot. As it is I make a face and gesture at my neck. "It's a little off centre, I think."

"Is that better?"

"A bit to the right," I say, gesturing with my finger.

"That's left." His brows pull down, and I smile at his confused expression.

"My left, not yours."

A few minutes later, the rest of the project team file in. There are representatives from legal, finance, and three of Callum's direct reports. A couple of them wave at me, recognising my face from the office, and they come over to introduce themselves.

"Amy, right? I'm John Adair. This is Mike." They both shake my hand and we make small talk about the department, all the while shooting nervous glances across the room.

When 3:00 p.m. arrives, reception calls up to let us know the potential clients are here. Being the most junior—and I suspect because I'm the only female—I'm dispatched to the ground floor to pick them up. The lift is mercifully empty and I lean against the wall, tapping on the handrail as I descend the floors.

As soon as I walk across the lobby I recognise the clients. Not because I've seen them before, or even because Callum's described them to me, but because of the easy-going, relaxed nature of their posture, coupled with the sharp tailoring of their suits. There are three of them—all men, sitting on the sofas in the waiting area—and as soon as I approach them, they turn to look at me.

"Mr Grant?" I turn my gaze on each man. I wait for the oldest to step forward, fully expecting him to be the CEO of Grant Industries.

But the older man hangs back, turning his gaze on the younger, blonde-haired thirty-something who turns to smile at me. "Call me Daniel," he says, reaching out his hand. I take it automatically.

"It's a pleasure to meet you, Daniel. I'm Amy Cartwright, Callum Ferguson's assistant."

"Lucky Mr Ferguson." He shakes vigorously. I wait for him to introduce me to his co-workers, but he doesn't.

"Would you like to follow me?" I say, pointing toward the lifts. "Mr Ferguson's team are ready for you."

"Sure, lead the way."

Daniel Grant is chatty. In the course of a short elevator ride I discover he's a Harvard graduate who built his company from scratch, using hedge funds in the early days but bailing out long before the 2007 crash. Though he lives in Manhattan his heart is still in Chicago, where his beloved Bears play come rain or shine. I also learn—though not from them—that the two men accompanying him are his chief financial officer and chief counsel. When Daniel says their names they raise their hands in salute but say nothing. I get the impression that Daniel talks enough for the three of them.

The lift arrives at the tenth floor, and we step out, Daniel walking beside me as I lead them to the main conference room. It's here that he undergoes a transformation, a straightening of the back and a roll of the neck that signals a metamorphosis. It's like watching an actor slip into the skin of a well-rehearsed role; even his face takes on the expression of someone older. Someone with gravitas.

I wonder if this is what we all do. Step into clothes that aren't our own and talk with voices an octave lower than we should. It's like wearing armour, protecting ourselves, because if somebody rejects that skin we are wearing they aren't rejecting *us*.

"Let's go." Daniel's tone is clipped, but when he catches my eye I swear I see something of the lift version there. I wonder why he didn't feel the need to hide his talkative side from me. Is it because I look new, or because I'm unimportant enough to be sent down to pick him up?

When I push the heavy door open, the team stand. Callum walks forward, introducing himself, shaking each man's hand in turn. He has the ease of someone who knows where he's come from and where he's going. It hits me as strikingly attractive.

My only destination has always been "not here". Until now my life has been less of a journey and more of an escape. I wonder what it must feel like to be so sure of yourself, so comfortable with who you are. Maybe it's something the rich feed their children, along with their daily vitamins and silver spoonfuls of castor oil, giving them a sense of self-worth along with their shiny hair.

"Coffee?" Callum asks, his voice breaking through my thoughts. I immediately flush, my pink cheeks matching the scarf I wound around my neck this morning.

"I'm sorry, what can I get you?"

He shakes his head slowly. "I was offering you a coffee, Amy. Would you like one?"

Beside me, Daniel says nothing. The others place their orders, as Callum walks over to the flasks the catering service brought in earlier. Pressing down on the lever, he fills four china cups with steaming black coffee. It's so strong the acrid smell fills the room.

"I'll take mine black." Daniel takes the proffered cup. "Thank you."

"Did you have a good flight?" Callum asks as he pours milk into the other cups. Then he passes them over one by one. The first to Brian Johnstone—the CFO, the second to Saul Shoemaker, Grant Industries' chief counsel. He hands the final one to me. It's muddy and sweet, painting my tongue and palate.

Five minutes of awkward small talk follow, and I step back, letting Callum and his team take the lead. The coffee is strong enough to give my blood a little fizz, energising me. Everybody finally takes a seat and Callum fires up the screens, filling them with brightly coloured slides that reflect in the window across the room. They flicker as he progresses through them, providing a voice over to the charts and projections, his words smooth and reassuring.

I realise that he's wearing a different persona too. His accent is smoother than normal, his tone lower. He's all smiles and good looks, appealing to them with words of praise and reassurance.

Every now and again I glance over at Daniel Grant. His elbows are on the table, his hands clasped, fingers steepled. I notice he rarely looks at the screen, in spite of the vast array of information that flashes there. Instead he concentrates on Callum, the two of them sharing eye contact in a way I'd find uncomfortable. They're scoping each other out.

Callum reaches the end of his introduction and hands over to one of his technical team, who begins to talk through the intricate specifications of the proposals. The poor guy is barely two minutes into his spiel, when Daniel waves his hand, and asks him to stop.

Immediately the techie looks over at Callum, looking for direction. This is clearly a part of the presentation none of them have rehearsed, and he looks lost, standing up there, his mouth opening and closing silently.

Strangely, it's Daniel who takes charge of the situation, turning to him with a reassuring smile. "I'm sorry, I know it's rude, but I don't need to go into details right now."

The man at the front visibly swallows. His Adam's apple bobs up and down, stretching the thin skin of his neck. "Are you sure? We have some really cool stuff..." he trails off, looking down at his highly polished shoes. I can't help but feel sorry for him. I know how much effort it takes to get ready for a presentation. The preparation, the nerves, the fear that slowly morphs into elation.

"Is there anything else you'd like to discuss?" Callum's accent is stronger this time, and he's unable to hide the disappointment that veils his words.

"Yeah, but I'd like us to chat somewhere else. Just you and me," Daniel says. "The technical specs are important, and my team will need to go into the finer detail, but that's not the game winner here."

Callum doesn't flinch. "What is the game winner?"

Nobody says a word. It's as if we're all watching the climax of a movie. Collective breaths are held.

"You," Daniel replies simply. "Whether I can work with you, whether I can trust you. An army is only as good as the general leading it. That's why I flew over to meet you, not to hear all the details, as exciting as they may be. I want to see if you're somebody I can do business with."

For some reason my heart's racing in my chest. All those times I've watched boys square up—hitting the shit out of each other in beer-fuelled fist fights—they have nothing on the testosterone fest I'm witnessing here. Two alpha males circling, sizing each other up. Trying to work out if they're enemies or friends. Though it only takes seconds, it feels like full, heavy minutes have passed before Callum smiles and shrugs his shoulders.

"Everybody can go. Thank you for your time." Nobody moves. Like me, they all assume he's talking to somebody else.

"John, Mike?" he prompts. Suddenly they're scrambling to disconnect laptops and gather up folders, sheaves of A4 paper fluttering to the carpeted floor. I bend down and help them, earning a grateful smile from Mike, then I pick up the phone and call catering, asking them to clear away the coffee cups. By the time I'm finished only Callum, Daniel and his two employees are left. I turn off the screens and retrieve my note pad.

"Can I get you anything else?" I ask Callum.

He gives a languid, half-curve kind of smile that makes him look sleepy and vital all at the same time. It's the sort of smile that leads into something else, like a partly-filled promise. It waits and it lingers.

Then he turns to Daniel. "Do you play racquetball?"

It seems an odd sort of question, yet Daniel doesn't blink. "I do."

"Can you call my club and reserve a court, Amy? The number's in my address book. Oh, and make sure they open the shop, we're going to need some gear." He glances at Daniel. "You up for a challenge?"

"If you're up for an ass-kicking." Daniel grins, then shoots some orders at Brian and Saul. They're both nonplussed, standing in a foreign boardroom, being dismissed while their boss leaves with a man he might possibly award a multi-million pound contract to. It's only now that I realise exactly why an internship is so integral to my degree, because all the lectures and textbooks in the world would never be able to accurately describe this.

Some deals are the result of blood, sweat and tears. It appears that this could be one of them.

8

Though it's light outside, I can see through the huge window in Callum's office that the dark blue of evening is slowly encroaching, stealing away the sharpness of day. There are a few clouds in the sky—the wispy, just-torn from a roll of cotton wool sort—and their edges are tinged with orange and pink. At 6:00p.m. my desk phone rings and I snatch it up, bringing it to my ear as I answer with a breathless hello.

"Amy, it's Callum. I need a favour."

"Of course," I reply. "What is it?"

"Have you got time to bring some papers over to the gym? I want to talk them through with Daniel before dinner. I'd come and pick them up but I'm covered with sweat and smelling like a dog. I need a shower."

I glance at my watch. The two of them must have been playing for almost an hour and a half, no wonder he sounds exhausted. "Tell me where to find them and I'll bring them over on my way home. I was just leaving anyway."

"You're a lifesaver. Thank you."

Half an hour later I'm walking into the Trafalgar Club, a private gym about a hundred yards from Embankment tube station. The building echoes to the sound of balls slamming against walls, and the muffled noise of the swimming pool. It's surprisingly unpretentious. I have to admit that when Callum gave me directions I was fully expecting one of those five-hundred pounds a month gyms where girls walk around wearing less clothes than they would in Ibiza.

But it's clearly a working gym. Though it has its fair share of slightly overweight businessmen missing every ball that's served to them, as I walk past the courts I'm impressed with most of the games I see. At the back of the building, I find the members' bar. Clutching a manila folder close to my chest I scan the room. Every table is taken, filled with after-work drinkers who look ready to kick back and relax.

"Amy," a voice calls from my left. I swing around in time to see Callum stand to greet me, a pint of bitter in his hand. "We're over here, come and join us."

We turns out to be Callum and Daniel, with no sign of his entourage. Both men have slightly flushed faces, their hair still damp from showering. But it isn't their cleanliness that draws my eye—and that of every other woman in the bar. It's their natural elegance and indifference to scrutiny. They seem to harness a raw, almost dangerous, confidence.

"Hi." I pass Callum the folder and he flicks through it casually. While he's checking the contents I turn to Daniel, who's drinking what looks like a pint of orange juice. "Who won?"

Daniel smiles. "It was a draw."

"Bollocks." Callum puts the folder on the table and grabs his wallet. "Would you like a drink?"

It takes a moment to realise he's talking to me. Then when I do, I feel a blush steal up my chest and neck. It only deepens when I look up and really see him for the first time. Water droplets cling to his dark red hair, dripping on to his unbuttoned collar. His jaw is shadowed with stubble that stops halfway down his throat, leading to pale, unblemished skin.

"A drink?" he prompts again.

"Yes... no, are you sure?" I babble. "You two probably have lots to talk about."

"Join us, please. I don't know about Callum, but I could do with a break from business talk." Daniel leans back, stretching his arm across the back of the chair. I notice a racquetball-shaped bruise on his left bicep and wince. I'm guessing they didn't go easy on each other.

"Okay," I say, taking a seat in the chair next to Callum. "Can I have a glass of white wine, please?"

"Coming up." Callum turns and walks to the bar, and from this vantage point I realise he's wearing jeans. I wonder if he keeps a spare set here or if somebody brought them over for him. That fires my imagination; I start to speculate whether he has a girlfriend or wife. There haven't been any female callers to the office, and there are no photographs on his desk, yet somehow I can't picture a man like him being alone. Instead I picture a tall, blonde girlfriend, an ice-queen with Slavic cheekbones and crystal blue eyes. A contrast to his muscles and dark red, messy hair.

"... college?"

I catch the last word of Daniel's question and turn to him in horror. "I'm sorry, I was miles away. What did you say?"

He bites down what looks like a smirk. "I asked you what you liked best, work or college. Callum told me you've just joined him as an intern."

"I'm not sure yet," I tell him. "It's been a bit of a baptism of fire if I'm honest. There's definitely something nice about putting all that theory into practice but..." I trail off, shrugging. "I kind of like learning the theory too, you know?"

We get into a discussion about the college system in the US, and Daniel confesses he never finished his final year. He tells me about the part-time stock market speculation that grew and grew until he couldn't find the time for school work. It's strange, because I'm sitting here talking to the sort of entrepreneur I've been studying, and yet he puts me totally at ease.

"So tell me." He leans closer. "What do you really think of Callum?"

"I... um..."

"She called me a fox." Callum hands me the wine glass, and grins broadly at me. "Did I get it right?"

"That wasn't me," I protest, remembering that stupid instant message I sent to Charlie. "It was somebody else."

He's still grinning as he sits down, grabbing his beer and taking a long mouthful. "I didn't see you disagreeing."

"A fox? As in a little ratty animal that..." Daniel prompts.

"Eats shit and empties dustbins." I finish for him.

"Well I was going to say trash can, but you're pretty much there."

We both turn to look at Callum. Two mouthfuls of wine have started to mellow me, lending a glow that suffuses my body. I like the way they're making me feel as though I'm their equal, even though hierarchy and experience tell me I'm anything but. In the morning, I might regret this, but for now I'm having fun.

Callum's staring at me. It isn't the casual glance of an acquaintance, or the quick flicker of a disinterested observer. His scrutiny feels stronger and deeper, as if he's assessing and calculating. "She also called me an elitist arsehole." His eyes don't waver as he speaks. I find myself watching his lips, the way they move and curve around each syllable.

"You called me mouthy and opinionated," I say, softly. It feels as if the whole room is burning, heat soaking into my skin. "Does that make us even?"

"When did I say that?"

"In your office the other day, when you were talking with your friend."

His eyes dip lower, to my mouth then my neck. "I thought you weren't listening."

He doesn't sound angry or even exasperated. Only interested.

"There's a lot you don't know about me."

"I'm beginning to see that."

Smiling, he takes another sip of beer, then he reaches across the sticky bar table for the folder I brought. Sorting through the documents, he discusses them with Daniel, while I sit back and watch the two of them talk. My skin is still rosy with a warmth that doesn't disappear even when I press my cool wineglass to my flushed cheeks. Instead it radiates inside me, whispering little truths I don't want to hear.

It's embarrassing and clichéd, not to mention downright forbidden, but there's something about Callum that I can't ignore. As he leans across the table, chatting with Daniel Grant about a million dollar project that's inches away from his grasp, I wonder if I might find my boss more than a wee bit attractive.

* * *

When I let myself into the house an hour later, I can hear raised voices coming from the kitchen. Dropping my bag onto the floor, I pull off my black suede flats, the soles of my feet throbbing in protest. Then I hear mum shouting, and I panic, memories of the strange man flashing in my brain.

Without thinking, I run down the hallway, my chest tight, my throat dry. By the time I fling open the kitchen door I'm breathless, though more from fear than exertion.

"Mum?" I say.

She's leaning against the oven, arms across her chest. Her lips are turned down, creases scratching out from the corner. She doesn't look scared, though. Dissatisfied, maybe. Angry, even.

I see my brother, leaning with his hands on the table. His tendons are taut beneath his skin, tattoos etched across his flesh. There's a tic in his cheek that dances as he stares at Mum.

"What's going on?" I ask. That's when my sister, Andie, steps out of the doorway between the kitchen and living area. Her eyes are red, mascara stains smudged beneath them.

Carrie Elks

Andie doesn't cry. She never has. Even when we were keeping vigil around my six-month-old nephew's hospital bed, she didn't shed a tear. That's why her dishevelment is unnerving.

"Mum." Alex's voice sounds like a warning. I slide my eyes to hers, but she's looking anywhere but at me. "Mum," he prompts again. "Do it."

"Shut up." She bites back. Her voice is tinged with acid. It burns through the air, eating into us all. I'm assailed by memories of days long past, of a teenage Alex staggering through the door, high as a kite with his first tattoo. She laid into him that night, a screaming match so bitter it cut into my ten-year-old soul. Just like then, I feel the need to retreat.

"Do what?" I say. Without thinking, I take a step backward. The movement unbalances me, enough to make my head spin. I reach out and grab the counter, feeling a sticky residue gluing my palm to the surface.

"Amy? Are you okay?" Andie always was part-sister, part-mother. She steps forward, reaching her arms around my waist.

"Wine." I give her a wan smile. "I had two glasses of wine. They've gone straight to my head."

Alex joins us, his shirtsleeves rolled up, his hair mussed from running his hand through it too many times. I frown, trying to work out what the heck it is that's going on. Again I'm taken back fifteen years, to that little girl who can't understand why everybody's shouting.

It used to be awful hearing them all screaming. I would lie in my bed, cuddling my Cuggie, screwing my eyes up as if it would block out the angry words. At times like those the house would pulse with fury.

Then I'd wake in the morning to a silence that was laced with hangovers and regrets. Apologies muttered across a breakfast of black coffee and ibuprofen, while I shovelled spoonfuls of frosted flakes into my mouth, trying to decide if everybody was still angry.

76

But that was years ago. As time passed, first Andie moved out, then Alex followed. Every visit home would reveal a new piece of skin covered with colour, but eventually Mum got used to it. The house changed, became quieter, more sedate, and those ugly rows were a thing of history.

Until now.

"Why are you arguing?" I ask. The three of them are silent. Andie releases me, shooting a glance at Mum.

"It's that man..." she begins, then stops almost as quickly. Rolling her bottom lip between her teeth, she looks over at Alex. Though Andie is the oldest, everybody always defers to Alex. Whether that's because he's the only boy, or by dint of his larger than life personality, I'm not sure. Alex treats the entire world as his stage, and sometimes forgets there are other actors trying to grab their own piece of the limelight.

"He's a nasty piece of work," Alex adds. "I don't want him near you."

"I told you he wasn't a problem. He won't talk to her again."

"You told us a lot of things," my brother bites back. "But most of them were a pack of lies."

I look at Mum. "Who is he? If you don't owe him money, and he's not after our stuff, why's he hanging around here?"

Mum looks down, her voice uncharacteristically quiet. "He's nobody. He won't hurt you, he won't come around here again. Those two are just being overprotective as usual."

"I'd still feel better if you stayed with us for a while," Alex says. "Lara doesn't mind and I can keep an eye on you."

I sigh. "I'm twenty three, Alex. I can look after myself. Anyway, there's not enough room to swing a cat in your flat. Where exactly will I sleep, in the bath?"

"Come and stay with me," Andie suggests. "You can sleep on my sofa bed." She has a one-bedroom flat near Brick Lane. It feels squashed when two people are in there.

"So I can sleep in Alex's bath or in your lounge?" I clarify. "No thanks, I think I'll stay in my nice cosy bedroom. Mum says he won't be around anymore and that's good enough for me."

I sound braver than I feel. I haven't forgotten the air of menace emanating from that man, or the way I was shaking when I walked through the door after our first encounter. But I've come across intimidating men like him before and survived, I just need to be extra cautious.

"Now if it's alright with you lot, I'm off to bed. Some of us have work in the morning." I hug Alex first, then Andie, and plant a kiss on my mum's cheek.

When I get up to my room, I'm dog-tired. Exhaustion makes my bones ache and my skin throb. I take my clothes off, letting them fall into a messy pile on the floor, then pull on my pyjamas, deciding I'll shower in the morning.

The three of them have always treated me like the baby of the family, and for a while I was happy to be exactly that. It made up for the times when Alex and Andie would leave to visit their dad, while I was left at home on my own. I've always envied them that; although their father was an alcoholic and his visits were intermittent at best, at least they had him. My own dad died after I was born, a casualty of the first Gulf War, and I can't remember him at all.

I think that's why Alex is so overprotective. He hates to see me hurt or worried, or going through anything a normal sister would. Every time I'm knocked over by life he tries to cushion my fall, and if he had his way he'd cover me with bubble wrap.

What once was sweet is becoming increasingly stifling, and tonight is yet more evidence of that. I'm still fretting about things when the fog of sleep overwhelms me, muddying my thoughts and weighing on my body like a blanket. My breathing slows, my eyes flickering beneath paper-thin lids, and finally I disappear into a restless slumber.

9

Callum is out of the office for most of Friday, and I busy myself with emptying my inbox, then finishing off his expenses. I print out the form and carry it into his office for him to sign when he returns, placing it on the top of his in tray.

His desk is as messy as always, strewn with printed emails and scribbled pages he's ripped out of notepads. Lines of codes and lists of things to do mingle in with reminders to pick up a present for his mum's birthday and to call his accountant about his tax return. I'm not the tidiest person in the world, but this cluttered chaos is enough to make my head spin. I'm tempted to scoop all the pieces of paper into his bin and reveal the polished cherry wood beneath it all.

As I go to leave, I walk into the top drawer he's left half-open. The wood scrapes my nylon-covered leg, and I reach down to rub it.

A glint of silver catches my eye, and I pull open the drawer to see a photograph frame lying in there. It's face-down, the metallic edges curving against the black leather back, and without thinking, I pick it up.

The glass covering the black and white photograph is dusty, and I run my finger across it until the tip is coated in white residue. It isn't the dirt that catches my eye, but the glamorous couple smiling behind the glass, their faces shining with a happiness that makes my breath stick in my throat.

It's a wedding photo. Callum stands there in a black jacket and tie, his legs covered in a blue and black tartan kilt. Beside him is a willowy blonde, her silvery hair caught in a chignon that spills out curls, her head resting on his shoulder.

They are model-beautiful, her slim figure a contrast to his broad frame, and I find myself staring at them for long minutes, wondering why he hasn't mentioned her. Frowning, I try to picture his left hand—the one that sports a thick, silver band in the photo—and try to remember if I've seen the same ring in real life.

Is he still married? Divorced? He's usually here when I arrive first thing in the morning and is still punching at his keyboard when I leave at night; he doesn't give the impression of a man racing home to spend time with his beautiful wife. For some reason I find that thought unnerving.

If I'm truly being honest with myself, looking at this blonde bombshell on his arm makes me sick with envy.

I'm not sure what that says about me.

When I hear the door click, I hastily replace the photograph, sliding the drawer shut with my dusty fingers. Then I walk out to find Charlie standing next to my desk wearing his wool pea coat, a satchel slung across his shoulder.

"Hey! I wasn't sure you were still here." His smile is wide, and my racing heart starts to calm. "How was your day?"

I wipe my fingertips on my hips. "Surprisingly good. I think I'm getting used to this working thing." In truth, this place has started to feel like my haven. Though there's a learning curve and my first days with Callum were hard work, there's something about this office that's becoming my happy place. "How was yours?"

"Well I didn't break anything so I'm counting it as a win." He curls his fingers around the back of my chair. "A few of us are going out for a quick drink, would you like to join us?"

I glance back at Callum's empty office. From its disarray I assume he's planning to pop back at some point this evening, and there's a part of me that wants to hang around when he does. Since our drink at the Trafalgar Club, he's definitely softened his approach towards me, and I've definitely started to warm to him.

Okay, maybe more than warm. Not quite a burn, though. Not yet.

"I'm meeting a couple of friends later, but I've got an hour or two," I say, glancing at my watch. Ellie and I arranged to meet at eight in Covent Garden, and she texted me this morning to say a reluctant Sophie would be joining us. I haven't spoken to Sophie since our argument about Luke, and the thought of some liquid courage beforehand is quite appealing.

Charlie waits for me as I log off and lock up my drawers. I loop a soft pink scarf around my neck and pull on my jacket, grabbing the handbag stashed under the desk.

"Where are we going?" I ask Charlie as we walk down the corridor. Half the offices are empty, abandoned early by occupants impatient for the weekend, and it makes the hour feel later than it is.

"Just around the corner to China's," Charlie says. We both reach out to press the lift call button, and I beat him by half a second. "It will be full of partners and consultants, but Caro chose it." He shrugs.

The lift arrives, doors sliding open with a slight creak. Then Callum walks out, his pace slowing as he sees me. A smile breaks out on his serious face, and I find myself returning it.

"You leaving?" he asks. I refrain from pointing out the obvious, and nod in agreement.

"Yes, we're off to the pub."

"Well, enjoy your weekend." Callum presses on the lift button to keep the doors open, and I see Charlie waiting just inside. "Thanks for your hard work this week."

I feel a strange twinge in the pit of my stomach. It's like somebody plucking a guitar string deep inside of me; it echoes and vibrates. "Thank you for putting up with me."

He puts his palm on my lower back, where my spine starts to curve. Even through two layers of fabric I feel my skin warm. The gentle pressure makes me step forward, into the waiting lift, and I turn to face the doors as he steps backward. When they close, the steel sheets obscure his face, but the memory of his stare remains on my retinas.

* * *

The bar is heaving. People stand hip to hip, their sharp business suits wilting in the face of the steamy atmosphere. Our group of five has been here for three hours. Caro's boss has been paid a big bonus and has generously put her black Amex card behind the bar, and we're making the most of it. Though I'm not Caro's biggest fan—and she certainly isn't mine—it's amazing how the lure of free champagne can pour oil on troubled waters.

"You want another?" Charlie's voice is thickened by intoxication. There's a twitch in his right eye that's becoming more pronounced with every mouthful. I hand him my glass and he upends the bottle, the trickle of bubbles only filling it halfway.

"Damn, I shall have to order more." In an attempt to curb his slurring, he over-pronounces every word. He's becoming posher, too. Raising his hand, he hails the cocktail waiter. "Bartender, my good man."

"Some people can't take their drink." Caro rolls her eyes. "Whereas you, Amy, can drink like a soldier."

When she looks at me she wrinkles her nose, enough for me to know it isn't a compliment. "Where's that lovely boss of yours anyway? I thought all the partners were here." Caro scans the room, searching this way and that. For the first time tonight I'm glad Callum isn't here. I don't think I'd be able to watch her flirt with him.

Just before seven, I get a text from Ellie, saying that Sophie has a headache and can't make our night out. After a rapid exchange of messages, we decide to skip dinner and clubbing in the West End in favour of an evening of free drinks right here in Canary Wharf. Ellie arrives at eight, her slim legs encased in a pair of shiny leggings and her midriff bare, revealing the butterfly she had tattooed on her hip last year. I try not to wince when everybody looks at her as she walks in, eyeing her outfit as if it's some kind of fancy-dress costume.

"Amy!" she calls, running over in her skyscraper heels, their height making her wobble as she crosses the room.

I shouldn't be embarrassed by my best friend, especially since she's been so supportive with the Luke situation. I ignore the stares and step forward, throwing my arms around her waist.

"You look gorgeous," I say loudly. To be fair she really does. It's just that among the crisp white shirts and wool jackets, she's some kind of exotic bird.

Out of place. Unexpected.

"Is this outfit okay?" She tugs at her top, but nothing she does is going to cover her stomach. "I thought people would be a bit more dressed up."

"It's perfect. You need to tell me where you got those leggings."

Ellie grins. We both know there's no way I'd wear leggings and a crop top, not with the curve in my spine. Tight clothes only make it more obvious; one of the reasons I've always preferred loose and floaty to slinky and fitted.

I make the introductions, ignoring Caro's smirk and her friend Miranda's wide eyes. Then Charlie saunters back, bottle of champagne in one hand and a tumbler of whisky in the other, his eyes restless and unable to focus.

"It's a pleasure to meet you," he says, offering Ellie a glass of champagne. "What department do you work in?"

Caro coughs a laugh, muttering, "Slut department." Luckily Ellie doesn't hear. Instead she starts up a conversation with Charlie about the joys of working in administration, and I silently thank him for being so bloody nice.

As the evening progresses, we all join Charlie in varying states of drunkenness. Miranda manages to spill a whole glass of red wine down the front of her dress, and runs to the bathroom to scrub it off. Caro joins a group of her teammates, flirting and flattering her way to the top, while Charlie, Ellie and I hang around at the bar, moving from champagne to bottled beer in an attempt to stop the room spinning.

The two of them are getting on famously, enough for me to feel no compunction when I head for the bathroom.

I'm almost there when somebody grabs my wrist, fingers slipping around me like a bracelet, the touch gentle but firm. I turn, a champagne-fuelled smile painted on my lips, and come face to face with a broad, white-cotton covered chest. I stare at it for a moment, taking in the way the fabric is thin and close to his skin, before my eyes climb past the unbuttoned neck that reveals a covering of light brown hairs, to a jawline that's both familiar yet new.

"Amy." Callum says my name quietly, and I have to lean forward to hear him over the music. I'm close enough to feel his warm breath fan against me. It's laced with liquor, the hint of whisky lingering in the air, and I breathe him in unthinkingly, liking the way he smells.

"Hi." My smile remains. "I didn't expect to see you here."

The pad of his thumb rubs circles into the sensitive underside of my arm, causing goose bumps to break out.

"Jonathan dragged me out," he confesses. "This isn't my usual scene. He heard Susan Davies put her card behind the bar and insisted we made an appearance." His eyes twinkle. "So here I am."

He has to stoop to talk to me, leaning down so he can catch my eye. I see him in soft focus, the drink stealing any sharpness from my vision, and I'm not sure if it's only the champagne that's warming my belly.

"It *is* Friday night," I say. "All work and no play makes Callum..." I trail off, not wanting to call him a dull boy.

"Rich?" he suggests, raising an eyebrow. His response makes me giggle, and I wobble a little, reaching out to steady myself against him. My palm spreads against his shirt, feeling the hard flesh beneath, as his fingers tighten on my wrist.

"Rich is better than dull," I agree.

"That's what they say." He doesn't pull away. "Although I suspect for a lot of women rich and dull is perfectly acceptable."

"Not for me." I slowly shake my head.

The corner of his lip twitches. "No, I didn't think so. You don't strike me as the sort to suffer fools."

This makes me laugh. "You haven't met my ex." I think about Luke and the way he treated me for years. I was the biggest fool of all.

"No I haven't," Callum murmurs. "I don't think I want to, either. Exes are usually exes for a reason."

"Well Luke's reason is he was a cheating arsehole." I don't know why I'm saying this, and to my boss of all people. But there's something about the way he's looking at me—and holding me—that makes me soften.

"Then he's a bloody fool."

Somebody barges into me from behind, pushing me closer to Callum. My hand slips, splaying across the middle of his chest, and I can feel his pulse beating rapidly. My own body beats in time, my breathing fast and my blood thick. Somewhere deep inside my subconscious tries to make itself heard. This is my boss and we're surrounded by work colleagues, but my body doesn't seem to be listening.

"Your heart is racing," I whisper.

"So is yours." His thumb presses into my vein, and the sensation sends a shiver down my spine. He lowers his head, staring straight into my eyes. "Why is that, do you think?"

His lips are so close to mine I can almost feel them. I'd only have to roll onto the balls of my feet to close that final inch, and feel the pressure of his kiss. Yet in spite of the alcohol running through my body I hesitate for a moment. My mouth is dry, my breath caught in my throat, yet I still can't pull my stare from his.

"That took fucking forever." A voice startles me from behind. "I think Simon Jenkins has set up a coke factory in the men's toilets."

I step back, pulling my hand from Callum's chest, and he lets go of my wrist. It falls to my side, my fingers curled into a fist as I try to work out what the hell just happened.

"Hi Amy." Jonathan Cooper smiles, his head angled to one side. "I didn't know you were here."

I pull at the neck of my blouse and try to look anywhere but at him. "I'm here with some friends. I was just going to the bathroom and..."

"She took pity on her lonely boss." This time Callum's smile is tight, painted on for appearance's sake. "Thanks, Amy."

"You're welcome," I murmur. "I'll just... go." I gesture in the direction of the toilets. "Have a good evening."

"You too." Callum's voice is low, but it caresses my ears anyway. "I'll see you on Monday."

"Monday," I say.

I give them a half wave and walk away, feeling the warmth of their gazes on the back of my neck. My heart is still hammering, and the first thing I do when I get to the toilets is splash my face with cold water. Then I walk into a stall, locking it behind me, and lean my head against the brightly painted wall. I'm torn between screaming and laughing, my emotions darting between elation and embarrassment.

When I think about the way he stared back at me, his eyes soft and warm, elation wins.

10

Saturday morning disappears beneath the fog of a hangover that pounds inside my head and curdles the contents of my stomach. I clutch my duvet with shaking hands and turn over, squeezing my eyes tight to ward off the cold light of day. Mum leaves for work at ten, banging the front door closed, and the noise makes me groan and bury myself deeper beneath the bedcovers, unwilling to do anything except go back to sleep.

At lunchtime my fight against the encroaching day is lost, and I drag my protesting body out of bed, half-crawling to the bathroom. It's then that memories of last night come flooding back, as if somebody's opened up a dam, and I blink as images flash inside my mind, each one somehow more mortifying than the last.

Charlie dancing on the table, flinging his jacket and tie in Caro's boss's face.

Ellie joining him, teaching him how to twerk, as a hundred consultants stared at them, open mouthed.

Miranda throwing up in the corner of the bar, vomit clinging to her hair as she staggered outside, mascara running down her cheeks.

Then I remember my encounter with Callum, and the rest of the evening pales into insignificance. Groaning, I step into the steaming shower, rubbing my face with the heels of my hands. But even when I press them so hard against my eyes that I see stars, I still can't dispel the images.

That afternoon I head over to Shoreditch where my brother and his wife live. Climbing the narrow staircase that leads to their floor, I attempt to pull myself together and shake off the final vestiges of my hangover. I don't want Alex and Lara to think I'm irresponsible, especially since they're going out and leaving me in charge of Max. Nor do I want my baby nephew to grow up thinking his Auntie Amy is a lush.

Alex pulls the door open before I even get a chance to knock. He's wearing a tight-fitting navy suit with a skinny black tie, his dark hair brushed off his face.

"Thank god you're here, we got the time wrong. We were supposed to be at the church five minutes ago."

"Is that Amy?" I hear my sister-in-law shout from the bedroom. "Can you show her where everything is?"

I roll my eyes. "I think I can cope." Max is sitting on a blanket in the middle of the floor, playing with some plastic rings. I scoop him up and swing him around high before blowing raspberries on his neck; my reward is a high-pitched squeal.

A harassed-looking Lara emerges from the bedroom. She's wearing a short floral dress and pretty heels, her hair swept into an updo, enhancing her impossibly high cheeks. She presses her glossy lips to Max's head then kisses the air next to me. "We've got to run, I'm so sorry. I swear the invitation said three o'clock."

I laugh, mostly because I'm glad it's not me who's panicking for a change. "It's okay, just go. Max and I will be fine."

"If you're sure..." For a moment she looks lost. Then Alex grabs her hand, folding it inside his, and her shoulders visibly relax. I flash her a reassuring smile and help Max wave his hand at her.

"Say bye bye, Mummy," I whisper. He babbles incomprehensibly then wriggles in my arms until I put him back on the floor. Alex and Lara leave as I kneel down on the blanket, helping Max put the brightly coloured rings in size order.

We play for a while until Max gets bored and starts throwing the rings away. Then he crawls to the table and pulls himself up, grabbing the magazine Lara's left open. Grinning broadly, his two front teeth showing, he rips out a page and scrunches it up in his chubby hand.

"Ba ba ba," he says.

"Naughty," I chide him, gently pulling the rest of the magazine from his grasp. "Leave Mummy's magazine alone."

Max grins then dips his head to chew on the wooden table, and I realise it's going to be a long afternoon.

Twenty minutes later, I'm feeding Max chocolate buttons in an attempt to distract him from his appetite for destruction. Brown goo covers my fingers and drips from his mouth, staining his otherwise clean vest. I'm about to wipe him when my phone buzzes in my pocket, and I reach in with my clean hand to check the caller.

The number isn't in my contacts, so I let it go through to voicemail. A minute later the screen lights up again, suggesting I may want to retrieve my message.

I put the phone to my ear, still feeding Max with my other hand. He makes a grab for the bag and pulls it down to his feet, chocolate buttons spilling out across his blanket.

He looks delighted with himself, but I can't tell him off because that's when the recording begins.

"Ah, Amy, it's Callum, sorry to call you at the weekend. Look, I really need a favour, so if you could call me back, that would be great. Thanks."

I sit there for a moment wondering why he's called. Then Max reaches out and grabs my left boob, smearing half-digested chocolate all over my shirt.

Once we've both cleaned up and I've given Max a teddy bear to play with, I press redial. Callum picks up before the second ring has finished echoing down the earpiece.

"Amy?" He sounds breathless.

"Hi. I got your message, is everything okay?" I think I might sound a little breathless, too.

"Yeah, I've just done something stupid. I've managed to lose the key to the filing cabinet and I need some papers from it. I want to give Daniel the draft contract before his flight leaves tonight. I don't suppose you have the spare key, do you?"

I glance over at my bag, which I've put on the bookshelf. Max has a bag fetish and if you leave it within his reach, he'll empty the contents everywhere. The last time he did it, a box of condoms spilled out. Alex wasn't impressed; no man wants the evidence of his sister's sex life thrown in his face. In this case, literally.

"Yeah, it's on my key ring."

"Thank Christ." He sighs. "Can I come over and pick it up?"

For some reason, I don't want Callum coming here. His jibes about me coming from the east end of London make me reluctant for him to see where I'm from. "I can bring them over," I suggest. "Where are you?"

"I'm at the office. Are you sure you don't mind? I have my car..."

"It's fine, I'll hop on the bus. I should be there in half an hour."

"Great." He sounds relieved. "I owe you one."

Over the next forty minutes I discover that getting a baby ready, strapping him into his pushchair and manoeuvring it onto the bus takes considerably longer than I'd anticipated. By the time I make it to Canary Wharf, I'm harassed, worn out, and regretting agreeing to meet Callum at all. Max fell asleep at some point in the bus journey, and his head lolls against the back of the buggy as I push it across the concrete square.

Turning the corner, I spot Callum pacing up and down in front of the office building. He looks up and sees me, and shock moulds his expression.

"Amy?" He doesn't sound so sure.

"I'm sorry it took so long," I say, talking quickly to cover my embarrassment. "I know he looks cute but I think Max might actually be the devil in disguise." I gesture at my sleeping nephew.

"I didn't realise... I'm sorry. I would never have asked you to come over here if I knew."

I shake my head, confused. "He only fell asleep on the journey. He was awake when we left."

"No, I meant I wouldn't have expected you to come at all. I didn't know you had a baby."

It dawns on me that Callum thinks Max is mine, which makes me blush madly. I open my mouth to put him straight when he drops on his haunches to gaze at Max.

"He's beautiful," he says quietly. "He looks just like you." His eyes flick to me when he says the last bit.

"Thank you," I reply, wondering if he realises he just paid me a compliment. "But he's my nephew, not my son."

It's Callum's turn to be embarrassed. He laughs and stands up, towering over me. I'm wearing a pair of skinny jeans with a pair of red flat shoes, so I'm a couple of inches shorter than when he usually sees me.

For some reason, I like the way he makes me feel petite.

"Well, he still looks like you."

"You should have seen him earlier when he was covered in chocolate." I smile at Callum. "He looked like a monster."

"He seems pretty cute now."

I reach into the pocket of my handbag. "I have your keys here." I pull my key ring out and remove the key to the filing cabinet, placing it in his hard, leathery palm. "Go get your contract."

"Thank you." His fingers curl around the metal. "If you wait here while I run upstairs I can give you both a lift home."

My eyes widen in alarm. His offer seems too... personal. "It's okay, I bought a return ticket."

"I insist. It's the least I can do." His expression softens. "To say thank you."

I'm torn. Part of me wants to take him up on his offer just to spend some more time with him. But then I remember last night and the tension between us, the way I felt when he touched my wrist. This infatuation with him is embarrassing, not to mention dangerous. Especially when I know it's one-sided.

"You don't have a car seat. It would be illegal." I shrug in an attempt to feign nonchalance. "We'll be fine."

Callum hesitates, his hand opening and closing around the key. "You're right," he replies, finally. "In that case I owe you a drink. Coffee, tea, gin, the choice is yours."

"It wasn't a problem, honestly, so there's no need to buy me anything. It's all in a day's work." I grab the buggy's handles. "I suppose I'd better get this little monkey home and give him some tea. Otherwise I won't be his favourite auntie anymore."

"I suppose you should." Callum doesn't move. He's still standing in front of me, as if he's reluctant to let me leave. "Are you babysitting all night?"

I tip my head to the side. "Why? Do you have a better offer?"

Somebody walks out of the office building, brushing past Callum. I watch him pass, relieved when I realise it's nobody I know. In spite of the innocence of our conversation, making small talk with my boss, somehow makes me feel guilty.

Callum swallows, making his Adam's apple bob. His tongue snakes across his dry lips. "I'll be spending the evening fine combing this contract with Daniel Grant and his team, so unless that constitutes a better offer..."

I wrinkle my nose up. "I think I'll stick with dirty nappies and puréed carrots."

He nods slowly. "A wise choice."

"Thank you." I mime a curtsy in a rare bout of playfulness. "I suppose I should go." I wave my hand in the direction of the bus stop. "Do you need anything else?"

This feels like one of those telephone conversations where neither of you wants to hang up. I linger, not wanting to leave, unable to find an excuse to stay.

Callum takes a step forward and brushes his palm against my arm. Even through two layers of clothing I swear I can feel his fingertips.

"Thank you. I mean it. I know I gave you a hard time when you started, but..." He shrugs. "This was above the call of duty and I appreciate it."

There isn't the slightest hint of sarcasm in his voice; nothing remains of the superiority I heard when we first met. I'm unsure if it's me who has changed or if it's him, but right now all I want to do is step into his arms.

That's why I stagger back, pulling the buggy with me. Because it isn't Callum I don't trust, with his friendly words and kind face, it's me. I've just ended one relationship and it's clear I'm rebounding on to my boss. It would be funny if it wasn't shameful. "It was no problem, honestly. I'll see you on Monday."

A gust of wind whips around me, brushing my heated cheeks and lifting my hair from my neck. Max's legs move in his sleep; his tiny, sock-covered feet kicking at the blanket. I give Callum a wave and turn the buggy around, walking towards the main road.

By the time I get to the bus stop I'm a big, messy bundle of hormones and desire.

* * *

Max goes to bed nicely, sucking at the tips of his fingers as he bundles up beneath the covers, his breathing rapid and loud. I stand there for a minute and stare, marvelling at the way his tiny eyelids flutter as he dreams. Every now and again he moans softly, wriggling until his covers pool around his ankles, and I lift them up again, draping them across his shoulders, running my fingers across his soft, plump face.

Callum was right; Max is beautiful. His skin is smooth and unmarked, his lips a perfect bow. His eyelashes—dark and thick like Alex's and mine—are so long they almost sweep his rosy cheeks. I hate the thought that one day somebody's going to break his heart. I want to claw their eyes out already.

Closing his door gently, I tiptoe back into the living room, curling up on the sofa and scrolling through my phone. My back twinges and I try to sit up straight, aware that I should have gone to yoga this morning.

I while away the next hour uploading pictures of Max to Instagram and listening to music through one headphone. The other dangles down as I keep an ear free to listen out for his cries.

At nine o'clock Luke adds a photograph to his account. He's standing outside a bar with a goofy grin on his face, his arm around the same girl he swore he wasn't sleeping with. In the background I can see Nick and Sophie, and it makes my chest hurt.

The fact I'm more upset about my friend's betrayal than that of my ex-boyfriend doesn't escape me. It feels reassuring, somehow. The wound is scabbing over, new skin growing beneath.

Alex and Lara get home a few minutes after midnight. From the noise they make on the stairs and the way Alex's voice echoes through the house, I can tell he's been drinking before they even walk in the door. I bite down a smile; Alex drunk is always a sight to be seen. He's silly, funny and completely larger than life.

The door opens, the handle banging against the plastered wall, and Alex walks in; his face flushed, his words slurred. "Amy! How's my favourite sister? Come here, gimme a kiss." He throws his arms around me, his bristled cheeks scratching against mine. The sensation makes me giggle.

"Don't let Andie hear you say that."

Alex steps back, holding me at arm's length. "She's my favourite older sister. You're my favourite baby sister. There's a difference."

Lara walks in. "Has he got to the 'I love yous'?" she asks.

"Not yet. But it's inevitable." I grin back at her.

Alex stumbles and I steady him. "I'd say it's bedtime."

Alex pouts. "But I want to talk to you. Are you okay? Has that guy bothered you again?"

"What guy?"

"The one... the one outside your house. Digger."

"Alex." Lara's voice is low. "It's time for bed."

"I'm just talking to my sister." He looks at me with concern. "You okay, sweetheart?"

I hug him tight. "I'm fine, which is more than you'll be when you wake up in the morning. Now go to bed."

"Et tu, Brutus?"

I bite down a laugh. "It's Brute. You've been watching too much Popeye." Alex always did spend too much time in front of the T.V. "I love you big brother."

He pulls me in tightly, burying his face in my hair. "Goodnight."

He stumbles down the hallway to their bedroom, leaving Lara and me alone in the living room. She takes off her shoes and wriggles her toes, then walks to the kitchen and flips on the kettle. "Have you got time for a cuppa, or do you want me to call a cab?"

"Tea sounds good." I smile. "I'm not in a rush."

Lara potters in the kitchen, pulling out mugs and tea bags, spoons and milk. When she looks up she catches my eye and grins. "Thank you for looking after Max," she says. "I still hate leaving him."

"He was a good boy. We had to go to Canary Wharf to give something to my boss and he was perfectly behaved."

"You had to work? What a slave driver, I hope you got paid overtime." She hands me a mug and I cup my fingers around the china.

Lara has this aura about her that makes people want to open up and spill their secrets. When I first met her I thought it was just me she had this effect on. But as time has passed and I've watched her interact with others—with family, with friends—I've come to realise she brings the best out in everybody. It's why she's so perfectly suited to her job as a counsellor. She listens without judging, which few people are able to do.

"I wanted to help him," I confess. "He's a nice guy."

Lara says nothing. Just looks at me with melted chocolate eyes as she takes a sip of warm tea.

"What?" I ask.

She shakes her head. "Nothing."

"You think I like him?"

"Do you?"

I put my tea down and run my hands through my hair. "Yes." Only three letters, yet I feel every one of them as the admission escapes me. They say the truth hurts, and they're right, because admitting I like my boss is like having my teeth pulled out.

"Yes I like him, but I shouldn't. For one thing he's my boss, and for another I think he might be married." I drop my head, my brow meeting my palms. "God, I'm such a loser,"

"You're not a loser," Lara counters. "Office romances happen all the time. It's not unusual."

"It is when you can lose your job for having a work relationship."

Lara looks at me. "Really?"

"Yeah."

"Wow." She raises her eyebrows. "I suppose it's an American company. They get funny about things like that."

"Yes they do." I sigh. "So it's just a stupid crush that I'm going to have to ignore." The words make it sound easy, but the little fire he ignited on Friday is threatening to burn out of control. I've spent most of the night thinking about him, wondering what he's doing, whether his dinner with Daniel Grant is going well. If truth be told I didn't mind going out to meet him this afternoon; quite the opposite.

"You're not planning on getting back with Luke, then?" she asks, sitting down on the sofa. "It's definitely over?"

I pull out my phone and show Lara the Instagram photo of Luke and the girl. Like before, I'm more struck by Sophie's betrayal than Luke's new love—the fact she's made a miraculous recovery since last night hasn't escaped me, either.

"We've been over for a long time," I admit. "I know you kept telling me he was wrong for me, but it took me a while to realise." I look down, picking a piece of lint off my jeans. "I wouldn't go back even if he came crawling to beg." I tell her about the night at Sophie's and the cruel things he said in the car. She reaches out, squeezing my hand, sympathy shaping her features.

"It sounds trite, but these things happen for a reason. I know the two of you share a lot of history, but he treated you like shit. The number of times I've had to pull Alex away to stop him hitting Luke..." Lara trails off, glancing over at the bedroom door.

I swallow, thinking of the ways I let Luke walk all over me. After all this time together, maybe I should be sad it's over. But the truth is I'm more consumed with relief than anything else.

Get a degree, get a job and get the hell out of here, I remind myself. That's my goal, and I can't afford to let anybody get in the way. Not Luke and his wandering eye, not Sophie and her fake illness, and certainly not Callum Ferguson with his strong, hard chest and gorgeous smile.

If only my heart believed that.

11

When I get into the office on Monday morning Callum's nowhere to be seen. I slide into my chair to check my emails, and the first one I see is from the HR department. An emergency meeting has been called for all the new interns, and attendance is mandatory.

Something has riled Diana Joseph, and I'm pretty sure it's our drunken Friday night. Groaning, I put my computer to sleep and head down to the conference room, stopping on the way to grab myself a coffee from the canteen.

Charlie Simpson is already in the conference room when I arrive, his pale blonde hair hanging over his eyes, his skin tinged with grey. I slide into the seat next to him, offering one of the biscuits I grabbed from the tin, and he smiles wanly, taking the proffered cookie.

"You look as excited as I feel," I comment. "You okay?"

He shakes his head. "I've never had a forty-eight hour hangover before and I never want one again. I can't even remember what happened on Friday night." He turns and grabs my hand suddenly. "Did I do anything stupid?"

I frown when I remember the twerking, not to mention the round of body shots he insisted on taking off Ellie's bare abdomen. When I talked to her last night she was equally as sheepish, but I think she might have a little crush on him.

"Um," I roll my lips together, waggling my eyebrows. "Define stupid."

He drops his head into his hands, muttering incoherently. I reach out and rub his shoulder in an attempt to be consoling, but he shrugs me off.

"You shouldn't sit next to me, you'll be guilty by association."

"You didn't do anything wrong. Okay, so you dirty danced and told every woman in the room you loved them, but you did it with style."

He shakes his head. "Not helping."

The room fills up as the rest of the interns arrive, coffees in hand. Caro Hawes sweeps in holding a cup from Cafe Nero, then wrinkles her nose when she sees Charlie and me.

I wrinkle right back.

"Charlie Simpson? Miranda Vesey?" One of the HR administration assistants pops her head around the door. "Can you come with me, please?" The tone of her voice makes it clear it isn't a question. Charlie stands up reluctantly, grabs his half-empty coffee cup and walks over to the door.

"Wish me luck," he says, under his breath.

"Good luck."

He walks out, closely followed by Miranda, who looks as if she's going to faint. I can't say I blame her; she spent most of Friday night pebble dashing the bar floor with vomit, and half the partners saw her doing it.

After they've left, the room is silent for a moment, as we all stare at the door wondering what is happening. I feel sick myself when I think they might be asking Charlie to leave; I'm not sure I can face working in this place without him.

"You should be there too, you know." Caro sits down next to me. She looks angry. "You drank as much champagne as they did."

I don't bother telling her I can obviously hold it better than they can, because I feel guilty as hell. The three of us egged each other on, matched each other drink for drink. It's only my metabolism—and the fact I started drinking at the tender age of fifteen—that's prevented me from being taken out with Charlie and Miranda.

"I didn't do anything." *So fuck off.* The final words remain unspoken, but I'm pretty sure Caro gets the message. She flicks her hair over her shoulder and glares at me anyway.

"You won't get away with it. I know your type. If Miranda is sacked I'll make sure you pay for it. I should never have trusted you to look after her."

My voice is thick. "She's old enough to look after herself."

"She's younger than you." She sounds accusatory. "And don't think I didn't see you, draped all over your boss. You're not exactly smelling of bloody roses."

I blush enough to make her smirk. She's got me and she knows it. I can swear to the bible that Callum is only a boss, but my physiology's betraying me. "Nothing happened. You're being a bitch."

She leans close, enough for me to feel her hot breath. "You've no fucking idea what a bitch I can be. I don't like you, Amy Cartwright, and I'd be happy to see your arse walking out the door." Her expression is anything but pleasant. "So watch yourself, because I'll make sure I am."

By the time Miranda and Charlie walk back in, their eyes downcast, I'm feeling awkward and worried. Then the HR manager sweeps in, her face stormy, her voice harsh, and she reminds us all why we should re-read the code of conduct, with the black veil of dismissal hanging over us all.

* * *

"Hey." Callum looks up when I walk back into the office. His expression is light and open. There's a part of me that feels pulled to it, that aches to be as at ease as him. He looks amazing as usual. Comfortable in his skin and in his expertly tailored suit, his hair hanging over his brow, his eyes bright.

I feel like a blurred photograph hanging next to a Warhol.

"Hi." My voice is as flat as I feel. I walked back to the office with Charlie, who revealed he's had a final warning about his conduct. One more wrong step and he's out. The thought frightens me. He's the only person I look forward to talking with when I walk in the building—well him and Callum—but he's the only one I *should* be talking to.

"You okay?" Callum asks.

"We just got a telling off from HR. Apparently we aren't allowed to have fun."

He tries not to smile and I hate the way he looks appealing and sexy. *Frustrating bastard.*

"What happened?"

I sigh loudly and sink into my chair. Callum stands up and walks around his desk, out of his office and into my space. His proximity warms me, in spite of myself. I hate and love the way he makes me feel.

"According to them we embarrassed the whole company on Friday. We've been reminded that we shouldn't be drinking alcohol, enjoying ourselves or even speaking. We should be seen but not heard." I may be exaggerating but the sting of their reprimand still lingers. Callum stares at me, perplexed.

"What?"

"We're all banned from China's." It's true. I don't think I've been banned from anywhere before. It's humiliating. "Until further notice."

Callum's stuck somewhere between amusement and annoyance. I watch as the two emotions battle for supremacy, his expression morphing until he finally settles on bemusement. "Seriously?"

"Yes. They seem to think we're all toddlers. I can't believe they've banned us." My cheeks flame as brightly as a tomato.

Callum sits on the corner of my desk, picking up a sheaf of papers and idly leafing through them. "Ignore it, they'll forget about it before you do. I remember when I was at Oxford..."

I snap. "You tore up somebody's teddy bear?"

He tips his head to the side. "You really think I'm an elitist arsehole, don't you?"

I nervously rake my hands through my hair. "No. Well maybe... no." I prevaricate long enough to make us both confused. "I'm sorry, it's just that you wouldn't understand."

"Try me." His voice is a whisper.

The frustration crescendos inside me. "You've had it easy all of your life, I had to fight my way here, and the fact it could be stolen from me..." I squeeze my eyes shut. "It frightens me."

"You think I've had it easy?" he questions, his tone strained. "What makes you think you know anything about me?"

My eyes snap open. I stare at him, taking in the way he exudes wealth. "What? Did the silver spoon bend a little in your mouth? Did you get a paper cut on the wad of money your parents gave you?" I sound bitter because I am. I've grown up knowing there are people who are much better off than me, but to have him talking it down in front of me is wrong.

His Scottish burr becomes prominent when he's angry. "You know nothing. You think you're the only one that's suffered? You think money prevents people from feeling pain? Maybe you should walk a few miles in my shoes."

"What?" I scoff. "Did your nanny spit in your porridge? Did the boys at boarding school shove your head down the toilet?"

He backs away as if I'm full of venom. "Don't say anything else."

But I'm on a roll. An anti-elitist, no-bullshit roll. "When you've had the bailiffs knocking at your door because you can't pay their exorbitant fucking interest, maybe you can lecture me," I storm. "When you're afraid to go home because some bloody weirdo might be waiting for you, then you can tell me I'm wrong."

He frowns. "What weirdo?"

I shake my head, but he steps forward, his face marred with concern. "What fucking weirdo? Tell me."

When I speak, my voice feels raw, as if I've been flayed. "It's just a guy."

"Tell me."

He's so reassuring it frightens me, and I'm aware that's a contradiction. But I've never relied on anybody except Alex and Andy, and the fact he's trying to involve himself in my problems is alarming.

"It's nothing."

"Bullshit," he says. "What fucking weirdo is waiting for you?"

I don't know whether I want Callum to back off or hold on. "There was some guy hanging around my house last week. He knew my name."

"Did you call the police?" he asks with clipped words. It's obvious that in his easy, clean-cut world, involving the law would be the only thing to do.

"My mum..." I feel like I'm cracking. "She doesn't always stay on the right side of the law. Where I live we don't call the police."

Callum leans towards me. "You should."

I shake my head. "We don't involve the police. We have our own sense of justice. An eye for an eye..."

"Amy, if this guy bothers you again you need to call me."

"That's what my brother said."

"Thank God somebody's talking some sense. Promise you'll phone next time."

I say nothing, looking at him through wide eyes.

"Promise me, Amy."

I nod. "Okay." It comes out as a sigh.

"Good. Now get some work done and then we'll go out for lunch."

"What?"

"I still owe you that drink, remember?"

I sit back, staring at my boss. He's looking at me through pretty green irises, his mouth wearing a half-frown. I'm torn between touching him and drawing away, unsure of myself, unsure of him. When I answer him, it feels as if I'm reliving a nightmare. Painful. Awkward.

"I remember."

* * *

Callum spends the next hour in a teleconference. His door is closed and I'm thankful for it, because he's confusing me, making me feel emotions I don't want to feel. I don't need to be protected; I don't need to feel safe. I don't need to feel this ache deep inside.

I spend every second of those sixty minutes trying to centre myself, remembering why I'm here. Degree, job and get out of here. Everything else is simply distraction.

I achieve nothing, apart from watching the words on my laptop screen float and dance in front of my eyes, the black letters blurring into a single mass. I hate feeling like this, all open and vulnerable, when I've worked so hard to grow a shell around me, but I feel powerless.

One step forward, two steps back.

Callum steps out of his office just after twelve. His hair is messy, his shirt half-pulled out of his waistband, his tie askew.

He looks glorious, despite my determination to stay strong.

"Give me five minutes and then we'll head out." He smiles at me and my traitorous pulse speeds.

"There's no need, honestly. I've brought lunch with me." I pick up the foil-wrapped cheese and pickle sandwich I scraped together this morning. It folds limply in my hand and I put it down. "Yeah, it's appetising."

He grins, revealing white, even teeth. "Come on, we deserve it. I promise not to take you to China's."

"Good job, I'm banned," I remind him.

Callum grins. "I just got the email from HR. I have to admit I'm tempted to take you anyway, see what they do when we walk through the door."

"That's easy for you to say, it's not your job on the line," I huff.

"Which is exactly why we're heading for The Don."

I look up at him, surprised. "Seriously?" The Don is a swanky restaurant in the City of London, in a small courtyard on St. Swithin's Lane. It's a taxi ride away, far enough to take longer than my allotted 45 minutes for lunch, and part of me is afraid I'm going to get told off. Again.

"Seriously," he repeats. "Grab your coat and we'll get a cab."

Ten minutes later we're climbing into a black taxi, Callum taking the back seat while I pull down one of the chairs opposite. I suppose I could have sat next to him, but somehow that feels too presumptuous. I remain straight as a rod as we drive along the river, past the Rotherhithe tunnel and Tower of London, before the taxi comes to a stop just past the restaurant. Callum leans forward, his hand brushing my shoulder, and hands the driver a twenty-pound note. He climbs out, holding the door open and offering his hand as I step onto the pavement.

"Thank you."

He squeezes my fingers. "You're welcome."

There's an atmosphere growing between us I don't quite understand. It makes my spine tingle and my breath shorten as we walk into the restaurant, my hand opening and closing as it brushes against his.

I linger behind as he talks to the maître d', his bearing relaxed and assured. They both laugh and speak rapidly, before Callum reaches out for me. "Are you ready?"

I stare at his outstretched hand. It feels as if I'm standing on the edge, scared to step onward, afraid to move back. I nod tightly, ignoring his hand, and the host leads us down some stairs to a low-ceilinged vaulted room. It's empty except for the three of us.

"Where's everybody else?" I ask. It's half past twelve, late enough for the restaurant to be full.

"This is the private dining room," Callum tells me. "I thought you'd be more comfortable here."

Oddly, he's right. It does feel more welcoming, less in the spotlight than the glitzy restaurant upstairs. I'm touched by his kindness, with the knowledge he thought of me when booking a table.

"Thank you." The maître d' pulls out my chair and I slide into it, letting him push me back in. Callum sits opposite me, nodding at the waiter who brings over the wine list. He glances at it for a moment before reeling off a request that flies right over my head.

I get the impression the waiter knows Callum well. It's in the way he takes his instructions, the way they talk.

Leaning forward, I cup my chin in my palms. "So," I say. "Do you come here often?"

He chokes out a laugh. "Smooth."

I grin. "Thank you. I pride myself on my chat-up lines."

"You're very good at it." His voice drops. "Have you been practising?"

The waiter opens the bottle of Fleurie, pouring a dash for Callum to taste. He smells it, swilling the red liquid around in his glass, and gestures for the waiter to fill up our glasses. Callum stares at me, enough to make me feel heated and awkward.

"I've just come out of a long term relationship," I blurt out, grabbing my wine glass and swallowing a mouthful. "I can't even remember how to flirt."

He takes a sip of his own glass. "Tell me about him."

"My ex?" I ask, my voice raised. "Why do you want to hear about him?"

Callum shrugs. "Maybe I'm a masochist. Indulge me."

The waiter slides menus into our hands without trying, while I attempt to form the words to explain my life.

"I met Luke when we were fifteen," I say. "We were in the same science classes and ended up sitting next to each other. I was pretty low at that point. I'd just been diagnosed with scoliosis and told I'd have to wear a back brace, and I was pretty sure that nobody would want me. But Luke was..." I search for the right way to put it. "He was understanding and sweet and made me feel good about myself."

The waiter comes over to take our order and Callum murmurs to him quietly, not taking his eyes from mine. He makes me feel safe and on edge at the same time.

"You were grateful?" Callum asks.

"Looking back he made me think that way, too. As if I should be pleased he was paying me attention, regardless of my problems. I think he played on my insecurities."

In fact I know he did. He'd pay me backhanded compliments, telling me I had a good body in spite of my spine, that I was pretty for a girl with a disability. But I didn't see it at the time. I was too grateful for his attention, too desperate to feel normal. He was an expert at making me feel indebted.

"The first time he was unfaithful I knew it was my fault." My voice breaks. I thought I was over this, but saying it out loud dredges up painful memories.

"He's an arsehole," he says. "You know that, right?"

"I know that now. But back then I really thought it was my fault. If I was prettier, if I was normal, maybe I'd be able to keep him."

"You are normal. As normal as any of us are. And what the hell is normal anyway?" Callum asks.

"It's what I always wanted to be. When I was a kid and everybody's dad came to their school plays and I only had my mum. When I was a teenager and everybody could wear tight clothes and I had to wear baggy dresses." My eyes glisten with unshed tears. "Even now I feel out of place. I've got too much ambition for my friends at home, but I don't belong at Richards and Morgan either."

"Of course you do."

"I'm the only intern who isn't from Oxford or Cambridge," I tell him. "They only took me on as a token gesture. Trying to show how liberal they are."

"You're better than the rest of them put together." He slides his hands up mine, grabbing hold of my wrist. The movement sends shoots of pleasure down to the tips of my toes. "You're not a token gesture."

The waiter brings our starters—two steaming bowls of soup. Callum releases my arm and I immediately feel the loss.

"You said you didn't have a dad. Are your parents divorced?" he asks.

I spoon some soup between my lips, the broth burning the tip of my tongue. "He's dead. Was killed in the first Gulf war when I was a baby."

"He was a soldier?"

"Yes." I feel the need to wipe away any sheen of romanticism. "He hooked up with my mum a few times then walked out of our lives. Don't feel sorry for me, I never knew him."

"I know what it's like to lose somebody." Callum pushes his half-eaten bowl of soup away. "So I'll feel the way I want to."

I look up at him through my lashes. The air between us is laden with something intangible, drawing us together whether I want it to or not. "You've lost somebody?"

"My wife. She died two years ago."

The soup in my stomach feels thick and viscous, curdling inside me. I remember that photograph, the way he looked so happy standing next to that beautiful blonde. His wife. His dead wife.

"I'm sorry." I play idly with my spoon, twisting and turning it inside my soup bowl. It's clear neither of us has much of an appetite. "That must have been awful."

He catches my gaze with his beautiful eyes. "It was." He blinks, lashes thick. Then he steals my words. "Don't feel sorry for me."

He pours us both another glass of wine, and I'm surprised at how fast the first glass has disappeared. I can feel the alcohol working its magic, making my muscles loose and fluid. "Should we drink this much at lunchtime?"

"Probably not," he admits. "But I think we need it, don't you?"

As if to underline his point I swallow another mouthful. "How did she die?"

"She had a heart attack in the middle of the night. Cocaine-induced." He drains his glass, drops of red wine clinging to his lips. "By the time I woke up she was dead."

I try to imagine the horror. It's one thing to have a father killed in combat in a country thousands of miles away, another to lose the love of your life at such a young age.

Especially when she was so beautiful. So vibrant.

"That's terrible."

"Yes."

Tears sting at my eyes and I squeeze them shut, unwilling to let him see them fall. But the thought of him going through that, seeing her lying dead next to him, is enough to strike me dumb. This time it's me who reaches out and threads my fingers between his. I circle his knuckles with my palm, warming his skin with my own. His touch makes me shiver.

"Don't cry." He reaches out with his free hand, capturing a rogue tear. It beads on his finger and he stares at it for a moment.

It's that confusion that steals my breath. The way he stares at my tear as if he can't understand what it is. For the first time I realise we don't just share an employer. Both of us are more damaged than we're willing to admit.

Silence descends as our main courses arrive, but it crackles like static. As I chew on a steak that melts in my mouth, I realise that I'm not just falling for my boss.

I've already fallen. And it hurts.

12

The following Friday evening Charlie walks into the office, his coat buttoned to the top and a striped scarf hanging around his neck. He slumps onto the sofa on the other side of the room, groaning loudly as he drops his head into the backrest, closing his eyes.

"Hi," I say, amused. I've noticed he has a tendency to the dramatic. "Have you got problems?"

"Ninety nine," he replies, cracking open an eyelid. "But the bitch ain't one."

I pull open my drawer and slide my laptop inside. "Well, on the bright side it's Friday," I say lightly. "Time to kick back and relax."

I glance at Callum's office. Though the door is closed I can see him pacing behind the frosted glass, no doubt talking rapidly into his headset. Things have been strained since our alcohol-fuelled lunch, as if neither of us is sure how we're supposed to treat each other any more. Our mutual confessions left me feeling as if we are more than just boss and subordinate, but I know there's nothing else we can be.

I think he's been avoiding me, and in many ways that's left me relieved. It's always easier to avoid than confront.

"Do you fancy a drink?" Charlie asks, his voice cutting through my murky thoughts.

"As long as it's not China's you're on. Just the one though, I want to make it to Yoga tomorrow." I managed to get there twice this week and I want to keep the momentum going. It's better for me, both body and soul.

"You will go to the ball, Cinderella." Charlie walks over to the exit as I shrug my coat on, pushing buttons through their loops. For a moment I wonder if I should tell Callum I'm leaving, but from the way he's leaning on the table, his arms tense and outstretched, I'm not sure I'm brave enough to bother him. So I take my bag and sling it over my shoulder, striding towards Charlie and the start of the weekend.

We join a mass-exodus of workers leaving Canada Square, and have to wait for the second elevator because the first's too busy. Stepping inside I feel like a sardine in a can. When we reach the ground floor it's a relief to be out of there. Charlie and I join the wave of people heading for the sliding exit doors.

I don't notice him at first. Perhaps I'm too wrapped up, my head full of work and thoughts of Callum. Or maybe it's because Canary Wharf is so far away from home that I don't even consider he might find me here. Regardless of the reason, I stand stock still as everybody pushes past, staring at the man about thirty yards away. Though I've only seen him once before, I recognise him immediately, from the broken nose and the scarred cheek, his eyes as vibrant as I remember them. They rise up to meet mine and he startles in recognition. He begins to walk towards me, pushing through the oncoming crowds, and panic stabs me like a knife.

My feet are glued to the concrete slabs, my body stiff and unyielding. It isn't until he's less than ten feet away that I finally find the strength to move, turning around and running back to the building. I barge my way through the workers, and run across the lobby. The doors are closing on an empty lift and I squeeze through the gap, punching the button for floor ten as the elevator begins to ascend. Only then do I let the air escape my lungs, whimpering as I balance against the mirrored wall.

I've left Charlie behind. He's probably standing outside, wondering where I am, but I can't bring myself to care. I'm still gasping as the lift arrives at floor ten and I have to push through another wall of people.

When I reach my office, I pull the door shut behind me, panting loudly. I search through my bag, looking for my phone, desperate to call Alex and tell him Digger was here.

"I thought you'd gone," Callum says, popping his head round the door. He takes one look at my face before walking over. "Jesus, what's happened? You look like you've seen a ghost."

I'm too scared to talk so I shake my head, trying to bite back the tears. They flow anyway, hot and fast, and before I know it Callum's wrapping me in his arms, pulling me tightly against him. He's warm and he's safe and he smells amazingly good as I bury my face in his chest. I hold on to his shoulders with a death grip.

"Amy, try to calm down," he says softly, his mouth right next to my ear. "Take some deep breaths, okay? You're safe here."

That makes me cry harder. He starts to stroke my hair, tangling his fingers in the strands, and it feels so damn good. We stand there for a moment, him stroking, me sobbing, until I finally gain control. He pulls away and I feel bereft, seconds away from throwing myself back into his arms.

"Are you hurt?" He takes my chin in his hand, lifting my face until we're staring straight at each other. "Amy, has somebody hurt you?"

He keeps saying my name. More than he would normally. Somewhere in the back of my mind I remember Lara telling me it's a technique she uses when her clients are having panic attacks. A way of grounding them, reminding them who they are. I wonder if Callum's trying to do the same.

"That man I told you about," I say. "The one who was hanging around my house. He was outside the building when I left, it looked as though he was waiting for me."

"Bloody hell, Amy." He drops his head until our foreheads touch. When he blinks, his eyelashes brush my cheeks. "What did he do?"

"He started to walk over to me." Our lips are so close I can practically feel them touch. It's thrilling. "Then I turned and ran back here."

"He's still out there?" Callum frowns, loosening his grasp on my chin. He tries to step back, but I hold on to him without thinking, not wanting to let him go.

My hand moves up from his shoulder, my palm cupping the back of his neck. My fingers burrow into the thick hair that falls over his collar.

"Amy." This time it doesn't ground me, it sends me soaring. Then his lips touch mine and we're flying together.

We kiss, our mouths moving as one, his hand pressing into the base of my spine. I arch against him, tugging his hair when his tongue slides against mine. His breath is hot, tasting of coffee and mints. My skin tingles and all thoughts are replaced by the desperate need to feel him. I cup his jaw, feeling it move beneath my palm as he kisses me harder, then he moans softly.

Pulling away, I bury my face in his chest, afraid to look at him. Because that was possibly the best kiss of my life, and I'm not ready to regret it. Not yet.

He presses his hand against me, angling my head. His touch is firm but gentle, and it excites me.

Before I was scared, now I'm absolutely petrified. Not only did I see a crazy man outside the building, but I also kissed my boss.

I kissed my boss.

It doesn't matter how many times I repeat it, it still sounds absurd. So patently unlike me.

"Are you okay?" he whispers, and I realise his face is buried in my hair. The thought sends pleasure through my spine. I still can't bring myself to look at him. The realist in me knows that at some point we're going to have to move, but the child inside is begging me not to do it yet. Just a few more moments of not having to deal with it, that's all I want.

"I'm okay." I mumble into his shirt. I lower my grasp onto his toned hips, but that means I'm still touching him. He's touching me, too; one hand on my cheek, the other wrapped around my waist. Somehow I force my eyes open and I'm immediately struck by the urge to kiss him again. It snakes around my body, making me ache for him. His lips part and a breath escapes, and I'm pretty sure he's thinking the same thing.

Then the door opens and we jump apart. There's only a foot between us when Charlie walks into the room, scratching his head.

"What happened to you?" he asks, confused. "One minute you were there and then you were gone." He notices Callum. "Oh hello, Mr Ferguson."

Callum nods, saying nothing. I can still feel his fingers even though he's not holding me. Slowly, I bring my eyes to his, and I see the expression I've been trying to hide from.

A combination of excitement and regret.

Is it in my eyes, too? I'm not sure. My emotions are too shaken for me to single them out. I feel like I'm on the edge.

"I didn't feel well," I mumble. "I'm sorry, Charlie, I don't want to go out anymore."

"Are you sure?" He sounds confused and I can't say I blame him. Only minutes ago I was heading to the pub with him. How is he supposed to know everything has changed so quickly? That my world's just taken a one hundred and eighty degree turn.

"I just want to go home," I whisper. I'm not sure if I'm saying it to him or Callum. "I'll feel better then."

"Okay then." Charlie shrugs. "I'll walk you to the station."

My body stiffens at the thought of going out there again. Digger could still be waiting for me, and as much as I like Charlie, he isn't exactly built. In fact he's five eight and pretty scrawny. He wouldn't stand a chance in a fight.

"I'll take her," Callum says, putting his hand on my shoulder in what must look like a friendly gesture, except I can feel his thumb rubbing circles into my skin. "She's not well enough to go on the tube. I'll give her a lift."

I keep forgetting he has a car here. Only the senior partners are allocated a space in the underground parking lot. The plebs are expected to travel by public transport.

Charlie shrugs and waves, wishing us both a good weekend as he leaves the office. There's a quizzical expression on his face and I feel a twinge of guilt that I've let him down. But it's nothing compared to the knot of nausea that kissing Callum has caused.

* * *

We drive through the London rush hour in silence. Callum hasn't touched me since we left the office, nor have I touched him. I'm sitting on my hands to prove it.

We head to my brother's flat; I'm too wary to go home, knowing Digger is looking for me. At least he doesn't seem to know about Alex, and right now I need to feel safe.

Safe from what, I'm not sure.

It isn't until we crawl into Shoreditch that Callum finally speaks. "Security are looking at the CCTV recordings to see if they can spot him. They'll want to take a statement from you on Monday." So that's what he was doing when he went back into his office. "I'll go and see HR on Monday, too."

I turn in my seat. "HR? Why?"

He swallows, his eyes still fixed on the road ahead. We stop at some temporary traffic lights, and the oncoming traffic filters towards us. "I shouldn't have taken advantage of you like that. I need to go and tell them."

My chest feels as though it's gripped by an ice-cold hand. "Tell them what?"

"That I kissed you."

My voice sounds strangled. "It wasn't like that. You don't need to say anything."

He glances at me. "I'm your boss, Amy. You came to me for help and I..." He breaks off, running an agitated hand through his hair, "I kissed you. I'm pretty sure that's against the rules."

"It is, but I think you'll find I kissed you, too. And if it comes to a choice between a well-established senior partner and an intern who's been with the company for a few weeks, I'm pretty sure I know who they'll be throwing out."

"I won't let them get rid of you."

"That's easy to say. But even if they don't get rid of me I'll be known as the girl who kissed her boss. Everybody will look at me differently. I don't want people to look down on me. It's already hard enough as it is being from the East End, and not going to Oxford or Cambridge. There's no need to make it harder."

"I've fucked everything up, haven't I?" The lights change to green and he slides the stick into gear, pressing his foot down on the gas. "I'm sorry."

"It's not your fault."

We're quiet again until we reach the street where Alex and Lara live. Callum finds a parking space about fifty yards away, reversing his car into it with practiced ease. I unclasp my seatbelt and reach down for my bag, barely able to bring myself to look at him.

"Thanks for the lift."

He walks around the car, opening my door to let me out. He doesn't take my hand or meet my gaze, but somehow that makes me feel better.

"I'll walk you to the flat."

"There's no need," I say. "The street is empty, I'll be fine."

He walks with me anyway, his body half a foot away. I'm hyper-aware of his warmth, his muscles, and for some reason I want to shiver. Instead I keep my back as stiff as I can, not willing to show how he affects me.

"This is me," I say, inclining my head to Alex's building. I press the buzzer by the front door, waiting for a response. I want Callum to leave, there's no way I can cope with him meeting Alex. My brother can read me like a bloody book. The last thing I need is for him to see me mooning about my boss.

Lara answers and I speak into the microphone. The door clicks open and I reach for the handle, putting my weight onto the wooden frame. "Thank you for the lift."

I don't wait for Callum's reply, stepping inside the lobby and pulling the door closed behind me. It's rude and goes against the grain, but I can't deal with him walking in with me. He stands on the porch for a moment, visible through the frosted glass pane, before turning and retreating down the path, back to his car.

Sighing, I lean my head on the cool, painted wall, tightly squeezing my eyes shut. My mind is full of pounding thoughts and regrets, accusations and recriminations.

I've done stupid things before, but today I've reached new heights. There doesn't seem to be a way to make things right.

13

"Did Digger say anything to you?" Alex is agitated, stalking up and down the living room like a caged animal, barking out questions. "Did he touch you?"

I shake my head. "He didn't get a chance. I told you, Alex. I ran before he could get close."

Lara is watching both of us, Max sitting on her lap. Her mouth is twisted into a worried frown.

"He's gone too fucking far, I'm going to kill him." Alex stops, hands fisted by his hips. "I can't believe Mum let it come to this."

"It's not her fault," I protest. "She didn't know he was going to turn up at work. None of us did."

"She should have fucking told you," Alex shouts, his face red. "She's letting you walk into danger without warning you."

"What do you mean?" I ask. He's talking in circles. "What should she have told me?"

He stops in front of me, reaching out for my shoulders. His expression softens when he sees the anxiety written on my face. "Amy, babe, there's nothing for you to worry about. I'll sort this."

He'll sort it? Sort what? "Are you going to pay him?"

"Money doesn't talk to psychos like him. There's only one thing he understands."

"Alex, stop it." Lara's voice is light, but there's steel in it.

"You can't reason with an arsehole like him. He only understands violence, Lara. I can talk to him until I go blue in the face, and he'll still be stalking her."

"So what are you going to do?" Fear uncoils in my belly. "Hit him?"

Alex doesn't answer, grabbing his coat and slinging it on. "I'm going out."

"Out where?" I grab his arm, but he shakes me off easily. "Alex, where are you going?"

"To see Digger," he mutters, heading for the door. "He won't bother you again."

* * *

Lara wakes me with a shake of my shoulder, and when I sit up and unfurl my legs she hands me a cup of steaming sweet tea. Blinking the sleep from my eyes, I take a mouthful, the hot liquid warming me from the inside out.

"Is Alex back?" I feel disoriented; I don't remember going to sleep. It's as if I fell pretty much where Alex left me, the mixture of adrenaline and shock forming a lethal cocktail in my bloodstream.

"He went to your Mum's," she tells me. "I think Andie went over there, too."

I bring my gaze up to meet hers. "Is he okay?"

Lara nods. "He didn't find Digger. Apparently he wasn't in any of his old haunts." She takes a sip of tea. "Alex wants you to stay here, I'll make up the sofa."

"I haven't got my things here." My voice is still heavy with sleep. A weariness takes over my body. "I need to go home."

"Amy, it isn't safe. Alex wants to look after you. Just stay for tonight and tomorrow we'll make a plan."

"What kind of plan?" I ask. "Who is he anyway? Nobody would be going this crazy about a loan shark."

Lara looks down at her mug. Her voice is soft. "No they wouldn't."

"Then who is he? Why's he following me?"

Max cries softly from their bedroom. We stop talking, but he manages to calm himself, his sobs thinning out to silence.

"He's not a nice man, that's all I really know. You'll have to ask Alex about the rest."

"But nobody will tell me," I say, frustrated. "I'm so sick of people treating me like I'm some kind of special snowflake. First Alex then Callum..."

"What's Callum done?" Lara leans forward, clasping her hands together. I remember our previous conversation, the one where I confessed that I liked him. That seems like such a weak word for how I feel.

"He kissed me." If I close my eyes I can still feel the pressure of his lips against mine. The way his tongue pushed inside, claiming me when I was already his. *God.*

"He did?" She looks surprised. "How, why? What happened?"

She listens while I run through the events of the day. Silent and unjudging. I start to cry and she gently takes my half-empty teacup and places it on the table.

"You've fallen for him," she whispers.

I don't bother to correct her, because she's right. I've fallen for him, hook, line and sinker. The problem is, I think I've shattered on impact.

* * *

Alex arrives home a few minutes after eleven. Though his hair is dishevelled, a brief scan of his face reveals no bruises or cuts, no signs of an altercation.

"Baby." My mum follows him in, and she seeks me out immediately. She runs across their small living room, scooping me up into a hug. "I'm so, so sorry." Her voice breaks on her apology, and when I look at her I'm shocked to see a tear rolling down her cheek.

"Why are you sorry? It's not your fault some psycho's stalking me." I'm almost flippant when I say it, though the fear remains.

"We should sit down," she suggests. I notice Alex and Lara have made themselves scarce, closing their bedroom door softly behind them. It makes me feel nervous.

"What's going on?" I twist to look at her, but Mum refuses to meet my gaze. Though she's still holding my hand, it's as if she's building a barrier around herself.

"First of all, I want you to know I only ever wanted to protect you. If I'd have thought for one minute he'd show his face again, I never would have told you what I did."

"Told me what?" My voice is clipped, mainly because I'm so sick of being kept in the dark.

"Told you about Digger." She still isn't looking at me. "Told you..."

"For goodness sake, Mum, just spit it out."

"Told you about your dad. There, are you happy now?"

"What about my dad?"

I think I know where this is going. All these secrets and lies, they've been festering for years and I've been wilfully ignoring them. In spite of all evidence to the contrary, I'm not an idiot. My lungs contract as I wait for her to answer.

"Your dad didn't die in Iraq. He isn't dead at all. But as far as I was concerned he was dead to us, and I never expected to see him again."

"That guy... Digger. He's my dad?" I lean back from her, snatching my hand from hers. Nausea mixes with anger as I realise I'm the last person to know.

That my dad isn't dead.

"I didn't want you to find out like this," she whispers. "I begged him to stay away. But he keeps insisting on seeing you, he reckons he's better, but I don't know."

It's like reading a novel when half the pages are torn out. I'm getting the gist of the plot but the motivation remains a mystery. "Why did you tell me he's dead?" I bite my lip, remembering all those times I wished I had a dad. Seeing other kids at the park with their fathers, lingering in the card shop every June, staring at greetings I could never purchase.

All this time he's been alive? There's a man out there carrying half my DNA and I never even knew it.

"I ran away from him," I whisper. "I ran away because you told me he's a bad man. I turned my back on my dad."

Mum sits back, rubbing her face with the palms of her hands. Her week-old manicure is starting to chip, bright red lacquer peeling away to reveal yellowing nails. "He is a bad man. That's why I told you..." Her voice cracks. "You should stay away from him, Amy. We all should."

The door to Alex and Lara's bedroom cracks open and Alex looks out, catching my eye. "You all right?" he silently mouths. I shake my head.

Is it all right to lie to your daughter for twenty years?

Is it okay to pretend her father's dead?

Alex leans on the doorjamb, face soft with concern. He always hates it when Mum and I row.

"Why is he bad?" I swing my eyes back to Mum. She still won't look back at me. She pulls her pink fluffy cardigan tightly across her chest, as if there's a chill in the room.

"Start from the beginning," Alex suggests, pushing himself off the doorway and walking into the living room. He collapses into the armchair opposite, crossing his ankles as he rests his feet on the coffee table. There's a twitch in the corner of his cheek, as if he's clenching his jaw too hard, and I know he's desperate to make this all go away. He was like this when I was a frightened kid, standing up for me when challenged. Though part of me still longs to be hiding behind my brother while Doctor Who is on the T.V., I know I can't let him do this any more. It's time to stand on my own two feet.

Finally, Mum looks up. "I met your dad in a pub I was working in. It was just after Operation Desert Storm. He was heading to Iraq, and I was lonely and sad." Her eyes flicker over to Alex. "We hit it off right away."

In my mind I'm picturing my mum twenty three years ago, flirting across the bar with a short-haired soldier. The image is so vivid I can hear her tinkling laugh as he knocks back a pint.

"What happened next?"

"I thought it was a fling. We only spent a few weeks together before he shipped out. But somehow he found my address and started writing to me, and I wrote back." She pulls at the sleeves of her cardigan. "I found out I was pregnant with you that Christmas. You were a little surprise for all of us. One minute I was pouring brandy over the pudding, the next I had my head down the toilet."

"Uncle Les reckoned you'd drunk too much Babycham," Alex remarks. "He let us watch James Bond while Mum crawled into bed."

"Did you tell him about me?" I ask.

"I sent him a letter. I wasn't sure how he'd react but he was delighted. He wrote back with a whole list of plans. He wanted us to get married and adopt Alex and Andie. It all sounded too good to be true."

Alex laughs, short and harsh. "You can say that again."

Mum shoots him a nasty look. "He sent me some money and told me to spend it on baby things. It was enough to kit out a little nursery for you."

Her words are making me emotional, and there's a lump in my throat the size of a rock. I imagine her with a baby bump, buying a cot and pram, her face glowing from hormones. It could all have been so different, I could have had a mum and a dad who loved me. We could have been a normal family, so what the hell went wrong?

She's staring into the distance, locked inside her memories. Her voice takes on a wistful edge. "You were born six months later. Uncle Les managed to let Digger know, and he was allowed home to see you. I've never seen somebody so in love. You took to him right away, and as soon as he picked you up you'd stop crying, your face quiet and serious. I was a bit jealous, I think, but when he got down on one knee and proposed, I was so excited."

"He flew back to Kuwait, but by that time it was clear that things were calming down. A few weeks before he was due to come back he was travelling in a convoy, heading toward Iraq. They drove over a land mine."

I can't breathe, I can barely think.

"They managed to pull him from the wreckage, said it was a miracle he survived. Nearly everybody else was killed, including his best friend."

"He was injured?" I ask. I barely recognise my own voice.

"They rushed him to an army hospital. His ribs were broken as well as both his legs, and there was a piece of shrapnel embedded in the side of his face. He had five operations before they were able to stabilise him, and it wasn't until two months after that he was well enough to be flown home."

"I remember you going to see him," Alex says. "You took Amy with you."

"He was in a bad way. It wasn't just the physical injuries, though they were bad enough. He was closed off emotionally. He barely looked at you, and didn't talk for the three hours we were there. That was the first time he really scared me."

"Why?"

She winces. "Because when you started crying he shouted at you to shut up."

The way she says it sends a shiver down my spine. "What happened next?"

"Eventually he was discharged, and with his legs it was clear his career in the army was over. He had no job, no home, and no family to speak of. So..."

"He moved in with us."

She nods. "But he was different, you know. Intolerant. He'd shout at Alex for kicking a ball too loudly against the garden wall, and tell Andie she was stupid when she asked for help with her homework. I suppose now they'd diagnose him with PTSD, but he refused to get any help. And I thought..." She falters. "I thought I could heal him."

It's the story of her life. She thinks a man will change just for her. Sometimes they do, but the transformation is only ever superficial. She's perpetually disappointed in love.

"It got to the point where Alex and Andie were scared to come home from school. I lost my job because I didn't like leaving you all alone with him, and that made things worse because we had no money at all. Then one night I went to Andie's parents evening. It was only for half an hour, and I put you to bed before I left, so I didn't think there'd be any trouble. But you'd started teething, and you got all grizzly, enough to wind him up."

It feels like my skin is burning all over. I don't want to hear the next part of her story, yet I'm helpless to stop it.

"I could hear you screaming from halfway up the road. Andie and I started to run, and we met Alex on our way to the house. He was crying and his cheek was puffy and red as if he'd been slapped, but he wouldn't tell me what happened. Just begged me to come and save you."

"What did happen?" I turn to Alex. He's turned pale, his eyes flashing with tears. I picture him as a frightened seven-year-old, terrorised by his mum's fiancé. Trying and failing to protect his baby sister.

"He broke your arm." Alex's voice is flat. "Snapped it in two when he couldn't stop you crying. I tried to stop him, Amy, I swear I did, but the bastard was too strong for me."

The bile that's been lingering in my stomach rises without warning. Covering my mouth, I run to the bathroom, barely making it to the toilet before I vomit. I bend over the bowl, retching until my stomach is empty, muscles spasming in an attempt to purge.

It's Lara who comes in, her voice soft, and her touch softer. She helps me clean up then leads me back to the living room with an arm around my shoulder. She holds me while I cry, stroking my hair and murmuring sweet words, telling me it's okay, that I'm so brave.

Except I don't feel brave. I feel sick and guilty and angry all at the same time.

"What did you do?" I ask Mum. "What did you do when you went back into the house?"

"I picked you up and we all ran into the bathroom. There was a bolt on the inside and I slid it shut, and we sat down on the floor. You were still screaming, and Alex and Andie were crying, and the only thing I could think of was I had to protect you. I had some hairdressing scissors in the bathroom cabinet, so I got them out and held them in my hand. If he broke through that door I was ready to stab him in the eye."

"He didn't break in," I say. "I've seen him, he has both eyes."

"One of the neighbours called the police. About an hour later they got inside the house. Digger had drunk himself into oblivion, but they arrested him anyway and took him down to the station. The rest of us went to the hospital, and we stayed there until the morning."

"They put a cast on me." I've seen photos of me as a baby, a white plaster cast encasing my wrist. Mum told me I'd broken it falling down the stairs.

"Yes. You hated it, too. It was so heavy you could barely lift your arm." Though Lara's still holding me, Mum reaches for my hand. "They charged your dad and he pleaded guilty. He ended up in jail for a year. When he got out I applied for a restraining order, and told him never to come near us again."

"Why's he come back now?"

"After he left prison, he ended up in psychiatric care. He was diagnosed with PTSD. I think he was in some kind of treatment for more than three years before they finally discharged him. That's when he moved to Australia."

"He moved away?" I don't know why that surprises me.

"He ended up in Melbourne. Got married eventually to a local girl."

"Did he have kids?"

She shakes her head. "No. And that's why I think he's back. He came to see me, told me he'd changed, that he's devastated over the way he treated us. He asked to meet you so he could apologise himself."

"But you told him to take a running jump," Alex interjects.

"I told him to leave you alone, that you thought he was dead. I expected him to get angry about that, but he didn't. I thought he'd got the message but then he turned up at the house and, well, you know the rest."

"He wants to see me?" I ask. I'm like an over-stimulated child, darting this way and that. The confusion hurts my head.

"You don't need to," Alex says, and for a moment he looks like that scared little boy again. "You don't need to talk to him at all. I'll make sure he stays away."

I lean back, exhausted.

"I'm tired."

"I should let you sleep." Mum sounds hesitant. "Do you want to come home?"

"She can stay here for the weekend," Alex interjects. "I'll take her to work on Monday."

"You'll be late for your own job." I raise my eyebrows at him. "I'll be fine." I wonder if I sound more certain than I feel.

"I'll take you," he says, and his certainty is enough for both of us.

An hour later, I lay awake on the sofa bed, white cotton sheets draped around my hips as I stare up at the shadowed ceiling. Though my body aches, my mind is much too busy to give in to sleep. I think back twenty three years ago, to a time when there was no Internet, when people phoned each other instead of messaging, when a young ex-soldier thought it was okay to break his baby's arm.

Just before 5:00 a.m. Max wakes up, his sobs loud and heavy as Lara attempts to hush him. I imagine somebody hurting him, snapping his bones until he screams, and tears roll down my cheeks.

I lie there wide awake, and the bleak light of morning finds me long before sleep does.

14

As promised, Alex takes the tube with me to work on Monday morning. Though I moan loudly about him treating me like a kid, I'm grateful for his protection. We stand on the train, clutching the rail that hangs over our heads, and he does his best to make me smile.

"How's the job going?" he asks. "Managed to burn anybody yet?" It's a standing joke in our family: when I was fourteen I got a Saturday job in our local cafe. It lasted exactly 32 minutes, the time it took to pour a cup of tea over my first customer.

"Not yet," I say dryly. "But I'm not ruling it out."

He walks me to the office block, an arm protectively slung around my shoulders. And though the circumstances could be so much better, I'm glad we at least get to spend some minutes together.

We part outside the electronic doors, after Alex gives me a short, sharp hug. I feel his hands curl into fists, digging into my back.

"If he turns up, you call me, okay?" His voice is gritty. "I'm working over in Tower Hamlets, I can be here in a few minutes."

I wrap my hand around his still-tight fist. "I'll be fine." I'm not scared of a man who broke a three-month-old baby's bone. Disgusted, maybe, but not frightened.

The more I think about him, the harder it is to categorise my emotions. They swing back and forth like a pendulum, from shocked to angry, sad to disbelieving. When I lay in bed last night, my mind flitted from my mum's lies to my father's violence and at one point I wanted no more to do with either of them. But there's a difference between telling falsehoods to protect the one you love and deliberately harming a child.

"What time do you finish?" Alex interrupts my thoughts. I squint at him, the morning sun making me blink before it slides between two clouds.

"I'm not sure. I'll be fine, Al. I promise I'll be careful."

"I don't know..." He looks torn. "I'll come and pick you up."

"Alex," I say gently. "I'll be okay. You can't spend your life taking me back and forth to work. You've got a family of your own, a job... you can't be responsible for me as well." When he hesitates, I attempt to reassure him. "I'll get somebody to walk me to the station after work."

It won't be difficult, there are so many co-workers leaving the office at the same time as me.

He breathes out, rubbing his head. "All right."

Stepping inside One Canada Square lends me strength I didn't know I needed. It makes me feel normal, like everybody else who waits impatiently for the lift, feet tapping and chests huffing. I'm so busy soaking it in that it takes me a moment to realise somebody's talking.

"Can you drop by my office at ten? There's something I need to discuss with you," Diana Joseph asks. She flicks her hair out of her eyes and I look at them, trying to read the rationale behind her request. I may have only been working here for a matter of weeks, but I've already learned that a meeting with HR usually means one of two things. Either you're out of a job, or you've got a promotion. She definitely isn't there to hand out tea and sympathy.

"What for?" An image from Friday night flashes through my mind. Callum holding me, his mouth millimetres away from mine, his warm breath bathing my face.

He said he'd go to HR and confess what we did. I wonder if he has.

"There's something I want to tell you." Diana purses her lips like an old woman and it's clear I'm going to get nothing out of her here. At times like this I'm not sure if she's a stickler for confidentiality or on a power trip.

She says nothing more until we both step out of the elevator on the tenth floor, and even then it's just a terse reminder of our meeting time. I stand in the corridor, watching her stalk her way towards the HR office, and come to the conclusion that I don't like her very much.

I suspect the feeling is mutual.

When I walk into the office, Callum's door is open. He glances up from his computer and my body lights up. His expression is unreadable as he tilts his head to the side, making me wonder what's going on in his mind.

"Good weekend?" he asks. I hear a ping as an email arrives on his computer but he doesn't look down.

"It was..." I screw up my face, trying to find the right word to encapsulate a weekend full of revelations and recriminations. "It was interesting."

I can cope with this, I tell myself. Callum behind his desk, me behind mine. I can fight off the urge to touch him, to feel his skin touching mine.

Then he stands up and walks out from his office into mine, and he's all muscle and presence. I want to tell him to go away and I want to tell him to come closer. Everything about him is confusing.

And lovely.

It only takes two strides of his long legs to reach my desk, where he leans on the corner. "Did that guy show his face again?"

I shake my head.

"Have you been to security?"

I shake once more and a look of exasperation crosses his face. "You need to go and see them, Amy. What if he turns up again?"

"He's my father," I blurt out. Then I immediately regret it. After the events of this weekend I'd been determined to make a new start—another one. My cool and professional persona lasted for all of ten minutes.

"I'm sorry," Callum replies, his brow creasing into a frown. "Have I just stepped onto the set of a soap opera?"

His levity bursts the tension. A shocked laugh escapes my lips and I clamp my hand over my mouth.

"Or is it Star Wars?" he asks. "Luke, I am your father."

"Stop it," I reprimand him, grinning. "This isn't a laughing situation." It is though—at least for now. "I'm not even kidding."

"You need to fill me in, the suspense is killing me."

Callum plays with my pen pot as I tell him about the weekend's events, sorting my biros into a colour-coded bundle. Every now and then he interrupts to ask a question, listening carefully when I respond, craning forward as if to catch every word. It isn't melodramatic or clichéd or anything like an episode of Eastenders, it's just the story of my life. The story I didn't know until now.

"So he wants to see you," he murmurs, rolling a red pen on my desk. "Do you want to see him?"

"I don't know," I admit. "I still can't get my head around everything. I know Mum doesn't want me to see him, and my brother just wants to kick his head in." I shrug. "I don't want to upset them."

"But this isn't about them is it? It's about you and what you want."

I look at him, rolling my lip between my teeth. "You're not an only child by any chance are you?"

"What's that got to do with it?" He tries to hide the grin that's pulling at his mouth.

"You are, aren't you?" I laugh. "Well I'm not. I'm the youngest of three. Nothing's ever just about me."

He blinks slowly, eyes heavy lidded. "Something should be."

The moment twists, the humour dissolving in the frisson that grows between us. I feel it crackling and buzzing against my skin, and all I can think about is that kiss.

Soft, sure. A brief moment of everything.

"Something?" I ask, a little breathlessly.

He catches my gaze, holding it without trying. In that instant I know for sure that whatever I'm feeling for him isn't one-sided. It weaves between us, soft as silk, unbreakable as iron. It makes me feel delighted and downright scared. I can cope with a crush, enjoy it even. Treat him like the eye-candy he is, a piece of deliciousness to look forward to when I enter the office. But mutual attraction? That's dangerous. It's a lingering force that threatens everything; my job, my degree, my hopes for the future.

Here be dragons, but rather than run away from the flames, I'm letting them consume me.

* * *

"Amy, please take a seat." Diana Joseph's office is exactly how I imagined it. Impersonal, neat, everything locked away. She takes a sip of sparkling water, lip gloss barely even smudging the glass. "How are you getting on?"

For a sliver of a second I'm tempted to unleash the truth on her, purely to see her reaction. A returned-from-the-dead father and a brief entanglement with my boss, they must be the things that fuel her black HR heart. But I keep my counsel, shrugging, muttering something non-committal, and she nods rapidly, ignoring every word.

"Good, good. Well I've been speaking with your tutor this morning, giving her an update. She insisted you need to be put on a project as soon as possible."

I stifle a smile. Good old Professor DiMarco. She might be gruff but she's always on her students' sides. "Okay," I say.

"Luckily I'd already identified a project. It wasn't easy to persuade the manager you're suitable for the job, and it will be a long slog to see the first phase through to completion." She looks self-satisfied, and I wonder if I'm supposed to congratulate her for doing her job. Finally.

I don't give her the satisfaction. Instead I sit there, patiently, waiting for her to continue. It takes a few moments, but finally she gets frustrated enough to speak.

"Technology Integration have just been awarded the Grant project. They need somebody to project manage the requirements capture phase, and I suggested you."

A grin breaks over my face. All that work, all that schmoozing. Callum won the contract and he didn't even let on. Part of me wants to run back to our office and throw my arms around him.

Bad idea, Amy. Very bad idea.

"I thought you'd be pleased," Diana says smugly.

Pleased is an understatement. I'm absolutely delighted. Not just for Callum, although that's fantastic enough, I know what a juicy project this is. The project manager is the glue that holds something like this together; who develops the schedules, coordinates the work packages, makes sure everybody is doing what they need to.

Okay, so it's just the requirements phase. I won't be around to see the project come to completion, but if I do well at this it will be like getting the keys to the city.

A guaranteed job.

"It sounds good." I manage to keep my voice smooth in spite of the adrenaline bubbling inside me. I want to jump up right away and start making lists.

"You'll be under the close supervision of Jonathan Cooper," she says, referring to Callum's friend. "You'll also need to make weekly reports into the Head of Technology Integration."

"I can do that."

The smile she flashes is brief. "Good. Now I just need to identify a new PA for Mr Ferguson. It's not going to be easy."

I think of the piles of receipts, his strange requests when booking hotels. His gas-guzzling monster of a car.

The way he kisses.

"No it won't," I agree. "But I've left things shipshape and I'll be around if they have any questions." I feel a flash of sympathy for the new PA. Having been there myself I know what a mess Callum can be. The way he's flippant yet exacting, a curious mixture of arrogant and nice that makes my pulse beat a little strangely. I'm a little envious, too. For weeks I've been able to spend most of my day with him, listening to him talk on the phone, watching him pace his office like a panther on the prowl. I'm going to miss that. Too much, probably.

Which is exactly why this new job will be good for both of us.

* * *

The next week passes in a blur; I'm buried in paperwork, fixated on Gantt charts and completion plans. I spend half my time on the phone introducing myself, leading to late nights at work, so that I catch the Americans at a suitable time. I revel in the buzz of making contacts, letting my work life make up for a personal life that's a footstep away from dire. The office becomes my sanctuary and my drug, comforting yet exciting, and I spend too much time here.

I finish a conference call at eight o'clock and pull the headset from my ears, laying it down wearily on the desk. The office is deserted; the only lights still burning are the ones above my desk, the others idle when they detect no motion. When I finally grab my coat and head out to the lifts, the lights switch on one by one as I walk under them, and it's like being in a music video. I shimmy a little, grinning to myself, then walk straight into the frame of Callum Ferguson.

"Oh shi... I mean sorry." I back away before my body can react to his touch. "I didn't see you there."

"Clearly." I'd forgotten how lovely his voice sounds. Broad and burred, sexy as hell. "Did you have a good day?" He reaches across to press the lift button, but this time I don't step away. His hand brushes the front of my jacket and I get the stupidest thrill from it.

"Busy but good. What about you?"

Callum leans on the wall next to the lift, his arms crossed loosely. "It's quiet without you. My new PA brought me coffee before nine and I couldn't find the energy to shout at her."

That thought warms me. "You must be losing your touch," I say lightly. "You've got a reputation to keep up, Scrooge McDuck. Next you'll be giving all the staff Christmas Day off."

The lift arrives and he ushers me in, his chest almost touching my back. It's unusual to have so few people in the elevator; a side effect of working late.

"Am I that bad?" he asks.

"I bought you a coffee and you shouted at me."

"Ah, but that was a sign of affection."

"You called my university shitty."

"How many times are you going to throw that back in my face?"

The lift doors open and we step out into the ground floor lobby. It's already dark outside, and the interior lighting casts a moody glow, adding to the dystopian atmosphere. The security guard barely notices us when we walk past. Like always, I get a twinge when I step through the doors, wondering if tonight's the night that my dad shows up.

Like the office block, the plaza outside is empty. I stay close to Callum anyway, feeling his finger brush against mine as his arm swings. I try to pretend it doesn't affect me.

"Are you heading home?" he asks. "Or do you fancy a drink?"

I don't miss a beat. "A drink sounds good."

Ten minutes later we're nursing beers in the corner of a non-descript bar, surrounded by dozens of suits doing exactly the same thing. I lift the bottle to my lips, and swallow a mouthful of beer.

"How are you getting on?" he asks, staring at me.

"It's great," I tell him, still feeling breathless. "I think we've almost hit the first milestone. I just need to speak to a few more people."

He looks pleased. Proud, even. "Everybody tells me how well you're doing. I feel like my protégé's all grown up." Though his words are teasing his voice isn't. It's sexy.

"I'm definitely grown up."

"I can see that, Amy." His eyes sweep down, his scrutiny making my nipples harden. If he can do that only with a look, who knows what he can do with his hands?

"It's not the same without you around though. Going through the day without being shouted at is boring." I tease him in an attempt to lighten the mood. "I even buy coffee before nine nowadays."

"You're a heathen."

"I believe you've told me that before." I smile at him.

"The place isn't the same without you either," he says.

There's something sparking between us that I can almost taste. "You know I can come down and make your life a misery every now and then if you'd like."

His lips quirk up. "Ah, just the thought of it makes my skin crawl."

"I thought it might."

The noise of the crowd is drowned out by the sound of my pulse.

"Have you heard from your father?"

I quickly shake my head, welcoming the change of subject. "No, I'm still trying to decide whether to see him or not."

"You're considering it?" He frowns. "After all he did to you? Jesus Amy, you can't see him."

It's as if I'm talking to Alex again. "I'm a big girl. If I want to see my dad, I'll see my dad. And if I don't want to, well that's my decision, too. And I'm the only one who gets to make it."

His expression is warm. "I understand that. But if you do decide to see him... well I'd like to know. Just so I can keep an eye out for you, okay?"

I take another swig of beer, trying to ignore the way my heart races every time I look at him. His offer is sweet, caring, and it's puzzling the hell out of me. I've no idea where we stand, especially now he's not my boss. All I know is something between us springs to life every time we're in the same room. It pulses and it sizzles and it makes me want everything I shouldn't.

It's becoming almost impossible to ignore.

15

A few weeks later I'm sitting at the kitchen table in my pyjamas on a Sunday morning, furiously cursing at a spread sheet that doesn't seem to add up. Before I check it for the third time, I refill my coffee cup. Pulling out my chair, I slump back down and stare at the numbers.

The laptop pings. I'd forgotten I was logged into the network. Normally I download what I need and then log straight out in an effort not to look too much like a girly swot who spends her whole weekends working. I guess on this occasion I forgot.

Ferguson, C: Working on a Sunday? Tut, tut, Amy. All work and no play...

I try to stifle my smile at the way he's turned my own words back on me.

Cartwright, A: Pot, meet kettle. Have you nothing better to do on a Sunday?

Ferguson, C: Sadly not. I've a meeting in New York and my lovely PA isn't answering her phone. Any idea how to book a return ticket for tomorrow?

He's going away? That sends a shot of disappointment through me.

Cartwright, A: I do, but I've just been told that working on a Sunday makes me dull. I'd love to help but...

Ferguson, C: I see I'm going to have to grovel. How about if I promise to bring you back a present?

That gets my attention.

Cartwright, A: What kind of present?

Ferguson, C: So easily tempted, Amy. Name your poison, chocolates, wine; I can even stretch to a sick bag.

Cartwright, A: Ooh, a sick bag? In that case, what time do you want to leave?

I spend the next ten minutes organising his flights and sending his itinerary, checking his visa status and other delightful details. Mum wanders into the kitchen, sending me a strange look when she notices the inane grin stretched across my face.

"Working again?" she asks. I can tell from her tone she disapproves. "Aren't you supposed to have the weekend off?"

"I'm doing it by choice, Mum," I reply, messaging Callum at the same time, letting him know it's all booked up. "I want to get ahead, so..." I shrug.

She mumbles something about being taken advantage of, then walks into the living room with a mug of tea, pulling her pink bathrobe closed across her chest. A minute later I hear the TV come alive, and turn back to the laptop.

At lunchtime, Mum and I take the underground into the West End. It's Lara's birthday, and Alex has arranged a meal for family and friends in a small Italian restaurant in Covent Garden. It's one of their favourites, unpretentious and authentic, with Cannelloni to die for.

We walk in and see them sat around a huge table in the corner. Alex is spooning something disgustingly brown and gloopy into Max's smiling mouth while Lara stands and talks with guests, handing out glasses of sparkling Prosecco.

"Happy birthday." I press my lips to her cheek, handing her the gift bag I've carried all the way from Plaistow. "We didn't know what to get you so I hope you like it."

She pulls out the dove-grey and white-butterfly printed scarf, rubbing the silky fabric between her finger and thumb. "It's so beautiful," she sighs, holding it up to her neck. "Thank you."

"There's some money in that card," Mum says, stealing her own kiss. "You and Alex go out somewhere nice with it. Amy will babysit."

I turn and raise my eyebrows pointedly. It's the first I've heard of it.

"What?" she asks. "It's not as if you've got anything better to do."

"Well thanks for that," I huff. It's one thing to have no social life, quite another for your mum to rub your nose in it. Even if she's right.

Lara grins. "Come and say hello to Beth. You remember her don't you?"

"Of course I do." I smile and reach out for Beth's hand. "How's Brighton?"

"It's fantastic." Beth used to work with Lara at the Drug Rehabilitation Clinic, but moved to the coast since she adopted her nine-year-old daughter, Allegra. Allegra's mum died of a heroin overdose, and getting her away from that lifestyle was Beth's number one priority.

"Hey baby." Beth's number two priority, the luscious Niall Gallagher, walks forward and slings his arm around her. "Allegra wants the nuggets."

Niall is tall, dark and has a ridiculously sexy Irish accent. Though I've met him a couple of times, I still find myself closing my eyes when he talks. It's like a reflex action.

"Tell her no chips." Beth screws up her nose. "She had a bellyful last night."

Niall grins. "So did you, greedy girl."

Andie is the last to arrive, by which time we're all seated around the large table. Max is playing contentedly with a book, while Allegra is telling everybody about a film she saw last week. Lara sits there happily, staring at everybody, and it reminds me just how far she and Alex have come. Only a few months ago they were on the edge of separation, but now he's holding her hand and they are clearly still in love.

"Sorry I'm late." Andie sits down in the only empty chair, between Beth and Lara's father. "Happy birthday, Lara." She looks over at me and smiles, mouthing an "okay?" I nod rapidly. We've talked on the phone a couple of times since my dad showed up, but she hasn't been to Mum's house for Sunday lunch in a couple of weeks. Truth be told, I'm worried about her. She doesn't quite seem herself.

"How's the job going?" Lara asks me. "Alex said you've been given a project to manage."

"A bloody millstone more like," Mum grumbles. "I used to think her college work was bad, but this is ten times worse. At least back then she'd go out sometimes, and of course she had Luke..." she trails off, covering her hand with her mouth.

I laugh and shake my head. "You can say his name. I'm not going to curl up into a ball and cry or anything."

"I can never tell with you. You're a closed book."

I'm taken aback by that. I'm anything but shut off. "I think I was over him before we even split," I say. "I just didn't know it."

Lara catches my eye, and I know she's thinking about my kiss with Callum. I am, too. Remembering the way his lips brushed against mine, the soft sweep of his tongue, it's probably fair to say I'm obsessed by the memory.

Maybe him going to New York is a good thing. He's made it clear we can only be friends, and to do anything else would put my job in jeopardy.

That kiss, though...

"What are you thinking about?" Alex grins at me from across the table. "You look like the cat that got the cream."

Lara frowns "Do you mean canary?"

"Don't be silly, babe. Canaries don't eat cream."

There follows a meaningless debate about cats versus canaries, and I sit back and take a mouthful of sparkly wine. Being surrounded by family and friends makes me feel warm from the inside out. Maybe all work and no play really does make Amy a dull girl. I should call Ellie and arrange for a girls' night out.

After the waiter clears away our main courses, Alex pulls out his chair and bangs on his glass with the end of his spoon. The chatter dies down as we all turn to look at him. He seems nervous, twirling the spoon between his thumb and finger. That isn't like Alex; usually he thrives on being the centre of attention.

"I wanted to thank you all for coming to celebrate the birthday of my beautiful wife," he says, and we all gush in response. "Seven years ago she married me and I thought I was the luckiest man in the world. Then she gave birth to our beautiful son and I knew I was."

Lara grabs his hand and squeezes, tears glinting. My eyes feel a little damp, too.

"As you know, we had a bad summer, and nearly lost our gorgeous boy. So I'm delighted you can all be with us to see just how well he's recovered. And that's all down to Lara, who isn't just a fantastic wife, but an amazing mother, too." Alex slides his hand into the pocket of his black trousers, pulling out a small, blue box. "And if I wasn't already married to her, I'd be down on my knee right now."

"Do it!" Niall yells. Alex laughs, shaking his head.

"So I'm going to do the second best thing." He opens the small box, revealing a diamond encrusted eternity ring that catches the light. "Lara Cartwright, love of my life, mother of my child, will you do me the honour of renewing our vows?"

Lara covers her mouth with her hand, hiccupping back a sob. Alex has to gently prise it away to slide the ring on to her elegant finger. She holds it outstretched, moving it this way and that, admiring the way it looks. "Of course I will," she says, still choked. Then we all surround the two of them, hugging them both and wishing them well, until Max breaks up the party by throwing a chicken nugget at Alex's head.

* * *

The next morning I'm desperately clinging on to sleep when the shrill ring of my phone cuts through the early morning silence. I sit up, rubbing the last vestiges of sleep from my eyes, squinting to read the caller id. *McDuck, S* flashes impatiently, and I bite my lip in an attempt to stave off my grin.

My teeth do nothing to stop the excitement swirling in my belly, though.

"Hello?" My voice is lower when I wake up. I wonder if I sound like a man.

"I can't find my passport."

Groaning, I lean across to my bedside table, flicking on my lamp. "Why are you more demanding now I'm not your PA than you ever used to be?"

"I always want what I can't have."

And bang, I feel the impact of his words right down to my toes. Touché, Callum, that makes two of us.

"Have you looked in your top left drawer at work? Under the photo?" I ask, my throat suddenly dry. I want to drop my head into my hands and slap myself soundly.

"Under the photo?" he says softly. "I didn't look there."

"Well you should." I try to sound nonchalant and chipper, but it doesn't work. The memory of that picture leaves a bitter taste in my mouth. "You need to check in within an hour."

"I'll pick it up now. Thank you, Amy." His voice is deep, smooth and completely unreadable. Does he know I've seen the picture of his wife?

"Have a safe flight," I say, falling back on the bed. "Bon voyage."

"Take care." He rings off and I close my eyes. Why is it that every interaction with Callum Ferguson leaves me feeling more confused?

* * *

When I get to the office a little after eight on Monday, a box of chocolates and a gift card for the local coffee shop are on my desk. He's scribbled a thank you on a yellow post-it note, his writing as illegible as ever. In spite of the early hour I rip the cellophane from the box and greedily stuff a chocolate Brazil nut into my mouth, letting the gooey goodness swirl around my tongue.

"What are you grinning at?" Charlie sits down on the edge of my desk. "It's Monday morning, nobody should be that happy."

"Correction, it's Monday morning with a box full of chocolates," I shove the carton at him. "Help yourself."

"I've only just brushed my teeth." He stares at me with disgust. "I don't know how you can face chocolate this early in the morning."

I shrug and pop another in my mouth; this time a caramel creme. "Your loss."

Charlie picks up the gift card and turns it over. Then he reads the post-it note. If it were anybody but him, I'd get annoyed, but you can't shout at Charlie. It would be like telling off an old, much-loved dog.

"How come you get chocolates when your boss calls you on a Sunday, and I get a flea in my ear for not picking up the phone quickly enough?" he complains. "That doesn't seem very fair."

I take the card from his hands. "Because he's not my boss anymore and I did him a favour. Plus I respond really well to positive reinforcement."

"So do I," Charlie whines. "But nobody ever gives me any."

"Is there a reason for this visit," I ask. "Or did you just want to have a general moan? Because if you haven't noticed, I'm a very busy, important person." I grab another chocolate. "Lots to do, you know?"

"Are you free on Friday?"

I bat my eyelashes. "Why, Mr Simpson, are you asking me on a date?"

He grins. "Yep, a date for ten. It's my birthday and we're heading over to The Salty Dog. Legend has it there's going to be a DJ, too. Music, grub and all the champagne we can drink."

The Salty Dog is a bar on the edge of the wharf, its name harking back to the days when it was a real, working dock. Since all the interns were banned from China's, this is where we congregate. I've noticed some of the partners prefer its more earthy nature, too. In spite of the stupid name it's a lot less pretentious than China's.

"Is that a good idea?" I ask gently. "After what happened last time we drank champagne?"

"That was a long time ago," he scoffs. "I was a child then. Twenty one is such a difficult age."

"It was six weeks ago," I point out, folding my arms. "And seriously Charlie, remember what Diana said? Two strikes and you're out."

He mirrors me, crossing his own arms. "Seriously, Amy, I promise to behave myself. And if you see me getting drunk you have my full permission to cut the alcohol off. In fact I insist, it can be your birthday gift to me."

"I haven't said I'm coming yet."

"You haven't said you're not, either," he replies. "And now you have to be there, it might be the only way to save my job."

"I can save your job by tying you to your desk."

"It really is my birthday." He waggles his eyebrows. "Honestly, Amy, I really will be sensible. A few drinks and a good dance, okay?"

Though every sceptical bone in my body protests, I nod my head and try to look agreeable. "Okay, I'll be there." Whether it's a birthday party or his last hurrah, only time will tell.

16

"Two Peronis, a vodka tonic and a glass of water, please." I lean across the bar, a twenty pound note between my middle and fore fingers. The bartender has to stoop to hear my voice, which is croaky from hours of shouting above the noise. The DJ is playing tracks at ear-pounding volume, and by this point in the night the choice is dance or go home. I'm tempted by the latter option.

I shove the open beer bottles into my waistband and scoop up the glasses, pushing my way through the throng of people. It's sweaty, the temperature a few degrees above unbearable, and my hair curls damply around my neck and back.

When I reach the side of the dance floor Charlie is holding court, so I push the glass of water into his hands. He raises it to his mouth, top lip beaded with perspiration, and takes a long, cool sip.

"Thanks."

In a moment of unprecedented maturity, I cut off his champagne two rounds ago, and Charlie was surprisingly relaxed about my intervention. He gave up after one tiny attempt at arguing, even agreeing to alternate between beer and water. It's only when I look at the lights reflecting off his face that I realise why. There's a tell-tale residue of white powder on the rims of his nostrils, which he wipes away with the back of his hand.

Shit. I immediately feel my skin crawl when I realise how naive I must look. After all, I've seen drugs before. Luke used to regularly light up on a Friday night—much to my disgust—but none of my friends have ever been into coke.

Until now.

I've heard stories, of course. Tales of long, boozy lunches with clients followed by a nice sobering snifter of blow. Or the anonymous partner who has a courier deliver his weekend stash every Friday afternoon, and pays for it by bank transfer. It's not quite accepted in the city—and I'm pretty certain Diana Joseph would have a conniption fit—but it's pervasive and it's easy to get hold of. All a matter of who you know.

It would also explain why Charlie's able to stand up straight and speak without slurring.

"Are you amped?" I whisper into his ear. Charlie turns, a quizzical expression on his face.

"Why, do you want some?"

"No I bloody don't. And nor should you. This place is heaving with people from work, if they catch you you'll be dust."

He laughs. "Dust. See what you did there."

"Seriously, Charlie."

He mimics me, in a high tone. "Seriously Charlie."

People continue to brush past us, dancing and gyrating, and in spite of the vodka my buzz has well and truly worn off. Then Caro Hawes bumps into me as she reaches out to Charlie, and he passes her a tiny bag of powder without a word.

When I was at school, we read a short story by HG Wells, about a man who enters a country full of blind people. He's certain he's going to become their ruler, because he can see and they can't. But then, the blind people capture him and remove his eyes, believing they're cancerous lumps. I feel a bit like that guy now. I seem to be the only sensible one around here. It's hard work swimming against the undertow when everyone else is having fun beneath the surface.

"I'm heading out." I shout in order for Charlie to hear me. He inclines his head toward me, a bead of sweat running down the bridge of his nose.

"Don't leave yet. It's not even twelve."

"It's been a long week and I have to babysit tomorrow. I'll see you on Monday."

"C'mon, just share one little line with me." He grabs my hand, pulling me into him. His shirt is sticking to his chest, outlining a surprisingly firm torso. I vaguely remember him saying he was on the row team at university.

"I don't do drugs." I hate the way that makes me sound like a whiny goody-two-shoes. "Thank you anyway." Oh, and polite, too.

"Let me buy you another drink then. Or we can dance. Whatever you want to do." He sweeps the hair out of his eyes and it stays slicked back from his forehead. "Just stay here for five minutes, okay?"

I close my eyes, feeling the blood pumping through my veins in time to the beat of the music. I wasn't lying when I said it had been a long week. The late nights in the office were exacerbated by Callum's absence, which has been more poignant than I care to admit.

I miss him.

"I'm going to call a cab," I tell Charlie, unwilling to face the underground alone at this time of night. "Walk with me, okay?"

He trails me to the entrance, and the cool breeze of the night-time air hits us as soon as we walk past the bouncers. It takes my ears a moment to adapt to the sudden drop in volume, and for a minute all I can hear is the pulsing in my head.

When I take out my phone and slide the screen open, I see two missed calls and a text. Fearing the worst, I glance at the numbers, wondering if something's wrong at home.

They're from Callum. Of course my reckless heart does some kind of galloping dance, hammering against my chest and making me breathless. I assume it's a similar sensation to the one Charlie's been getting from his secret stash, except this is all natural.

"You want me to call one for you?" Charlie asks. "I've got a number here I think." He reaches into his pocket, tugging out his iPhone, and a tiny bag flies out, the contents dusting the pavement like a miniature snowstorm. "Oh shit. Fuck." He drops to his knees, frantically scooping the white dust in a futile attempt to get it back in the bag. I look behind to see one of the bouncers frowning at us.

"Charlie," I whisper-shout. "We need to move."

He says nothing, still running his palms across the concrete.

"Charlie, people are watching."

He continues to ignore me. Sighing loudly, I reach down and pick up the cellophane bag, curling my hand around it. With my other hand I grab his shoulder in an attempt to pull him away. "Let's go, okay?"

Finally he stands up, the expression on his face distraught. "Fucking hell, that cost me a grand."

I'm about to answer when I feel somebody standing behind us. The hairs on the back of my neck rise, and my breath escapes in a whistle.

The half-spilled baggie of coke is still in my hand.

I twist my head in a slow, torturous fashion, afraid that it's a security guard, or even worse a policeman, who's spotted us scrabbling around on the floor.

But instead of a navy-blue uniform, I see a pair of cool, mossy green eyes.

"What the fuck's going on?" Callum's accent gets stronger when he's angry. His lips twist as he stares down at the powder-coated paving slab, taking in the detritus Charlie's left behind. "What's that?"

"I don't know," Charlie says, his voice tremulous. I think it's finally dawned on him what an idiot he's been, and the possible consequences of his action.

"Amy." Callum's tone is quiet, but it's edged with steel. There's a coldness to it I haven't heard before. "Is that yours?"

My muscles seize up. I can't breathe, I can't move. I definitely can't work out how to answer his question without landing one of us in it. That's why I stay silent, gripping the baggie tightly.

"Are you going to say something, or do I need to call the police?"

I look over at Charlie, who's staring back at me. His face is almost as white as the powdered floor. He shakes his head slowly at me.

"Don't call the police," I say, my hand aching from holding the packet so tightly. Any minute now it's going to cramp, and everything will be revealed.

For a moment I think about throwing Charlie under the bus. I could tell Callum exactly who's responsible for this clusterfuck of epic proportions. But then I remember Charlie's kindness, the way he's included me in evenings out while the other interns have mostly ignored me. He's a decent guy. Easily led, but nice.

Somehow I find the strength to raise my eyes to Callum's. "It's not ours. We just found it here."

"Liar."

He's looking at me as if he hates me. There's a twitch on the side of his jaw that is rapidly pushing at his cheek.

"Callum, I..."

He grabs my wrist, his fingers digging into my skin. His ferocity scares me.

"You're doing drugs," he hisses. "Do you know how stupidly fucked up that is? I thought you were better than that."

Tears spring to my eyes. "You're hurting me."

He steps back, wincing as if I've slapped him. My wrist throbs from its newfound freedom. Charlie is completely silent, looking back and forth at the two of us. He seems totally out of his depth.

Callum exhales slowly, rubbing his face with agitation. "Just tell me what the fuck's going on."

I'm not sure what makes me do it. It could be the haunted look on his face or the desperate tone of his voice. Whatever it is I find my fingers slowly unfurling, revealing the crumpled, now-damp bag of coke. Callum follows my gaze, and his expression hardens into something unrecognisable.

The next minute he's grabbing hold of my sleeve and dragging me away, while Charlie mutters something about going back inside. Then Callum takes the baggie from me, his breath coming in shallow, irregular gulps.

He pulls me around the corner of the building, then stops, pushing me against the cool, brick wall. Leaning close, he rasps out a question.

"How long have you been taking it?"

I shake my head, my voice surprisingly strong. "I'm not."

"Don't fucking lie to me," he roars. "Tell me how long you've been inhaling this shit and then we can do something about it."

"Like call the police?" I scoff. "Well, thanks, but I don't need your kind of help." The fact I haven't explained myself hasn't escaped me, but his accusations are cutting. My fear of a few moments ago is morphing into a white-hot anger that matches him scowl for scowl.

"Do you know how irresponsible you are? People die from this shit. You don't know where it's come from, you don't know what's in it, yet you're stuffing it up your nose on a regular basis."

"You know nothing," I yell back. "With your stupid assumptions and blind accusations. I told you it isn't mine, and it isn't. So you can fuck off."

I rarely use that word, but it tumbles out before I can swallow it down. Callum holds the bag in front of me, shaking it so the scant contents fall down the cellophane.

"If it's not yours, what the hell are you doing with it?"

"I don't have to explain myself to you."

"That's what a liar would say."

I straighten my back as much as I can. Then I open my mouth, my eyes flashing with ire, and attempt to speak without wanting to kick him in the balls.

"It's your choice. If you believe I spend my Friday nights snorting coke off a toilet seat, then maybe you don't know me at all."

He's still agitated, tugging at his hair with his fist. I watch as his expression changes from angry to confused.

"I know you," he whispers.

I nod. "You do."

He leans closer. "But why have you got the coke?"

I shake my head. "I can't tell you."

"Was it Charlie's?"

"I can't tell you."

He comes closer still, until his face is inches away from mine. His skin is pale in the glow of the moonlight, his eyes fierce and bright, and he's never looked more beautiful.

"Then tell me it's not yours."

I exhale slowly. "It's not mine."

"Thank God."

He's silent, and near enough that if I move a step forward our lips would touch. Instead we stare at each other, still as statues, our heart rates slowing. It's only then, as the moment calms into something less frantic, that I remember his wife, the way she died.

No wonder he was so angry. I look up at him, my expression soft, an apology about to tumble out.

"Fuck it." He closes the gap, pressing his mouth to mine, his lips moving as if in silent prayer. It's tough and angry and everything I'm feeling inside, and I kiss him back twice as hard.

"I'm sorry," he whispers into my mouth. "I'm so sorry." I don't know if he's apologising for his accusations or for kissing me, but it doesn't really matter. His tongue runs along the seam of my lips and I part them, moaning softly. Then he slides inside and it turns everything upside down. I wrap my hands around his neck, pulling him closer, until his hard body is pressed against mine. Little pulses of pleasure shoot down my body, making me ache with need, and I curve myself against him, feeling his growing excitement as the length of him presses against my stomach.

"Christ, Amy." He pulls back, still cradling my head with his hands. "What the hell are you doing to me?"

I grab his tie and jerk him back down, desperate to taste him again.

There are kisses and then there are *kisses*. Callum Ferguson knows how to move his lips until every cell in my body sings. My toes curl up and my fingers tingle and another sigh escapes. This time he captures it, letting my breath linger in his mouth, his tongue sliding against mine, sweetly.

His firm, thick thigh parts my legs, and I unashamedly rub myself against him. I'm slick and hot, aching for sensation, and judging from the frantic glint in his eyes, so is he.

"You're beautiful," he says, when we pause to catch our breath. "I've thought about you every fucking day I've been away."

"I've thought about you every night."

He groans. "Don't say that."

"Why not?"

"Because it makes me want to strip every single piece of clothing off your body."

I look up at him, unsmiling. "And that's wrong, because..."

He blinks twice, as if he's trying to work me out. "Because." His voice is strangled, disappearing into nothing as his mouth crashes to mine again.

I fall back against the wall, the cool bricks scratching me through my clothes as he digs his fingers into my waist. They burrow beneath my shirt as he kisses me frantically. He's hard, and I grind a little, enough to feel him gasp into my mouth.

I hitch a leg around his hip. He grabs my calf, fingers tracing a line of fire past my knee and inside my thigh, before he thrusts against my core.

The next moment he lifts me higher, until both my legs are wrapped around his waist. He takes my weight in his hands, the added height letting him press exactly where I want him.

Callum runs his lips down my exposed neck, nipping and kissing his way to the dip at the base of my throat. The sensation spears straight through me, forcing a moan from my lips as he pins me to the wall.

I feel a strange mixture of vulnerability and safety. He drops his head onto my shoulder, nose pressed into my throat. I feel his breath on my skin, hot and harsh, and it brings goose bumps out on me. Then he's kissing me again, more gently than before, his lips tender and soft. It makes me ache from the inside out, my body pulsing with need.

Slowly, he pulls my legs from his hips, lowering me to the ground. His fingers are still stroking my thighs.

"I should take you home," he whispers, kissing the sensitive spot between my throat and my ear.

"Yes," I murmur breathlessly.

"To *my* home."

"Yes."

17

"This is me," Callum says between kisses. He slides a key into the lock. The front door is as smart as the rest of the house—as the street—perfectly painted in a glossy black.

"Nice." I nip at his bottom lip. He pulls me against him until I feel him harden through his trousers. My breath hitches with desire.

"Mmhmm." The door opens, and we half-tumble inside. My heels click against the polished hardwood floor, and for a moment I wonder if I should take them off. But I'm so short in my bare feet that I'll end up with my face in his chest and I'm not ready for that. Yet.

Callum hooks his hands beneath my jacket, sliding it off my shoulders. It falls to the floor in a pool of black fabric, and I step over it as he pushes me along the hallway. His fingers brush my bare shoulders, rough and demanding against my sensitive skin. Then he scoops the hair away from my neck, holding it in his fist, and presses his lips against my throat.

I might moan. A lot. He's finding sensitive spots I didn't realise existed, laying claim to them one by one. Every kiss is a brand on my skin, staking his ownership, and the sensation is overwhelming.

"So fucking beautiful." His mouth reaches my shoulder. "Every inch of you."

I swallow hard as his lips brush down to my clavicle. He reaches behind me, fingers finding my zip and tugging. That's when nervousness overtakes me, as I realise we're really doing this thing. That I'm going to get naked in front of my ex-boss.

My spine stiffens as soon as I think about it. He's going to see everything; the way my right hip curves much more than my left, the way my shoulder is off-centre, making me lopsided. His hands freeze halfway down my back.

"Are you okay?"

Blood pools beneath my cheeks. I nod, but say nothing. He cups the back of my head, his voice as soft as his eyes.

"Do you want to stop? You only have to say the word..."

Disappointment floods through my veins. "Do you want to stop?"

He steps backwards, and I immediately miss his proximity.

"Hell no, babe. But if you're not ready for this, there's no way I'm going to force you." Moonlight floods in from the window next to him, illuminating his face. He looks worried, vulnerable, and his hesitation is enough to give me strength.

"I don't want to stop," I tell him, taking a deep breath. "But I'm...I'm embarrassed to let you see my body. I'm not perfect and you're going to see that."

He frowns, eyes scanning from my face right down to my legs. "What do you mean 'not perfect'? You're fucking gorgeous."

"I've got a curved spine. I lean to the left a bit. I'm not symmetrical."

The smallest of smiles shapes his mouth. "Not symmetrical?"

"One side of me is curvier than the other."

He reaches out and traces my side, running from the edge of my breast to my waist. "Symmetrical is pretty fucking overrated."

He kisses me again, his hands pushing into my hair as he angles my head, his tongue dipping and sliding into my mouth. Then he lifts me up and I wrap my legs around his waist as he carries me down the hallway. If he wasn't so big and I wasn't so light, it might be a disaster. But as it is, his strength is a turn on, and I kiss him back just as hard.

He kicks open the door to his bedroom before walking across the cream rug and laying me down on his bed. The covers are fresh and soft, and they fluff around me as I hit the mattress.

"Nobody's perfect, sweetheart." He pulls his tie off, then deftly unbuttons his shirt, pulling it open to expose his chest. He shrugs it off and he's naked from the waist up. He has the strength of an athlete, his pale skin defined by the thick muscles beneath. His chest is covered by a smattering of light brown hair that leads down to his navel, before sharpening into a line. He stands there, exposed and vulnerable, and all I want to do is touch him. So I scramble to my knees and crawl across the mattress until I reach the edge, then get down and stand next to him.

"Sit down," I say, my voice thick with need. I push him down, his shoulder flexing beneath my palm. Reaching behind me, I pull the zip the rest of the way until my dress is gaping open at the back. Then I slide it down, past my hips, past my thighs, and step out of it.

I'm naked save for my bra and panties. Callum stares at me from the edge of the bed, his eyes sweeping every inch of my body. The tip of his tongue pokes out to moisten his dry lips, his breath ragged. My need for him escapes from every pore.

"I lied. You *are* perfect." He doesn't take his eyes off me.

I shake my head. "That's not what Luke says."

He swallows, the action making his throat bob. "There are two things you need to know about me, sweetheart. The first is I don't lie." He reaches out and runs his finger across my hip. "And the second is you really shouldn't mention your ex-boyfriend when you're half naked in my bedroom." He smiles at the last part, making me giggle. I move forward and straddle him on the bed, my bare legs on either side of his suit-clad thighs.

Callum wraps his hands around my hips, pulling me down until my panties slide against his cock. He's hot and hard and makes my toes curl in delight, my body grinding against his. He reaches behind me to unclasp my bra and my breasts spill out, the cool air making my nipples pebble before he cups them.

"Exquisite." He rubs his thumbs across them, making pleasure spit and spark in my belly. "Flawless, beautiful." Callum captures my nipple between his lips, teeth grazing, tongue bathing.

The air catches in my throat, straining my voice. "Did you eat a dictionary?"

His lips curl around me, and I can feel his smile. "It's not a dictionary I want to eat."

"No?"

"No."

He leans back until he's flat on the bed, and I follow him, my body on top of his. He tugs me up until we're aligned, his chest pressed to mine, his dick hard against me. Just a gentle roll of his hips is enough to make me gasp, and I realise how excited I am. Every cell in my body is buzzing with desire, and the need to *really* feel him is tugging at me.

He kisses me, grabbing my arse as he grinds against me again. Then his fingers slip inside my panties, trailing down until they reach the hot, ready part of me that's begging for his touch.

"You're wet," he whispers. "So fucking wet." He slides a finger inside me, and I nearly jump with how good it feels.

Desperate, I fumble at his belt, sliding it open and unbuttoning his trousers. I press my hand inside, beneath his boxers.

His hips buck at my touch. He's hot in my palm, soft skin stretched across his hard thickness, and it throbs against me. I drag my hand along him, making him gasp, the sound making the pulse between my legs crescendo.

Callum shuffles out of his trousers and shorts, lying naked beneath me, and I can't tear my eyes away. Taut, toned and masculine, he makes me feel tiny and petite.

"Beautiful." I press my lips to his chest, my fingers still wrapped around him. Dragging my teeth against his nipple, I smile as I feel him react, his heart hammering against his chest.

"These need to come off," he mutters, pulling at my panties. They catch on my hips and he lets out a frustrated growl, before I get to my knees and shimmy out of them.

"A real man would have torn them off," I tease.

"I like them too much for that." He seems to have a thing for my throat, spending long minutes nipping and licking before he moves down to my breasts.

Then he's flipping me over so I'm on my back, his body tensing above me, muscles taut and defined. His hips lower until he's brushing against me, and like a reflex action, I open my legs.

He fits perfectly.

I wrap my thighs around him, squeezing my eyes shut as I feel him come even closer. He stills, reaching for his trouser pocket and grabbing a condom from his wallet.

There's a tear as he extracts the latex, and I quietly watch him roll on the condom. Then he's lying on me, skin to skin, and I'm aching from the inside out.

"Callum," I whisper. He flexes his arse, dimpling beneath my palms, and the movement sends shots of delight through my body.

"Mmm?" he mumbles into my throat.

"Please..." I'm almost too sensitive. Raw and exposed beneath this hulk of a man. I'm aching for him to fill me, needy for his touch, my body arching and circling. He flexes again, hips pressed to mine, and I can feel him nudging against me. The next moment he's inside me, all of him. Any thoughts in my mind are replaced by the primal need to be taken. When he pulls out, the emptiness makes me sigh, and I look up for reassurance. There's something indecipherable in his eyes, something deep and expressive that I'm trying to decode, but then he pushes again and I'm all sensation and desire.

* * *

An hour later I'm laying on my side, my head nestled into the crook of his arm. I can feel the insistent beat of his heart beneath my cheek and the thin sheen of perspiration that's coating his skin. He breathes in, his chest expanding, and I snuggle in closer, inhaling him.

"Are you okay?" He kisses the top of my head.

"Mmm." I'm anaesthetised by pleasure, my whole body leaden. My eyes are closed and I'm more relaxed than I've been in a long time. As if I'm safe here.

I don't want the feeling to end.

"I'm sorry if I hurt you," he says. There's a tone of regret in his voice that makes me look at him in alarm.

"You didn't hurt me. That was... that was... amazing."

He laughs. "I didn't mean that, although thank you for the compliment. I meant earlier, outside the pub."

I shift in his arms, resting my chin on his chest. We're looking right into each other's eyes. "You didn't hurt me, well not much. I was shocked more than anything." I frown. "I understand why you were so upset when you saw the coke."

Callum closes his eyes, and I miss the green. "I've seen what drugs can do."

I stare at him, seeing the pain in his face. "You mean what they did to your wife?"

He won't look at me, and I hate the lack of connection.

"She died too young, and it was avoidable and I—" His voice cracks. "I hate the thought of you risking yourself like that."

"I've never taken coke. I think I've had a smoke of something twice. I'm not like that."

"I know," he says, his voice low. "And that's why I'm sorry. I shouldn't have accused you of that."

"It's okay." I let my head drop again. The need to feel his skin against mine is too compelling. I could get used to this feeling.

We lay there for a while, and I think about his wife. There's a twinge of jealousy when I remember how happy he looked in his wedding photo. I feel like an interloper, a magpie. Stealing shiny baubles from somebody else's nest.

This shouldn't have happened. I shouldn't be here in my ex-boss's bed. I shouldn't be aching whenever he touches me. The intense happiness of a few moments ago dissolves, replaced by the nagging fear that I've done something spectacularly naïve.

Whatever happened to get my degree, get a job and get the hell away from home? I seem to have forsaken it at the first flash of bicep, and my traitorous body is still humming in contentment at that trade.

My mind, though, is reeling.

"Hey, I lost you for a minute." Callum tightens his arms around me. I can feel the knots of his muscles pushing into my skin. "What's going on in there?" He brushes his lips against my temple.

It feels good. *Too good.* I'm aware that if I give in to the fog of comfort that wants to envelope me, everything will be lost. How can this be anything more than a fling to him? I'm an intern, ten years younger, and with a hell of a lot to lose. If anybody ever found out...

"I should go home." I sit up, all too aware of my nudity. My clothes are scattered on his shiny wooden floor. Like Callum, his bedroom is intensely masculine, dark woods and grey linen, the art colourful against the stark white of his walls. I feel awkward and out of place here, so I clamber to my knees in an effort to escape.

"Come here," Callum croons, as if reassuring a frightened animal. He wraps his arms around my waist, and it takes every ounce of my strength not to melt into his body. "What happened here? We had a good time didn't we?" He frowns. "You did come, right?"

Blushing, I remember the three amazing orgasms he gave me. "It's not that."

"Then what is it?"

I brush the hair out of my face. Callum is frowning at me, two vertical lines furrowed between his eyebrows. I reach out to smooth them away, but pull back as if I've been burned.

Maybe I have.

"This can't happen." I gesture between the two of us. "We can't do this."

In spite of my protestations, he gathers me into his embrace. "I've got news for you, sweetheart, it just did."

"I know," I wail. "And it shouldn't have. I almost work for you, you should be giving me orders, not orgasms."

He smirks, and it's sexy enough to make me want to slap him. "I can give you both, if that's what you're into."

An image of Callum standing over me naked, and barking out demands, flashes through my mind. "I'm not into that." It's a complete lie. I could be *so* into that. I could be into anything he wants. But I shouldn't be, and the whole damn thing is so confusing. "I should go."

"Look, babe, you're tired, you're overwrought, and you need to get some sleep. I can take you home if you want but I'd much rather you stayed here with me."

There go those biceps again, flexing deliciously. They cage me in—a muscle-bound prison—and it would be so easy to relent.

"I need to get home. My mum will be wondering where I am."

Callum says nothing, just gets out of bed and starts to pull on his clothes. The intimacy disappears, and we're little more than strangers sharing a dressing room. Though I know it's my fault, there's nothing else I can do, we're already skating on thin ice.

When we're dressed, I start making his bed, lifting the sheet and billowing it up. Callum stops me.

"You won't say anything?" I ask. "At work, I mean?"

He scowls. "Why the hell are you so afraid, Amy?"

"I don't want to lose my job." I whip my head around, matching him grimace for grimace. "And if I get thrown out I'll also flunk my degree and end up at square one."

"You won't lose your job," he says calmly. "I wouldn't let that happen."

He's so sure of himself I almost cave. But then I remember the contract I signed on my first day at work. There's no way I can risk it.

We walk out into his hallway and I scoop my jacket off the floor. Shrugging it on, I turn to look at him. "Can you call me a cab?"

He reaches for my hand. "Stay."

I start to waiver. "Callum…"

Scowling, he grabs his phone from the jacket hanging in the entranceway and slides his fingers across the screen. A moment later he's ordering a taxi, his eyes still on me. My mouth tastes of bitterness and regret. Though I try hard to make it disappear, the flavour still lingers.

When the taxi arrives he opens his front door and waves at the driver, before wrapping his arms around me. He holds me tightly, pressing his lips to my hot forehead, and I want to crawl back into bed with him.

"I won't give up on you," he warns, releasing me outside his front door. "I know you're scared, and I know this has come as a surprise, but I like you, Amy, and I think you like me, too."

He's right on all counts. I *am* scared and I *do* like him, and that's why it's so difficult. I'm still a mess of emotion as I climb into the taxi and he gently closes the door behind me, tapping twice on the roof to let the driver know he's good to go. As we accelerate away, I twist in the seat, my eyes seeking Callum as he walks back into his house. At the last second he turns, his gaze meeting mine.

He lifts his hand to wave, and I mirror him, waving back. Then I sit back, closing my eyes, as the taxi driver traverses the late night streets of London.

18

When I wake up in the morning, my mouth is glued together by a mixture of dried-up alcohol and cold hard regret. Through my half-open eyes, the red digits of my alarm clock show it's almost ten in the morning. I sit up, panicking before realising it's Saturday. With a sigh of relief, I allow myself to slump back on the bed. At least I'm not going to be late for work.

There's a blissfully empty moment before the memories begin to take shape in my mind. The feeling is fleeting, replaced by images that flicker in my brain like a Pathé newsreel of my worst moments, as I remember the way I practically crawled all over Callum, stuffing my hands down the front of his trousers.

Groaning, I haul myself out of bed, grabbing my robe and tying the sash around my waist, pausing in the bathroom to splash ice-cold water on my face before I drag myself downstairs. The kitchen light is too bright, the kettle too loud, and the tinny sound of the radio makes my teeth grind.

"Did you have a good night?" Mum glances up from her phone. Mascara is smudged beneath her eyes, blending into the grey that shadows her cheeks. Her skin is sallow without her usual foundation and blusher.

"Mmm." I take a glass from the cupboard and a carton of orange juice from the fridge.

"You came home late."

I can tell from the smirk on her face that she knows exactly how late—or how early—I got home this morning. Though I try to ignore it, Callum's face flashes in my mind, and I remember his confused expression as the taxi pulled away from his flat.

Oh God, what have I done?

"It was full on." I collapse into the plastic chair opposite Mum, my legs refusing to hold my weight any longer. "We partied hard."

"It looks like it." She swallows a mouthful of tea. "I'm glad you had fun. You deserve it."

Surprised, I catch her eye. "Really?"

"Yes, you've been working hard. And after everything that's happened..."

We're quiet for a moment. The DJ introduces another song, and we both sip at our drinks. The orange juice sticks to my teeth, coating them in sugar, and I run my tongue along the enamel, trying to clean them off.

"How was work?" I finally ask in an attempt to change the subject. Mum tends the bar at the local pub on a Friday night. She loves being surrounded by friends and noise.

"Same as usual. At least until your dad came in."

Alarmed, I look at her. My eyes are dry and wide. "You saw him?"

She picks up the cereal box in front of her, suddenly preoccupied by the text printed on the back. Her eyes dart back and forth, judiciously avoiding mine.

"Yes," she says slowly, each letter lingering on her tongue. "He came in to ask about you." Red spots form on the apples of her cheeks, their pinkness a contrast against her pale skin. "He really wants to see you, Amy."

"What did you tell him?"

"I told him how beautiful you are. How clever. I said how proud I was to have you as a daughter."

I don't often hear words of praise tumbling from her lips. "What did he say?"

Finally she drags her gaze from the cereal box. "He wants to meet you, he's desperate to. He's changed, I promise you. Digger isn't the angry man he used to be. He's calmer, I don't know, more mature?"

There's something in her voice that both panics and reassures me. A firmness leaving me in no doubt she believes what she's saying, coupled with a lightness that makes me wonder if there was more to last night than just a chat. Her eyes sparkle, lending them a vibrancy that's all too familiar. Mum's in man-hunting mode, her eyes set firmly on the prize.

She grabs me, the same wrist he once snapped in two. Instinctively, I pull away. Though the pain is long gone, her touch makes me cringe.

"What did I do?" she asks, confused.

"I don't know," I admit, still rubbing my arm. "He just scares me, that's all."

"He's sorry for that, too. All he wants to do is talk, nothing else. I promise you, Amy, I wouldn't say anything if I didn't believe him."

My throat feels congested. "Why do you believe him?"

"Because he's a broken man. He's not the cocky, arrogant sod I first met, and he's not that angry ex-soldier either. He's just a middle-aged man who's desperately sorry for the things he's done, and he wants to find a way to make up for it."

"He wants atonement?" I ask, softly.

"Something like that."

I run my finger around the top of my glass. "But why now?"

Mum shrugs, and her robe slips down from her shoulder. "He broke up with his wife and flew back to England after years of being away. I think the things he did are coming back to him, making him feel ashamed. I honestly think he's sorry for it all. Now he wants to meet his only child."

That's when it finally hits me. This man is part of me, my flesh and blood, the reason I'm alive. Regardless of his actions, he's still replicated in every cell I have.

He's my dad.

"What's his name?" I ask. "His real name, I mean."

"Douglas Bolt. Doug. That's why he's called Digger, you know, like a spade."

"Douglas." I test it out loud. Then I think of saying "dad", but can't voice it out loud. It feels too alien.

"He's changed," she repeats. "He really has. You don't have to meet him here, it can be in public, anywhere you feel safe. I can be there too if you like."

"Okay," I say, wavering. "I'll meet him, but I can't promise anything else."

Her fingers wrap around mine, squeezing tightly. "That's all he wants," she says.

I hope she's right.

* * *

"No fucking way." Alex stomps across his living room, scowling. "You're not meeting him and that's final."

Lara touches his arm, but he twists from her grasp. I haven't seen him this furious in a long while. Although I like this daddy-bear side to him, and the protectiveness he's showing, the fact he's making decisions on my behalf is also extremely irritating.

"I'm meeting him at the café near work," I tell Alex. "It'll be the middle of the day, we'll be surrounded by people, what can possibly happen?"

"You're so fucking naive, Amy," Alex shouts, coming to a stop in front of me. His muscles vibrate with anger. "People get killed in broad daylight. Kids get abducted, guys get beaten up. Digger's a fucking psychopath. He crushed your bones with his bare hands. There's no way he's coming near you."

"I want to meet him," I say quietly. "He's my dad, Alex."

"He's a bloody sperm donor, not your dad. Just one in a queue of men mum opened her legs for. Are you really going to believe her when she's told so many lies? For fucks sake..."

I open my mouth then shut it again, any words stolen by shock. Alex never talks like this—at least in front of me—and it's like a slap in the face.

"Alex." Lara's voice is low. "Calm down. You're overreacting."

"Overreacting?" He laughs mirthlessly. "I was eight years old when I watched that man crack her bones. I heard it, Lara, heard her wrist break, heard the way she screamed. I'll never fucking forget it." Tears fill his eyes, and he wipes them away furiously. "And now you want me to be okay with this?"

Lara reaches out again. This time, he doesn't shrug her off. It doesn't calm him, though. He's still as tense as a big cat ready to pounce.

"But this isn't about you. It's about Amy, and what she wants."

"She doesn't know what she wants." He faces me. "If you knew what a devious bastard he was you wouldn't do this."

"He's my dad."

"Fucking hell!" Alex kicks out at the wall, his boot crashing into the plaster. Flakes of paint stick to the black leather as he pulls his leg away, leaving a dent behind.

"Alex, calm down!" Lara raises her voice. "You're scaring Amy and quite frankly you're scaring me. And Max is asleep."

Alex drags his hand through his ink-black hair, tugging at the strands. "How can I calm down when she's being so stupid? He's going to ruin her life. Again."

"He won't," I say, my voice calm even though I'm shaking inside. "I won't let him."

"Well I'm sorry if I don't trust your judgement, but you seem to rebound from one fucking crisis to another. If you do this, don't expect me to be there to mop up your tears this time."

I step back, offended. "I'm not a little kid, Alex, I know what I'm doing. You need to back off."

"You're *my* little kid. I'm the one who was there for you, the one who looked after you. Don't expect me not to care." He grabs his jacket from the arm of the sofa. "I'm going to the pub before I say something I regret."

With that, he storms out, leaving Lara and me standing with our mouths agape. It takes a few moments for me to find my voice, and when I do it's thin and shaky.

"I'm sorry, I didn't mean to cause trouble."

Lara smiles, then hugs me close. "You haven't. It's not your fault."

I close my eyes, resting my cheek on her shoulder. "But Alex was so angry..."

"He was." She leads me to the sofa and we sit down. "But you know what he's like, he blows up and then he calms down. He'll be back full of apologies I expect."

"Why doesn't he trust me?" I ask, looking up at her. She tucks a lock of hair behind her ear and rests her face on the palm of her hand.

"He's very protective of you," Lara says. "You've always been his little girl. You have to remember he's used to being the man of the house, he thinks it's his job to look after you."

"But I can look after myself."

"I know you can." She smiles. "It's just going to take Alex a while to realize that. As far as he's concerned, you're still a fifteen-year-old school girl."

"Ugh." I rub my face with my hands. "Sometimes I wish I was still at school. Life seemed so much easier then."

Lara twists around. Through a gap between my fingers I can see her staring at me. "Does this have anything to do with the text I got from your mum last night?" she asks.

"What text?"

"The one asking if I knew where you were, and why you still weren't home at two in the morning."

"She sent you a text?" I sit up straight, suddenly panicked. "You didn't tell Alex did you?"

Lara laughs. "Not likely. She sent me another one when you got in. Where were you all night, anyway?"

"Umm. A few of us went to a bar."

"And then?" She looks amused. "Wait, do I need a cup of tea for this? Or something stronger?"

I lick my dry lips. The remnants of my hangover have disappeared, leaving behind an arid taste and an intense thirst. "Tea sounds perfect."

Ten minutes later I'm clutching a chipped mug that's emblazoned with the Union Flag. Steam escapes from the opening, swirling through the air in a misty haze. Lara listens quietly as I recount the whole sorry tale, her face sympathetic. When I finish, she offers me the packet of biscuits she brought out with the tea. I stuff a chocolate Hobnob into my mouth.

"Wow," she says. "Now I'm really glad I didn't tell Alex about that text."

"So am I," I agree. "I've made him angry enough as it is, I don't need to add sex with my boss into the mix. You won't tell him, will you?"

Lara looks almost affronted. "Of course I won't. I'd never betray your confidence."

Frowning, I wipe some crumbs from my lips. "But won't keeping secrets from him cause problems?"

"Not half as many problems as telling him the truth would cause. You saw how he was today. Imagine what he'd be like if I told him your boss had taken advantage of you. He'd be running over to Canary Wharf for a fight."

I think of Callum, and his strong, lean, muscles. "I wouldn't fancy Alex's chances." Putting my now-empty mug on the coffee table, I try to get that image out of my mind. "Did you say Callum took advantage of me? You don't really believe that, do you?"

Lara tips her head. "Do you?"

Her words make me think. *Really* think. I close my eyes, remembering the events of last night, the way he touched me and held me. His words and his lips were soft, his fingers hard and demanding. But he didn't take advantage, or assume anything. More than once he asked if that was what I wanted.

And it was what I wanted, very much—at least until reality dawned.

"He didn't take advantage," I tell her. "If anything, it was the other way round. We had sex then I asked him not to tell anybody. I left him as if it meant nothing."

"*Did* it mean nothing?"

"Yes... no... Ugh, I don't know." I rest my elbows on my thighs. "It can't mean anything, can it? Not when I work for him. If anybody found out I'd lose my job, and I can't let that happen."

"What if you didn't work together?" she asks. "What if he was a guy you met in a bar? How would you feel then?"

"Completely different," I admit. "Because he's gorgeous and charming and everything I want." Not to mention the fact he's amazing in bed. "But I can't, so that's that."

"It's that easy?" There's still a hint of amusement to her voice. "You think you can just turn attraction on and off like a tap?"

I turn and stare at her. "I don't have a choice. It doesn't matter how much I like him."

"There's always a choice, Amy. Don't kid yourself, there's no black and white here."

I groan loudly, closing my eyes so tightly I see stars floating behind them. "But I want there to be. Because I've no idea what to do about this."

"Do you like him?"

I picture Callum's handsome face, and his strong body. Just thinking about him is enough to make me feel dizzy.

"Yes, I like him," I say, finally. "Much more than I should. I'm not sure there's anything I can do about that."

19

I manage to avoid Callum until Wednesday morning, when a project review meeting is arranged. Collecting the current data, I rapidly form it into a presentation which I hope will be enough to reassure the partners that everything is going to plan. My desk is cluttered with papers, as well as a vase of flowers that Charlie sent on Monday as some kind of peace offering. Though I reluctantly accepted the roses, I haven't quite accepted his apology yet.

Glancing at my watch I notice it's almost ten o'clock. The meeting is supposed to last for an hour and a half, which works out well as I'm due to meet Douglas for coffee at one. I can't quite bring myself to call him 'Dad'. I'm not sure I ever will.

Though Mum offered to come to join us, I turned her down. I figure a busy coffee shop in the middle of Canary Wharf is as safe as it gets, and I'm nervous enough about meeting him. She'd only make things worse with her fussing.

I'm still thinking about my family when I walk into the conference room. Distracted, I plug my laptop into the audio-visual system, playing around with the mouse until my presentation is on the screen.

Then I feel my hackles rise.

Callum walks in, followed by the rest of the technical team, and his eyes immediately catch mine. They're dark and narrowed, the shadows beneath them prominent, and his pale, chiselled beauty is hard to ignore. Flustered, I look away, feeling heat spreading across my face.

"All right, Amy?" Paul, one of the technical engineers, nods at me. I flash him a weak smile in return. I hate the way I react in Callum's presence.

When I sneak another glance, he's still staring. My heart stutters in my chest.

The catering staff come in, wheeling a trolley laden with coffee and biscuits. There's an immediate dash for the sideboard as the team fill white porcelain mugs with coffee, playfully fighting over the chocolate chip cookies.

When I walk over and take a cup, Callum's immediately beside me. He dwarfs me, his expression unreadable, his lips drawn into a thin, pale line. "You okay?"

I nod, because I can't find any words. Silently, I pour out two coffees, adding a splash of milk to his before passing it over. His fingers touch mine, warm and rough, and the sensation is enough to make me jump. I'm too damn jittery for my own good.

"Have lunch with me," Callum murmurs. "We need to talk."

"I can't." I half turn away, staring down at the rising vapour. "I'm meeting somebody."

"Who?" Is that a hint of jealousy I can hear? I'm not sure why but the thought gratifies me.

"My dad."

I hear his loud inhalation, followed by an ominous silence. He's still holding my arm, and I'm in no rush to pull away. A hum of conversation comes from the rest of the boardroom as the partners indulge is small talk. None of them seem to notice that I'm standing here in the corner, hemmed in by Callum's imposing body.

"You're meeting that man? Alone?"

"In a café," I correct him. "Surrounded by people."

He's staring down at me with a quizzical expression on his face, two vertical lines prominent between his eyebrows. I fight the urge to smooth them, aware that I have my hands full— literally and metaphorically—with him and my coffee cup.

"I don't like the sound of that."

"Who are you, my father?" I joke.

Slowly, he shakes his head. "No, Amy, I'm not your dad. I'm not the sort of guy who goes around scaring girls so much that they run into my office almost screaming. I'm just a… friend who's concerned about your safety."

I yank my arm out of his grip, and coffee sloshes over the side of my cup. It lands on my white shirt, staining it brown, and I sigh. "You know what, I'm so sick of this. First Alex and then you. I'm not some little kid who needs shielding from the big bad wolf. I'm a grown bloody woman."

My raised voice causes the room to quieten. Alarmed, I glance over my shoulder to see everybody staring at us. A blush steals its way up my neck, staining my cheeks in the same way the coffee stains my shirt. Perfect.

Callum steps smoothly around me, clearing his throat. "I'm sure you'll do fine. Of course I trust you to present your findings." His lips are so close to my ear that I can feel his breath warming my skin. "This isn't over," he whispers. "We'll discuss it later."

I shrug my shoulders and wrap my jacket around me to cover the stain, knowing that I'll be at the café long before Callum realises I've left the building. That's one of the good things about being an intern, nobody really notices when you're not there.

* * *

I spot Digger as soon as I walk into the café. He looks out of place. His jeans and t-shirt stick out like a sore thumb among the sharp suits and tailored dresses of the city workers. He's sat at a table near the centre of the room, almost as if he knew Alex and Callum would prefer us to be in full view of the surrounding diners. Making my way through the maze of tables and chairs, I step over laptop bags and huge designer purses, finally arriving at the empty chair opposite him.

A shyness descends over me when I get there, my fingers grasping the metallic back of the chair, looking at the scars that pockmark his face. Shrapnel, I remember Mum saying. The debris of a shattered bomb lodged in his skin.

"Amethyst." He gets up as soon as he sees me. The chair scrapes across the tiled floor. "You're here."

"Hello," I say softly. My voice sounds unfamiliar. It's tremulous, almost vibrato. We wait for an awkward moment, both mute, both staring. Then he gestures at my chair.

"Do you want to sit down?"

I nod and all but collapse into the seat. Even though the café is full of people there's a feeling of isolation. I don't know if it's fear or anticipation, or something else entirely that's making me feel so skittish.

Sitting in front of me is a man I thought was dead. The man who gave me life. The father who squeezed my tiny bones until they snapped. I'm not sure how I am supposed to feel. Elated or frightened?

"Can I get you something to eat?" he asks. It's one of those cafés where you order at the counter, no waitress service here. To be honest, it's little more than a glorified canteen, but for some reason it's popular among the city crowd. "And a coffee, maybe?"

His voice is quieter than I remember, but then I've only actually spoken to him once. Somewhere between that first meeting and this, he's become larger than life in my mind. A shadow that remains long after the sun goes down.

"Just a coffee please," I reply. "I'm not very hungry."

For the first time I see him smile. It takes ten years off his face, making him look almost boyish. That's when I notice his resemblance to me—or maybe my resemblance to him. He has the same dimple in his cheek, and his eyes crinkle just like mine.

"I'll grab us a couple of cakes, in case you change your mind."

While he's gone I whip out my phone and send a text to Mum to let her know I'm okay. I consider texting Alex too, but then I remember just how angry he was at the weekend. We haven't spoken since our argument because I know how long it takes him to calm down. When I slip my phone back into my bag, I notice a movement, as someone comes to claim the recently vacated table behind me.

A second later I realise exactly who that someone is.

"What are you doing here?" I whisper urgently.

Callum shrugs and pulls the plastic lid off his cup of coffee. "I was thirsty."

"There's a coffee shop in our building," I point out. "You didn't need to walk all the way over here for a drink."

He licks his lips languidly, and I follow the movement of his tongue. Then he raises the Styrofoam cup to his mouth, his eyes on mine. "I like the view better here."

"Are you spying on me?" I ask. "Did you follow me here? Because that's just…" I lose my train of thought. Instead I watch the way he holds his cup, remembering how I felt when he held me. His hands are big and strong, it's very distracting.

"I want to make sure you're safe," he answers.

I wrack my brain to think of a reply but come up with nothing. A slow, ragged breath escapes my lips and I offer him a half-smile. "Thank you."

He nods, looking over my shoulder. My father is back, sliding a tray full of coffee and cakes onto the stainless steel table, the legs beneath it wobbling. I twist back in my seat as he speaks. "I didn't know how you took it, so I've got some milk and sugar here. Is that okay?"

Glancing one last time at Callum, I turn my back on him and look at my dad. It takes a moment for me to collect my thoughts enough to answer.

"White, no sugar. That's how I take it."

My father slides the cup across to me, being careful to pull his fingers back before they can touch mine. I take a cake from the plate he offers, placing it on a napkin in front of me. Neither of us speak as we add milk—and in his case three sachets of sugar—to our coffee, using the white plastic stirrers to mix everything together.

Finally, he breaks the silence. "Thank you for coming. I know this must have been a shock. Tina—your mum—told me what she said. That she told you I was dead."

I bite my lip between my teeth, trying to remember the last time I felt this uneasy. Waking up next to Callum last weekend was a walk in the park compared to this. For reassurance I check that Callum's still there. He is, and it's enough to give me the courage I need to talk to this man who shares half my genes.

"She told me you died in Iraq. I thought you were a war hero."

He flinches, as if my words have the power to sting. "I'm no hero," he says. "But part of me did die out there. I wasn't the only one, a lot of us came home shadows of the men we were."

I pick at the napkin in front of me, tearing off pieces and dropping them on the table top. "It must have been awful," I murmur, more to break the silence than anything else.

"It doesn't excuse anything, Amethyst," he replies shortly. "I know that."

Finally I look up from the mess of tissue I've scattered all over the table top. "My name is Amy. Nobody calls me Amethyst." I don't tell him how much I hate my name or how mercilessly I was teased about it at school. He wasn't there to protect me when I needed him, because he was the one I needed protecting from.

I give a little shudder, trying to erase the image of a baby with a broken wrist.

"Amy," he says hesitantly, "either way it's a pretty name for a pretty girl."

He seems so eager to please, desperate to talk with me. The little girl inside of me who was always so needy for a father stirs. "Thank you," I reply.

"Tina says you're doing well at university, and that you've got a good job. Are you enjoying it?"

Behind me, I hear Callum shift in his chair. I'm desperate to look back again, to see what he's doing. Instead, I nod and try to hide my nervousness.

"It's a great opportunity," I tell him. "I'm hoping it will help me get a good position when I graduate."

"Have you always liked school?"

His question takes me by surprise. I pick up my cup, draining the dregs of my coffee before I reply. "I liked it until I was a teenager. After that..." I screw my nose up, remembering how awful it became after I was diagnosed with Scoliosis. For a year I had to wear a back brace and endure the taunts and jeers that only teenagers know how to deliver. It was only after I stopped growing—and no longer had to wear the huge, plastic molded contraption—that they finally calmed down. Even then, with one hip more pronounced than the other, and with posture that was always asymmetric, I still hated wearing tight clothes and swimsuits.

"After that?" he prompts.

"I didn't like it as much." That's why I left school and took a job as a legal secretary, wasting three years of my life when I could have gone to college. That and the fact Luke thought university was a waste of time. What a fool I was.

"You spent a bit of time in hospital," he prompts. "Your mum told me about your bad back."

For the first time I realise Mum has told him a lot. How much time have they been spending together?

The next ten minutes pass as we make painful small-talk. I turn the questions onto him, asking about his life in Australia and his plans now he's back in London. Neither of us mention his PTSD or the way he behaved when he came back from Iraq, but the knowledge of it underscores every word we utter. By the time the huge white clock suspended from the raftered ceiling clicks over to one o'clock the conversation has fizzled out to single word answers. I'm not sad to see that my lunch break is over.

"I should go," I say. "I need to get back to work."

His face falls for a minute. "I thought we could go for a walk."

The suggestion panics me, jolting me from the comfortable lull our conversation has created. It's one thing to talk to somebody you're afraid of when you're surrounded by diners, another to contemplate seeing them completely alone.

I'm not ready for that. Nowhere near.

I look behind me again, and Callum notices my wide eyes, his expression questioning. When I don't answer—mostly because I'm too busy trying to regulate my breath—Callum stands, rolling his napkin into a ball and dropping it into his empty cup. "Amy, I didn't realise that was you." His voice is over-loud and thick with brogue, as if he's hamming it up for effect. "Shouldn't you be back at the office by now?"

I nod mutely.

"I've got to go," I tell Digger. We stand together, both of us stepping back. It takes all the strength I have not to lean until my back is pressed against Callum's chest. I don't think I've ever wanted to be held more than I do right now.

"Who's that?" Digger asks, pointing at Callum. He looks smaller now, wiry and thin. Almost petite in comparison.

"My boss..." I stutter, "Well my ex-boss."

185

"Callum Ferguson." He offers his hand to Digger. There's nothing friendly about their handshake. Callum pulls his hand away, resting it lightly on my shoulder. Maybe I should be annoyed at this gesture, and the sense of ownership it conveys, but there's something so warm and reassuring about it. This time I allow myself to sink against him.

"Shall we go?" Callum asks me.

"We should," I agree. Safe in his protection, I turn to my father. "It was nice to meet you." I'm not sure if it was, but it seems the polite thing to say.

"You too, sweetheart." He glances up at Callum to see if he's noticed the term of endearment. From the way Callum pulls me closer, I'd say he has. "I'd like to see you again."

"Okay." I breathe the words out, but they don't feel light. "I'll call you."

Digger goes to kiss me, and I step back again, firmly into Callum's embrace. The strength of his muscles against my back flusters me, but the only way to pull away is to walk into my father's arms.

Rock, meet hard place.

Eventually, my father gives up, and I relax out of Callum's grip.

"I'll see you soon, then." Digger says, picking up his wallet and pushing it into his back pocket. "Say hello to your mum for me."

I watch him leave, as he half-swaggers through the café. He's out of the door before we start walking, and if I'm honest I can't say I'm sorry to see him go.

A wind whips around us as we emerge into the plaza, lifting my coat like a trickster.

"Well, that was intense," I remark as we corner the building.

"And that's an understatement." Callum stops, reaching for my hand, and his gesture brings me to a halt.

"What?" I ask. He says nothing, simply tips my chin with his hand, his eyes searching my face. "I'm okay, honestly."

186

"Will you just let me take care of you?" he mutters, his thumb rubbing my cheek. "For five fucking minutes?"

I lean against the brick wall at the back of the canteen, while Callum presses into my front. Though we are alone—except for the overflowing rubbish and recycling bins beside us—I still check guiltily for any observers.

"I don't need looking after."

"Well, maybe I need it," he shouts. "Maybe I need to take care of you. Maybe I need to protect you and know that you're okay."

"But why?" I'm genuinely confused. I peer at him, frowning, and try to ignore the stench that carries in the wind from the bins beside us.

His expression closes down, and I think back to the lunch we had when I was working for him. When he told me about his wife, about the way she died, and the memory is like a punch in the gut.

There's a part of me that warms at the thought of his protectiveness, at the thought of him trying to take care of me. But at the same time, I can't help wondering if I'm simply his way of gaining forgiveness for himself.

A replacement. A chance at redemption.

I want to tell him I understand, that it's all going to be okay, but the words curdle in my mouth like week-old milk. Instead I wrap my hand around his neck, feeling the sliver of skin between his jacket collar and hairline, my fingertips caressing and teasing. Then I roll onto my tiptoes, lifting my face to his, and communicate the only way I'm able to.

This kiss isn't hard and hot like our last one, it's all silky lips and warm breath. But there's something so sweet and yearning about the way the very tip of his tongue touches mine that I feel my legs beginning to shake.

For one glorious, awestruck moment, I forget about my family, my job and every other shitty thing that's happened in my life and let Callum Ferguson consume me.

20

I spend the rest of the afternoon in a fog, working through my churned-up emotions. I'm terrified by the thought that somebody might have seen us kissing. Every time the door to the office opens, I expect to see Diana from HR standing there.

There's some respite from my nerves at four o'clock when Charlie walks in, his right hand raking through his mop of blond hair. "Hello, stranger." He perches on the corner of my desk and takes my calculator, tapping at the rubber buttons. "Long time no see."

I lock the screen on my keyboard and slump into my chair. Though I hate to admit it, he's a welcome distraction to the maelstrom in my head. One of the best things about Charlie is that everything is simple with him.

"I've been too busy convincing my boss I'm not a coke-head," I tell him. "Telling the truth is exhausting."

"Oh, don't be like that." He pouts. "I said I was sorry."

Rolling my eyes, I pick up the 200g bar of Dairy Milk I found on my desk this morning. "Yep, nothing says I'm sorry like a bunch of half-dead roses and a petrol station chocolate bar."

"It was Sainsbury's Local, actually," he says, snatching the bar from my hands. "Why haven't you eaten it? Is there something wrong with my chocolate?"

"I wasn't in a chocolate mood," I say, taking it back. Running my thumbnail along the seam, I rip the packaging open, then offer it to Charlie. He snaps off a row, stuffing four squares into his mouth, and for one blessed moment it renders him silent.

"So," he says, his mouth full. "Did the big bad boss let you off?"

"Do you care?" I ask. "Because it didn't look like you gave a shit when your skinny arse was sneaking its way out of there. I could have been in a lot of trouble you know?"

"But you aren't," he says simply. "And if you were, I would have come clean. I'm a jerk, but I'm not an arsehole."

I raise an eyebrow. "There's a difference?"

Before he can answer, my phone starts dancing on the table like a man on hot coals, buzzing furiously. Callum's name is on the screen, and I immediately feel guilty. I'm lucky it's Charlie here, and not Caro Hawes or Diana from HR, they'd be able to read me like a book.

"Just a text," I say lightly. "I'll read it later. No biggie." Of course I'm desperate to find out what Callum wants. Will he mention the kiss, or will he apologise again? The thought of him regretting it makes me feel sick.

"I've got a meeting in ten minutes anyway," Charlie says, looking at his watch. "The monthly Health and Safety board. Somehow I've been elected as the student representative."

"Great," I reply, my mind still at the back of the café.

"So, um, there's something I wanted to tell you." He shifts on the desk, knocking off my note pad. Cursing, he bends down to pick it up, his hair flopping into his eyes. "A few of us are going out for Caro's birthday in a couple of weeks. Dinner followed by some clubbing."

As soon as he says her name my stomach drops further. At this rate it should reach the ground floor in five minutes.

"Sounds nice." I wait for him to invite me, already trying to think of excuses why I can't go. A night out with Caro Hawes doesn't sound very appealing.

"She's hired out a private room at a Japanese restaurant in Soho. Sushi followed by karaoke or some rubbish like that." He looks up at me, a sad expression on his face. "But it's really small. She wanted to invite you but there are already too many of us."

"Of course she didn't want to invite me," I say with a low voice. "She hates my guts."

Charlie doesn't try to deny it, instead he shuffles the business cards lined up by my keyboard. "Well I just thought you should know, in case you wondered where we are on a Friday night."

Slowly, I lick my dry lips. "Everybody's going?" I ask.

"Well not everybody."

"All the other interns," I clarify. "They've all been invited?"

Charlie nods. "And a few of the partners. Caro's dad's footing the bill."

It's pathetic, because I really don't want to go, but the fact I haven't been invited is humiliating. All the other trainees plus a host of partners will know I'm not there.

Then another thought grabs me, and even though I shouldn't ask, I can't help myself. "Is Callum Ferguson invited?"

His answer does nothing to calm my churning stomach. "Yes, and Jonathan Cooper. I think all the technical partners are going."

By the time Charlie leaves my mood has plummeted. Luckily, I remember the text from Callum. I unlock my screen, a smile playing at my lips as I read his words.

Can I take you to dinner tonight?

It takes me thirty seconds to tap out a reply. **Two meals in one day? People will talk.**

I'm only half-joking. But there's something so compelling about this need to be near him that I can barely bring myself to care.

A moment later, my phone vibrates again. **Maybe this time we can sit at the same table.**

My grin widens. All those doubts and worries seem to evaporate, replaced by an aching need to see him. For a girl who lives for work, suddenly I'm counting down the hours. Still, I can't help teasing him, marvelling at how easy it is to feel comfortable with a man I once worked for.

190

Does that mean I have to look at you while you eat?
Of course, his reply sends a blush to my cheeks and warmth
to my thighs. **If you're lucky, babe.**

* * *

When six o'clock arrives I'm not ready to leave. I've been stuck in
a video conference for the last two hours with a group of
managers from Grant Industries who have nothing better to do
than ask the same question in ten different ways. It's only
lunchtime in New York, and they're just gearing up, unaware that
I really, really want to go out to dinner with Callum bloody
Ferguson.

"Can you go over the timeline for the Exodus project?" one
of the managers asks with a nasally twang. Though I sigh
inside—I sent this information over in the pre-meeting pack—I
patiently talk them through the project plan. Jonathan Cooper sits
beside me, twirling a pencil between his fingers, and I sense he's
as frustrated with the repetitiveness of the questions as I am.

Jonathan is my assigned Supervisor for the project. Though
he's Callum's friend I get the sense he doesn't know there's
anything at all going on between us, and I plan to keep it that
way. I've grown to like and respect him, enough to care what he
thinks about me. Plus there's the small matter of the report he
has to write so that I can get my degree.

Grabbing the remote control, Jonathan turns the microphone
to mute. Even though the Americans can't hear us, he still
whispers.

"You think we're still going to be here at nine?" he asks.
"Maybe if I change into my pyjamas or start brushing my teeth
they might get the fucking hint."

My lips twitch, but I try not to laugh. It's okay for him to be
irreverent, but I'm nowhere near high enough up the food chain
to be rude about a client.

The meeting goes on in New York with the occasional input from us. Though Jonathan looks attentive, under the table he's scrolling through his Blackberry, answering emails. When they ask another question about delivery timescales, I keep a smile plastered on, showing them the charts which cover everything in detail.

I'm about to tell them about contingencies when the door to our videoconference room opens, and Callum walks in, his jacket slung across his shoulder. His jaw is dark where a day's growth of beard is starting to make itself known, and his shirt is unbuttoned so I can see the tender dip of his throat.

In short, he looks mouth-watering.

"Am I interrupting?" he asks, then sees the video is on, recognising some of the faces from Grant Industries' Manhattan office. He greets them with a salute, and a few of them say 'hi' back. He pulls out the chair beside Jonathan and sits down, stretching his long, muscled legs in front of him. I try not to look at the way the fabric tightens over his thighs, and how it's tight between his hips, but the view is so distracting I can't tear my eyes away, at least not until I'm asked another question.

"When will the first run be?"

"June twenty-fifth," I answer, remembering they like me to say the month before the day. "But if we decide to use the second protocol, we might be able to bring that forward."

Callum shifts in his seat, and the movement triggers my perception. Our eyes meet, and there's a dryness in my throat that wasn't there before.

"Let's call it a day for now," one of the Grant Industries executives suggests. "Maybe we can schedule another catch up for next week."

"Sure," Jonathan drawls, his thumb hovering over the 'off' button. "I'll ask my secretary to set something up." He presses the button, and the cameras whirr back into the wall. The screen turns off, leaving the room dark, and it makes me realise just how late it is.

"Well, that was a ten-minute meeting dragged into three fucking hours." Jonathan says, rubbing his face. "I don't know how many times we had to go over the bloody schedule, it's like they didn't believe us."

"I hope you're not pissing off my clients," Callum remarks sarcastically. "Anyway, since we charge by the hour next time try and drag it out for longer, okay?"

"Maybe you'd like me to dial in in my pyjamas?" Jonathan smiles. "Or perhaps I can send them a flash of my girlfriend's tits. Speaking of which, I was supposed to meet her at a restaurant half an hour ago, so if you'll excuse me." He stands up and grabs his papers, stacking them neatly into a pile. "Thanks for staying late, Amy, you did well to keep your temper." He looks over at Callum. "She's doing great."

"She is," he says softly.

Then it's just the two of us, and the room seems to shrink in size by about fifty per cent. Callum gently wraps his fingers around mine.

"I've been thinking about you all afternoon," he murmurs. His thumb brushes my wrist. I wonder if he can feel my pulse race. "Wondering when I can kiss you again."

"Not here," I say breathily. Though if he tried I don't think I could stop him. "Somebody might see,"

"Delayed gratification then. Let's go and grab something to eat, and we should probably have a talk."

Immediately, my stomach drops. "A talk?"

"After what happened last time I want to make sure we both know where we stand. I don't want to wake up in the morning to find you gone again."

I raise my eyebrows. "You seem very sure I'm going to stay over," I say. "What makes you think I'm not going home after dinner?"

He takes a step forward, holding my hand, until our arms are the only barriers between us. I still feel an intense need to press my chest against his. But somewhere in my horny, stirred up mind, I'm aware that I'm at work, and that a liaison with my boss is strictly forbidden.

"What makes me think it, Amy," he lifts both our hands up, using his finger to trace along my bottom lip. "Is the way you look at me with those pretty blue eyes, the way your lips plump up whenever you do."

"Maybe I have a new lipstick," I murmur.

"Then I'll kiss it off."

"Here?" I ask, a hint of alarm in my voice.

He shakes his head. "No, Amy, not here. When I kiss you—and I *will* kiss you—it's going to be so fucking hot it will blow the non-fraternization clause to smithereens. So I suggest we get out of here before I get us both sacked."

I nip his finger before licking it softly with my tongue. His eyes blaze in response, and he retreats as if he's been burned.

I know *I* have, and I like the feeling much more than I should.

* * *

When we come to a stop outside Callum's house I frown, glancing at him from the corner of my eyes. "I thought we were going to eat?"

"We are." Callum pulls his key from the ignition before unbuckling his seatbelt. His movements are calm, collected. A contrast to the nerves that seem to be my constant companion. "I wasn't planning on starving you."

"We're eating here?" I don't know why, but when he mentioned dinner and *a talk*, I pictured it happening in some dimly lit, expensive restaurant in the West End.

Not his house.

My question makes him smile. "That's the plan. Is it a problem for you?"

I find myself backtracking. "Not at all, I just didn't know you could cook." I unfasten my seatbelt. "You *can* cook can't you? You're not expecting me to whip something up or anything, because I have to tell you I can cremate water."

It's a true fact. Neither Alex, Andie or I inherited my mum's cooking skills, in spite of her many attempts to teach us. We'd starve without microwave dinners and Mum's Sunday roasts.

"No, Amy," Callum says slowly. "I'm not going to ask you to cook for me. I'm thirty-three years old, I think I can manage to cook us some dinner."

I don't tell him that cooking well isn't an age-related thing.

"Okay then." I open the car door and hop out onto the dull-grey pavement, sucking in a lungful of fresh air. Though the sun hasn't yet gone down, the moon is already out, an orphan half-visible in the wide blue expanse. I look at it for a moment, feeling somehow insignificant, but then Callum grabs my hand and we walk towards his house.

It feels strange, holding hands with him. His fingers weave through mine and his thumb brushes the inner skin of my wrist, and nice turns altogether dirtier.

I'm not sure why his hands fascinate me so much. It's not as if he uses them for much more than typing on a keyboard, yet they're strong and long and when I look at them I can't help but remember what they did to me that night.

In his house.

This house.

Oh God.

"Hang your coat up there," he says when we've walked into the hallway, pointing at a row of hooks. "I'll go and open a bottle of something and get started on dinner."

"Good, I'm starving." I've recovered my equilibrium enough to give him a cheeky grin. "Hop to it."

"Yes, ma'am," he calls from the kitchen, then under his breath he mutters, "Cheeky bitch."

"Oi, I heard that."

"You were supposed to," he replies, good humour lacing his voice. "Because you are a cheeky wee bitch."

"Wee?" I walk into his kitchen, my eyes raised. "Did you really just call me 'wee'? I'm not sure whether to be more offended by that, or the way you're a walking stereotype."

He puts down his knife, gently laying it on the chopping board. There's a glint in his narrowed eyes, a playful anger that sets my heart racing. Then slowly, deliberately, he walks toward me.

I back up until my hips are pressed against his black granite work surface. A minute later, he's against my front as he towers above me, so tall it feels like I'm craning my neck.

When he's this close it makes it hard to breathe. Though I'd never admit it, he does make me feel 'wee'.

"What?" I manage to get out.

The corner of his lip flickers, but otherwise his expression remains neutral. I wait for him to say something, but instead he stares, his dark-green eyes never wandering from my face. A lump forms in my throat, big and rough.

After a long moment, he wraps his hands around my waist and lifts me until I'm sitting on the work surface. Though the granite feels cold through the fabric of my skirt I don't complain, because all I can think of is the way he's pressing his hips into mine, and the long, hard ridge of his cock.

"What are you doing?" I murmur.

"This." He pushes again, the movement sending a thrill that makes my toes curl. Then his hand is on my chin, tipping it up until our lips meet. He pushes his tongue inside the seam of my lips at the same time as I wrap my legs around his back. We're kissing and rocking, hands everywhere they shouldn't be, the only sound in the room our loud, embarrassing gasps.

Callum stands straight, his hands underneath my bottom. For a second I think he's going to turn around and carry me into his bedroom, but instead he pushes his hand under the hem of my skirt, his fingers seeking out my warmth. He slides one inside me, then two, his thumb pressing against me in the most delicious way. I close my eyes tightly, my thighs flexing like a clamp around his hips.

"Amy," he whispers. I barely hear him. Blood rushes through my ears like a swollen river. I rock my hips, creating a rhythm that matches my heartbeat, unashamedly riding his fingers as my body reacts to his touch. Then he fumbles for his zip, releasing his hard, pulsing cock, and I reach for it. The next minute I'm pulling my knickers to the side, guiding him until his tip is brushing against my slickness. He pushes until I open up for him.

Callum steadies me, his hands holding me firmly, lifting me up and down until we're both panting loudly, breathing into each other as we kiss. I can feel the pleasure building and swirling at the pit of my stomach, radiating out with every thrust. Though we're both dressed—my skirt ruched around my waist, his trousers pooled at his feet—my nipples are hard enough to press through my thin bra and blouse, rubbing against his muscles.

That's when I feel it. The crescendo. The high. It takes me over, cell by cell, until I feel like I'm melting into him. Electricity courses through me, fizzing at my skin, and I freeze in his arms. My mouth is open and my voice silent as I ride the sensual, dizzying wave.

"Amy," he says again, his lips trailing down my throat, nipping at my skin. "You feel fucking amazing when you come on me."

He waits for my orgasm to settle before he moves again, reigniting the flame I thought had gone out. I squeeze around him and he moans, his thrusts becoming erratic and hard, and I can tell by the way his breath stutters that he's reaching his peak.

"Callum," I whisper in his ear. "I want to feel you come inside me."

He groans and angles his hips, fingers tightening on my behind, pressing in so hard I know he's going to leave marks. But I don't care, because nothing else matters apart from his pleasure, so I squeeze him tight until he mutters against my chest.

"Fuck, shit, fuck I'm going to come." His accent broadens, as if he can't even control that. His eyes are shut, his lips swollen and red, and all I want is to see his expression when he lets go.

My wish is fulfilled a minute later, when his hips slam into mine, a low groan escaping his mouth. He stills, his hands holding me tight, his face glorious as his orgasm overtakes him. At that moment I realise I could spend my whole life watching Callum Ferguson come.

It takes a moment or two for him to recover, but when he does, he pulls out of me, gently lowering me to the floor. A thin, white line of semen rolls down my inner thigh, and he watches it, licking his lips.

"That might be the sexiest thing I've seen," he says, his eyes still trained on my leg. "I might have to make you eat dinner just like that." He presses his finger to my thigh, spreading the wetness, then moves his hand up until he presses the pad against my mouth.

"Lick," he orders. For some reason I do exactly as I'm told, peeking my tongue out. His fingers tastes salty and wet—a curious mixture of him and me—and I suck it into my mouth.

"Are you trying to turn me on again?" he asks gruffly. "Because it's fucking working."

I smile. "No, I'm just bloody starving."

We spend the next few minutes cleaning up in his bathroom. He washes me gently with a flannel, lingering on my thighs, and pulls my skirt down, trying fruitlessly to smooth out the creases. His trousers are already fastened, but I'm pleased to see they look as messed up as my clothes.

The other thing I notice—which surprises me—is the lack of awkwardness between us. We talk easily as we leave the bathroom, laughing and giggling, and I love the way everything slots together so perfectly.

Pun absolutely intended.

Callum returns to peeling potatoes and chopping onions, passing me the glass of wine he poured out before we were distracted. I sit at the small glass table in the corner of his kitchen, sipping Sancerre and admiring the way his bottom looks beneath the dark blue wool of his trousers.

"I should have asked you about birth control," he says, slicing a red pepper into thin strips. "Although the words 'closing the stable door' and 'after the horse has bolted' spring to mind."

"Did you just compare yourself to a stallion?" I tease, still shocked by my lack of embarrassment. I remember how things were with Luke, when I could barely bring myself to say the word 'condom'. "And I'm on the pill, thanks for asking."

He turns around, knife still in hand, and fixes me a grin. "It's not my fault you're so fucking gorgeous I lose all common sense."

I roll my eyes. "The excuse of stupid men everywhere. This is why the planet's overpopulated."

He frowns. "Because you're gorgeous?"

"No!" I protest, laughing. "Stop trying to sweet talk me. All I'm saying is that birth control is a two-way thing. I knew I was covered, but you..."

"I just wanted to see me dripping down your legs," he says, his pleasant tone belying the dirtiness of his words. "And yes, I'm an idiot for not talking about protection before, but for the record I'm clean. I wouldn't put you in any danger."

I soften. "I'm clean too." I made sure of it after seeing the photo of Luke with that girl. "For what it's worth."

Even when he turns back to resume chopping, I can tell he's smiling from the tone of his voice. "Not from where I'm standing, babe. Everything you've done tonight suggests you're very fucking dirty indeed."

21

I'm not sure what wakes me up. Perhaps a strange middle-of-the-night creak, or the shaft of lamplight that sneaks through the velvet drapes covering Callum's sash windows. Whatever it is, I roll over in his unfamiliar bed, frowning when all I come in contact with is a cold, empty mattress.

It takes another moment to realise what's wrong. I'm used to sleeping alone—especially after breaking up with Luke—but I'm not used to doing it in a strange man's bed. I rub my eyes with balled-up fists, trying to wipe away the thick sleep that sticks my lids together.

"Callum?" The air is frigid enough to make me shiver. I pull the sheet around my chest, but the cotton does little to stave off the cold.

There's no answer. As my eyes adjust to the gloom, I realise he's not in here, and swing my legs around until my feet hit the wooden floor.

I pick up a t-shirt and pull it over my head, unwilling to walk naked through his house. It doesn't matter that we spent half the night unclothed and glistening with sweat, because right now, I feel vulnerable.

The hallway echoes to the sound of my bare feet slapping against the floor. A strange wistfulness weighs me down like a heavy blanket. I come to a stop in the doorway of the living room and look around, spotting him sitting in the large, leather wingback chair that's placed next to the open fireplace. He has a glass of whisky in his hand, the ice tinkling as he circles it around, and there's a serious look on his face.

A long minute passes until he notices me. His eyes rake up and down, taking in the thin, white t-shirt that's scarcely decent, and my bare thighs that emerge from the hem. Though there's a melancholy expression on his face, there's also a fire behind his eyes.

We stare at each other for longer than is comfortable. It's awkward yet compelling, pinking my cheeks and sending a shot of desire through my body. Then—almost without thinking—I walk across the room.

"I woke up and you were gone," I say, my voice wavering. "I didn't know where you were."

His thick, dark lashes brush his cheeks as he swallows the final mouthful of his whisky. "I had a bad dream."

For a moment he's almost child-like, awakening some dormant instinct deep inside me; the need to console is almost too strong to ignore.

I climb onto his lap, tucking my feet beneath me, and wrap my arms around his neck. He places his hands in the small of my back, burying his face in my shoulder.

Softly, I stroke his hair, murmuring sweet words into his ear. My fingers drag against his scalp, and I feel his breath hitch once, then twice.

What the hell is wrong? After a night of frantic lovemaking, it's almost frightening to realise he's so vulnerable, and I've no idea what to do.

"Tell me about your dream," I whisper, not loosening my hold on him.

He looks up at me, blinking. "It was a nightmare," he says. "The same one I always have. I wake up and she's there."

I start to feel sick. "She?" I ask.

"Jane. She's there, holding me, I can't get out." He's still so muted, his voice a monotone. "Her arm is pinning me down and no matter what I do, I can't get her off me."

His eyes are glassy, unfocused. I wonder how much he's been drinking. I've no idea what the time is. Although it feels closer to morning than night-time, the last thing I remember was falling asleep just after 1:00 a.m.

I cup his face with my hands, his half-beard scratching my palms. He looks at me as if I have all the answers, and I find myself wishing I did.

"Shh, it's okay," I croon, as if I'm talking to my baby nephew. "It was just a dream, I'm here. You're going to be okay."

When we kiss, there's a sweetness to it. His lips are soft, whisky-coated.

"Tell me about her," I say. "Tell me about your wife."

Callum says nothing, though his arms tighten. His wrists cut into my waist, almost hurting, but I can't ask him to stop. Instead I continue stroking his hair as if he's a little boy, breathing in the earthy, masculine scent which tells me he definitely isn't.

It feels like forever before he finally speaks. "I graduated from university in 2003 and walked straight into a job at Richards and Morgan. Back then they used to take on about fifty graduates a year, it was the boom times. So there were a lot of us competing for the best projects, and trying to see who could drink the most on a Friday night."

"Sounds familiar," I mumble.

"I met Jane in my second week. She'd graduated from Cambridge the year before, although she was the same age as me. Even so, she had this air of 'been there and done that' I liked. It seemed a simple step to ask her out, see where things went."

I don't want to hear this, but I think I need to. This girl—this woman—has played a huge role in his life, leaving scars I didn't know were there. I have to force myself to say, "Go on."

"As I said, we all worked hard and played hard. Stayed at the office until ten, and then headed straight to the bars. Sometimes we'd have enough time to stumble home, take a shower and drag ourselves back into the office. It wasn't sustainable, and it wasn't healthy, but it was what everybody did. So that's how I lived for four or five years."

I can remember Lara telling me the same thing about her experiences working in the financial district. There was constant pressure to excel at everything, whether that was getting the most prestigious projects or being able to handle alcohol. Somehow it's hard to picture Callum—this strong, big man—having to fight his way to the top. In my mind he was always there.

"But something changed?"

He clears his throat. "*I* changed." He pours another splash of whisky into his glass. "I got bored of doing the same thing, day in day out. I wanted to be awake at work; I wanted to give my clients everything I had. I didn't want to just coast along. A year later I was offered a promotion and a great job in the Edinburgh office, and I asked Jane to come up with me."

"Did she?"

He looks down. "She didn't want to. She liked being in London, she liked the party lifestyle. She found it a lot easier than I did to get up in the morning after a heavy night out. It took a long time for me to realise what she was doing to help her function."

My heart catches in my throat. I know exactly how people cope with alcohol consumption on a night out. I've seen it before—the traces of powder, the glassy eyes. Cocaine can be an excellent anti-hangover cure.

"She was a user?"

"She didn't see it that way. She thought it was a casual thing, something she did just to help her through the day. She swore she could stop whenever she wanted." He laughs harshly. "Idiotic isn't it? All addicts say the same thing, until somebody actually challenges them."

"Did she stop?"

His pupils dilate as they take in light. He blinks rapidly as if to acclimatise himself. "We agreed to make a fresh start in Edinburgh. We got engaged, bought a flat, and started our new jobs. I thought everything was fine, that she was happy. I'd forgotten how good she was at hiding things."

"But you got married," I prompt. "So things must have been okay?"

"As I said, I was oblivious. Too busy at work, too busy trying to get my next promotion. I didn't realise how unhappy Jane was, nor how she was trying to deal with her depression. We were both too ambitious to accept we could be anything less than perfect."

I close my eyes, picturing that wedding photograph. The beautiful couple, their beaming smiles. It's hard to believe that it wasn't genuine. How often do we hide our emotions behind a fake smile?

"Two years ago, things came to a head again," he continues. "I was running late for work and barged into the bathroom to clean my teeth. She was leaning over the sink, snorting a line of coke. I went fucking ballistic, told her it was over, that I couldn't take it any more. I said some things I regret, shouting I'd never have kids with her, that she'd be a shitty mother. By the time I left for work we were both boiling over." His voice cracks. Regret seems to seep from his every pore.

I relax my hold on him, moving my hands up to cup his face. "It's okay," I whisper.

It's as if he doesn't hear me. "When I came home from work that night she was nowhere to be seen. I did what I usually did, ate some dinner, cleared my emails, went to bed. I didn't bother calling her, didn't bother trying to find out where she was. As far as I was concerned, she wasn't my problem any more."

He pulls my head to his, until our foreheads are touching. "I took a couple of sleeping pills—prescribed by my doctor for anxiety—and fell asleep. According to the police, they think Jane came home around one in the morning. They had witnesses to say she was in a bar on Rose Street until midnight. They thought she took a taxi home, though the driver never came forward."

I shiver, in spite of the flames burning in the open fireplace next to us. Callum puts his hands over my own, holding them there, as if he's afraid I'll let him go. But I don't want to release him; I want to touch him until the anguish disappears. I want to make everything right, I just don't know how.

"I didn't wake up until the alarm went off, just before six. The clock was on Jane's side of the bed, and she always used to sleep through it. Normally I'd just roll over her and reach for the snooze button. But this time I couldn't move." He shudders, caught up in the memory. "The pathologist says I woke up at the worst time, just as rigor mortis was setting in. She'd been dead for four hours."

This time it's me who starts shaking. I can't begin to imagine waking up next to a dead body. Especially somebody you loved.

I press my lips to his cheek. "She died next to you?"

"Officially it was classed as Sudden Adult Death Syndrome, although cocaine usage was a secondary factor. The reason I couldn't move was because she was half-lying on me, her body weighing me down. It wasn't until I was fully awake that I realised she was gone."

"Is that why you woke up tonight?" I ask. "Because I was cuddling you?"

"It just reminded me..." He breaks off. "I didn't want to think of her with you lying next to me."

When he starts to cry I kiss away the tears, tasting their salty sweetness. I kiss him all over, on his mouth, his nose, his forehead. I stroke his face and murmur softly, telling him I'm here, that I'm not leaving.

That's where we stay for the rest of the night, until the morning creeps its way in, reminding us that even when our lives are rocked, the world still goes on. In the course of those pre-dawn hours, as we talk and caress, I realise I'm in love with Callum Ferguson.

22

There's something truly magical about realising you're in love with somebody. It's as if the world becomes a pretty backdrop made just for us, and the surrounding people are simply a cast of extras. For the past week, I've spent the days waiting until I can see him again, and the nights in his bed.

On Monday, Callum catches me as I'm walking to a meeting, dragging me into a breakout room for a heated kiss. We're getting careless but the lure is too strong. Falling for someone is funny like that. It makes you feel invincible, the resulting adrenaline an anaesthesia that protects. So we flirt and we kiss, and pretend we're living in our own universe, hoping nobody will notice the passion growing between us.

Of course, somebody always notices.

On Thursday, after a meeting where Callum seemed more intent on eye-fucking me than troubleshooting, he sends me a text asking me to meet him back at his place. I accept readily, stuffing my papers into my bag so I can leave the office on time. That's another thing that's changed—for now at least—we're both leaving earlier than we ever have. No more late nights squinting at the laptop or on endless video-calls to the US. We prefer to spend our evenings wrapped around each other.

I take the underground to his house, pushing my way through the evening commuters to emerge onto his street. Winter has finally set in, twisting her icy fingers around the city, and I pull my scarf around my face to stave off her chill. When I get to Callum's house, it's dark and empty, so I take out the key he pushed into my hand a few days ago, feeling excited and nervous about letting myself into his house. It makes everything feel real, knowing he wants me to be able to come and go, and I like the way the trust is building between us.

Everything changed after that night in his living room. The final door has been opened, and all our secrets have escaped. There's this man—this beautiful, strong, vulnerable man—and it makes my chest feel full to know he's mine.

The frostiness of the outside air follows me, and I keep my coat on when I step inside. Dropping my bag, I flick on the hall light, and make my way to his kitchen to put on the kettle.

Even the floors are freezing, but I'm not sure how to turn on the heating. I glance at my watch and hope he'll be home soon, that he'll build a fire like he has every day this week, laying the wooden logs in a carefully ordered fashion. There's something very sexy about his Boy Scout obsession with fire, and the way his face lights up with achievement when the flame starts to burn, that makes me want to throw myself at him every time.

Most of the time I do exactly that.

The kettle is coming to a rolling boil when I hear his key slip into the lock, and the front door open. I hear him drop his case on the floor, hang up his coat, and the thud of his dress shoes landing in his cupboard.

He walks into the kitchen, his tie loose around his neck and his top few shirt buttons open, revealing his chest. He leans on the granite work surface, tilting his head to the side, smiling at me as I take another mug from the cupboard.

"What?" I'm smiling too. "Don't you want a cup of tea?"

He folds his arms across his chest, his hip steadying himself against the wall, and nods. "Yeah, I'll have one."

"I can make you coffee if you want?" I take an exaggerated look at my watch. "Although it isn't quite nine o'clock yet, I don't want to make you angry."

Callum raises his eyebrows, silent for a moment. Finally, he steps towards me, his movements strong and intent, trapping me against the work surface, as he cages me in with his arms.

"Are you ever going to let me forget that?" he murmurs. "I just wanted to show you who was boss." He presses his lips to my neck, and I jump at the coldness of his skin.

"You're freezing," I protest. He laughs, pushing his hands beneath my shirt. Their iciness makes me squeal as I try to escape, but there's nowhere to run. "I'm not a bloody hot water bottle."

He laughs. "Says the girl who spent most of last night with her feet between my thighs."

"It's not my fault you're too miserly to have your heating on all night," I retort, trying hard to ignore the way his hands are feathering up and down my sides. When my nipples harden, it has nothing to do with the cold.

"If you think this is cold, you should try living in Scotland." He unbuttons my shirt as he talks. "Ice on the inside of the windows and snow drifts eight-feet high. This is Hawaii compared to that."

"I've never been to Scotland." My words catch as he reaches behind me and unclasps my bra. When he slides his hands inside the cups, his ice-cold fingers create a kind of pleasure-pain that makes me squeeze my eyes shut.

"We'll have to remedy that. We should fly up to Edinburgh for the weekend, I'll show you my old haunts."

I can't understand how he's so calm, so methodical, while I'm slowly being wound into a frenzy. He keeps the one-sided conversation going, telling me about the Royal Mile, about his apartment, the bars, the beautiful view from the Castle. He only quietens when he captures my nipple between his lips, sucking hard enough to make me arch my back.

The next minute we're running into his bedroom, burying ourselves beneath his white duvet, tearing each other's clothes off and throwing them on the floor. By the time he's inside me, all thoughts of ice and cold are forgotten, replaced by burning need and desire.

* * *

Later that night, we're sitting in front of the fireplace, eating pale fluffy omelettes and listening to his stereo. I take a sip from a large glass of red wine—decadent for a work night—and push my bare feet between his firm thighs.

"I told you," he says, capturing my feet between his hands. "Have you got some kind of thigh fetish?"

I smile because it's a Callum-fetish I'm suffering from. "Once again, Scrooge McDuck, I refer you to your miserliness. If you cranked up the heating I wouldn't need your body warmth."

"Where would the fun be in that?" he asks. His hands rub at my soles, the friction defrosting them. "Maybe I like having your feet close to my cock."

"Who's the one with the foot fetish now?" I murmur. Then I move my feet, feathering them against the hard ridge beneath his pyjama pants.

Callum grabs my toes again, this time stopping me from touching him. "Hey, I wanted to prove to you that we can have a conversation without it ending in sex."

I arch my eyebrows but don't struggle, repeating his words from a moment before. "Where would the fun be in that?"

We tease each other for the next hour, with our words as well as our touch. Then we climb back into bed—still unmade from our earlier, unplanned visit—and he holds me closely. The second night I slept here, the one after his confession, I'd tried to keep my distance so I wouldn't stir up his memories again. But he'd dragged me across the king-size bed and refused to let me go as we fell asleep.

Since then, I've draped myself around him every night, for the closeness as much as for the warmth. His nightmares, when he's had them, have been mercifully short and fast to dissipate.

"I meant what I said about taking you to Edinburgh," he whispers, running a hand lazily through my hair. I prop my chin up on my hand, as my elbow presses into the mattress.

"Okay." I can't hide my excitement. A dirty weekend with this gorgeous man in his home town? *Hell yes.*

"We could go next week, except there's that bloody party on Friday. Maybe we can travel on the Saturday morning after we get up."

Though there's a glow inside when I realise he's taking my staying over for granted, it's soon chased away by the thought of Caro Hawes's party. "I haven't been invited," I confess.

Callum frowns. "What?" he asks, his voice disbelieving.

"I haven't been invited, Caro hates me. I think it's because I wasn't born a duchess, or maybe my accent. I don't know, but she's had it in for me from the start."

He rolls his bottom lip between his teeth. "That's sorted then, we'll travel up on the Friday night. I'll book our flights in the morning."

"You're willing to miss out on the party of the year?" I ask him. "She won't be very pleased about that."

"I don't really give a fuck whether she's pleased or not. If she's being a bitch to you, then I'm more than happy to ruin her bloody party."

I hide my smile in his chest. "Then Edinburgh it is. Are you serious about booking the tickets tomorrow?"

"Yeah, sure. I'll ask my PA—" He stops abruptly. "Ach, yeah, probably best not to do that, right?"

"Best not to," I agree, still grinning. "I'll book them, you useless privileged bastard."

He rolls over on top of me, pinning me to the mattress. "Less of the useless, sweetheart." He presses his hips to mine. "I may be privileged, and I'm definitely a bastard, but I think you'll also find I'm very bloody useful indeed."

* * *

The day before we're due to fly to Edinburgh, I find myself cornered in the canteen by Caro and her sidekick, Miranda. I've just slid my tray onto the trolley reserved for dirty dishes when I turn to find them in front of me. For a minute I'm reminded of that scene in *The Shining* when the little boy sees the dead twin girls in a corridor. Only Caro and Miranda are much scarier than that.

"Amethyst," Caro says when I fail to speak first. "How are you?"

"I'm fine," I say, not bothering to inquire after her health. "On my way to a meeting, actually."

"In that case I won't keep you long. It's my birthday tomorrow and a few of us are going out for dinner. A space has come up and I know you'd love to join us."

She speaks as though she's doing me a favour, without the merest hint of irony. I keep my smirk to myself when I realise the spot she's referring to is Callum's, and only I know the reason for his change of mind.

"Oh that's a shame," I reply. "I'm already busy, otherwise I'd have loved to join you." I wonder if my sarcasm is laid on a little too thick. "Try to have a good time without me though, won't you?"

Caro frowns, three lines criss-crossing her dainty forehead. "I'm sure it's nothing you can't cancel. Everybody will be there, it would be really good for you to network." She leans in as if she's doing me the biggest favour. "You won't get a chance like this again."

It's difficult not to laugh. The knowledge I'm going to be spending the weekend with Callum buoys my confidence. "I'll have to survive somehow."

"Where are you going that's so important?" she asks. There's a sneer in her expression that I want to wipe off, I hate the way she talks down to me.

"My boyfriend's taking me away," I say. "It's been planned for weeks, so there's nothing I can do."

"I thought you'd broken up with him," she replies. "Or is it one of those tiresome on-again off-again relationships?" She exchanges an amused look with Miranda, who's been silent for the whole encounter. "I heard he cheated on you. It's sad that you have so little self-esteem that you'd take him back."

I'm tempted to tell her to stuff her opinions up her own behind. But I remind myself that I have so much more to lose than she does, and if I can lie enough to take her suspicions away, then that's what I'll do.

"I guess I'm just a glutton for punishment," I reply. *Maybe that's why I'm here, talking to you.*

"Well if you'd prefer a weekend with a cheater to an expensive night out with a work colleague, so be it." She rolls her eyes. "Next time I won't bother to ask you."

"I think that would be for the best." I keep my composure. "We're never going to be best friends, are we?"

She wrinkles her nose, as if I've suggested she eat a plate of dog food. "No, I don't think we will."

"In that case, I'd better get to my meeting." I look at my watch with an exaggerated gesture, trying not to reveal I'm talking about an imaginary appointment. "I'll catch you around."

With that I push past Caro, leaving her and Miranda behind with the dirty dishes and messed up trays. The image of her face, marked with disdain, puts the biggest smile on my face.

23

Our flight lands in Edinburgh a few minutes before eleven. Although it took little more than an hour and a half, my back is still aching from sitting in one position for too long. I rub it as we join the line to exit the aircraft while Callum pulls our bags from the overhead lockers. Even without looking at I feel him frown.

"Are you hurting?" he whispers. His accent sounds broader now we're back in his home country. I can't help but find his burr sexy.

"Just a bit stiff," I reply. "I'll be fine once I've stretched it out."

"Now that's something I can help with. I've always liked testing your flexibility."

We take a cab into the city, heading for his flat in Marchmont. Callum keeps up a steady spiel as we travel, telling me about the university, about growing up in Morningside, and promising he'll take me to meet his mum who still lives in a flat there.

When we stop at an imposing row of brown-brick houses, Callum climbs out, walking around to my side of the cab to open my door. I'm still full of questions but struck dumb by the opulence of the buildings, intimidated by their height and beauty, not to mention their age.

It's obvious this is one of the wealthiest parts of town.

"You said your mum is still in Morningside," I say as we climb the stairs to the glossy front door. "Is she still in the same place you lived in as a kid?"

He slides his key in the lock. "Yeah. After Dad died it was just me and Margaret in there."

"Margaret?"

"My mum. She liked me calling her by her first name. She's funny that way, a bit of an odd one. Not that she isn't lovely," he adds.

"It was just the two of you?" I clarify. "No brothers or sisters?"

"Nope, just us."

"Bliss." I smile.

Callum chuckles as we walk into the dark hallway. It's a garden flat, bought a few months after Jane died. "I always wanted brothers and sisters, I hated being an only child."

"That's easy to say until you have them," I tease. "Growing up in my house nothing was sacred. When I started my period the whole street knew thanks to Andie and Alex."

"I'd like to meet them," he says softly. "Your family, I mean."

I feel my chest tighten. As much as I'm desperate for the validation his meeting my family would give our relationship, the thought of Callum seeing my crazy family is enough to give me the jitters. "Soon," I say, hoping to placate him.

"If I show you mine, you have to show me yours."

"How old are you?" I ask. "Twelve?"

He grins. "You'd have liked me when I was twelve. I was horny as a dog with the stamina to go with it."

"Since I was two, I don't think I'd have been that impressed," I tell him.

He shakes his head and leads us into the flat, flicking the lights on as he goes. The building is as imposing in here as it is on the outside, with high ceilings, stripped floorboards and long, long windows. The wooden shutters are drawn across them, blocking out the night. I smile when I spot the cast-iron fireplace—black metal surrounded by ornate tiles—and wonder if he's remembered to buy enough wood to satisfy his pyromaniac tendencies.

I follow him through the rooms, each one more impressive than the last. We end up in a conservatory that leads onto a lush garden. The ceiling is strung with fairy lights, casting a mystical glow across the terracotta-tiled floor. I can tell from the comfortable sofas and blankets that this is the room he uses the most. There are shelves pushed against the back wall, stuffed with well-read books. I can picture him sitting in here on a Sunday afternoon, his feet up, reading a favourite story.

"This is beautiful," I say.

"It is," he says, staring at me. His eyes are dark, glinting beneath the hundreds of lights hanging above us.

"Do you ever think of moving back here for good?" I ask. "You must have kept this place for a reason."

He's silent for a moment. I sit down in an easy chair that looks out onto the moonlit garden and he hands me a beer from the fridge in the corner.

When he finally speaks, he's contemplative. "I can't see myself living in London forever. If I have kids I'd like to bring them up here."

He'd make a great dad, I know that much. While I'm not ready for babies, and don't anticipate having them for years, part of me wants to throw myself at his feet and offer my body for procreation purposes.

Is this what they mean by being crazy in love?

"I've heard Edinburgh's a beautiful city." I change the subject, ignoring my racing heart.

"And you'll see it tomorrow," he promises, scooping me onto his lap. "I'll give you the grand tour. The castle, the cathedral, the volcano. I guarantee you'll fall in love with Auld Reekie."

"Auld Reekie?" I question. "And wait a minute, volcano? There's no bloody volcano here is there?"

This time he grins. "There's a great huge one in the middle of Holyrood park, sweetheart. But don't worry, it's been extinct for about a million years."

"It would be my luck if this was the weekend it woke up," I grumble.

Callum coughs out a laugh. "I'm guessing geology isn't your strong point, then? I said extinct, not dormant."

"Same difference," I mutter.

He catches my hand, pressing my palm to his groin. "The difference between dormant and extinct, babe, is that with dormant you've got a chance of it waking up. As in my cock has been lying dormant for a number of hours, but right now there's definite signs of activity."

I press harder, feeling him stiffen against my palm. "Seems like there's a big chance of explosion," I whisper.

"Eruption, Amy," he retorts, his hand still firmly on mine. "Keep with the game."

Cocky Scottish bastard, I think, but I test out his theory anyway.

* * *

He drags me out of bed at stupid o'clock the next morning. The sun's barely risen when we're sipping coffee in the garden room, propping our feet up on stools and looking out to the lush vegetation surrounding the small gravelled courtyard. The bushes are strung with lights, and I imagine it must look magical at night time, as though a thousand fireflies have come to land.

"This would be a lovely place to sleep," I say. "If it wasn't so bloody cold. Maybe we should come in the summer, we could set up camp in here."

I don't even feel embarrassed suggesting we'll still be together next summer.

"I can tell you've never been to Scotland before," he remarks. "It's always bloody cold, even in the summer."

After breakfast we head out to do some shopping on George Street, where the higher-end boutiques are found. To my surprise Callum is a laid-back customer, rifling through racks and showing me things he likes. He buys me a leather jacket and a woollen scarf to make up for the fact I underestimated how much colder it would be here than in London. Then he drags me into an elegant shoe shop, where he makes me try on flat, comfortable shoes, assuring me I'll be glad of them before the day is out.

I don't doubt him for a second.

"I didn't picture you as a shopper," I tell him, as we head down Princes Street towards Holyrood Park. My arm is slipped inside his, and I'm luxuriating in the fact we don't know anybody here. It's so nice to be able to show him affection in public, to walk arm in arm just like any other couple.

"What do you mean?" he asks. "Everybody shops, don't they?"

"They do, but most men aren't as enthusiastic as you," I tease. "I think you actually enjoy it."

"Is that a bad thing? Don't all girls like shopping?"

"This girl does," I tell him. "And it's not a bad thing at all."

Holyrood Park takes my breath away. It's hard to believe such beauty can lie so close to a city centre. It's alive with grass and gorse, lochs and knolls. At the centre, rising majestically from a series of hills, is Arthur's Seat—the long extinct volcano Callum promised me. It's as though somebody dropped a little bit of the Highlands into the city, the wild nature co-existing peacefully with the old brownstone of the town.

"It's beautiful," I say.

Callum seems bemused by my response. "You're like a kid who's never seen the sea before," he says, putting his arm around me. "It's only a park."

I shake my head. "This isn't a park. London has parks. This is like a piece of magic. I can't believe you got to grow up so close to this. I'd have spent most of my life here if this was me."

He seems enchanted by my response to his hometown, pulling me to him and kissing me. I kiss him back eagerly, sliding my hands into the back pockets of his jeans, and more than one passer by clears their throat loudly at us.

"Are we making a spectacle of ourselves?" I ask, still clinging tightly to him.

"Who cares?"

When we get to the foot of Arthur's Seat, Callum suggests I replace my shoes with the flats we bought back in the boutique. Though I roll my eyes, I follow his suggestion. The volcano—extinct and all—looks higher here than it does from the distance.

We follow the main route around to the right—a gentle climb at first, which Callum assures me isn't strenuous. Passing through the broad valley of Hunter's Bog, we ascend upwards on the narrow dirt path. Though it only takes twenty minutes or so to get to the top, I'm already captured by the beauty.

When we sit on a crag overlooking the city, Callum pulls a bottle of Rioja from his rucksack. Handing me two plastic wine glasses, he fills them halfway.

He puts the bottle on the ground and takes a glass, tapping it against my own. "To us," he says, his accent broader than ever. "And a wonderful weekend."

I take a sip. The liquid sends a blush to my cheeks, the taste of blackberries lingering in my mouth.

"Thank you," I say quietly. "Thank you for bringing me here." My voice wobbles a little, enough for him to notice, and he slides across the rock until our hips are touching. His lips are red from a combination of wine and cold air, his eyes bright and clear. I feel everything inside me tighten.

"I'm in love with you." His voice is deep and strong. "I think I've loved you since the minute you walked through my door, all brazen and angry and railing at the world."

He sets light to me. "Tell me more."

"You want me to tell you that you're the first thing I think about in the morning?" he asks. "And the last name on my lips at night. You want me to explain that for the first time in years I feel as if I can actually fucking breathe again, and that life might actually be worth living outside of the office?"

I nod, and he gives me a half-smile.

"Maybe I could tell you that every time you walk in a room it's as if somebody's turned the lights on inside my soul. Or that when you leave it, I feel every muscle in my body ache, and I'm counting the seconds until I can see you again."

"You could," I whisper. I'm greedy, I want all his pretty words. I want to store them in my mind and replay them time after time. "You *should.*"

He continues talking as I clamber onto his lap, straddling his thighs. Our empty glasses lay abandoned in the grass, all thoughts of wine forgotten. "You tell me you think this place is beautiful," he whispers. "But when you're sitting here it looks like any other piece of scenery in any other town, because all I can see is you. I know it's not going to be easy, and I know that somehow we need to keep this under wraps, but I love you Amy Cartwright, and there's nothing wrong with that."

I grasp his cheeks with my hands, brushing my lips against his. Our noses touch, their tips cold from exposure, but we're grinning at each other anyway.

"That's the nicest thing anyone's ever said to me." My eyes are filled with tears at his beautiful words. "If I was half as eloquent as you, I'd be able to say it right back."

"Then do it." He strokes my hair. I shake my head, teasing, playing. He kisses me hard, enough to make my body rock against his.

"Say it," he demands again, tipping my head back and running his lips down my throat. "Say it, Amy."

When he kisses the sensitive skin beneath my ear, it takes everything I have not to gasp. Instead I search for my voice, ready to stop teasing him. "I love you," I say, my breath ragged. "I really love you, Callum James Ferguson."

He leans back until he's laying on the rock and I'm on top of him, and we're frantically kissing and repeating the words over and over. Though it feels perfect and blissful, I still have to squash down the niggling thought at the back of my head that's desperate to be heard.

Once you've reached the summit, the only way to go is down.

24

Callum's mum is nothing like I expected. Not that I know what I expected really. Perhaps a Dame Maggie Smith lookalike, along with the regal accent—but there's not a hint of the Professor McGonagall to this elegant blonde lady who is sipping her wine across the table from me. She's youthful, friendly, and delighted to meet me, her eyes twinkling as she talks.

"He's told me all about you," she tells me, as Callum rests on the bar, talking with the grizzled old man behind the counter. "I'm so glad you agreed to visit with him."

"Don't believe a word he says. It's all lies," I tell her. "He's been trouble ever since I walked into his office."

"Oh, I can believe that."

The pub is warm and cosy, the perfect respite from the Scottish winter. A fire blazes in the corner, orange flames licking up like a hungry cat. The walls are half-wood panelled, half-flocked wallpaper, and the dark wooden floorboards bear the scrapes and dents of a thousand footfalls. It's a typical British pub on a Sunday afternoon.

The door opens and a family hurries inside, their faces pink-cheeked from the bitterly cold Edinburgh wind. I watch as the mother fusses, sitting her children around the large square table, as her husband wanders over the bar to order their drinks.

Margaret must be watching, too, because the next minute she's asking, "Do you want children one day, Amy?"

I'm taken aback by her question. It's the second time in two days I've had this conversation. First with the son, then with the mother. Until yesterday, it wasn't something I'd thought about, other than as an abstract 'maybe one day' but somehow I don't think that's what she's asking.

She wants to know how serious I am about her son. It's the equivalent of a father asking a boy's intentions.

"I don't know," I reply. "I think so. But I'd expect the father to share the responsibility." For some reason I find myself saying more than I intend. "I was brought up in a single parent home, I wouldn't want that for my children."

Margaret nods. "That's understandable, nobody wants to bring their kids up alone. But sometimes we don't get any choice."

"Callum told me about his dad," I say softly. "I'm sorry you lost him."

She offers me a small smile. "He was taken too young. I never intended to be a widow at thirty-three, and I had no idea how to raise a boy on my own. But somehow I managed, and I think I did an okay job."

"You did more than okay." I mean it. He's complicated and occasionally irascible but there's a goodness in Callum that shines through. Standing at the bar, he laughs as he talks with another customer, sipping at his beer and shooting the breeze. Slowly he turns, looking over at me, his expression changing as he stares. I can feel heat flooding through my body and I start to worry how we are ever going to hide this passion back at work.

"Has he told you about Jane?" Margaret asks quietly.

I nod. "I was sorry to hear that, too." I was, even though it sounds contradictory; because if she hadn't died I wouldn't be here, would I?

"What was she like?"

Margaret takes a long sip of her wine. "You're asking a mother. I'm afraid I'm biased."

I want to ask her if she's biased for or against. Does it make me a bad person to hope it's the latter?

"I want to understand why he stayed with her for so long. From everything he's told me, the two of them had a toxic relationship."

"That's a good way of describing it, though I don't think it was Callum's fault. He did everything he could to help her. But some people won't be told, and some problems can't be solved." Margaret looks up, her wine glass drained. "I've never told him this but a part of me was glad she died without them having children. As much as I wanted to be a grandmother, it was a blessing they were spared that."

"Did he want children?" I ask, my voice small. The smell of roast beef wafting from the table next to us is making me feel nauseous. I watch Callum from the corner of my eye, buying another glass of wine for each of us, and I know this conversation needs to conclude very soon.

Part of me wants to know everything, and the rest wants to hide away. The contradiction seems to be pulling me from the inside out.

"I know he wants children, but I don't think he ever considered having them with Jane. He always had this hope that she'd get better, that they'd both be able to settle down, but he would never have brought a child into that situation. For all his height and strength he's a big softy. He wants to take care of his wife and children. It's something he never had—a father to look after us—and I think he wants to be able to make up for that."

Her words make me want to cry. I imagine Callum as a little boy, longing for a father and desperate for siblings, yet somehow having to be the man of the house. With every new piece of information I learn, I'm coming to realise we're more alike than I thought.

I silence the rest of my questions when Callum carries our drinks over, sliding them onto the battered wooden table. "Everything okay?" He sits next to me on the bench, his thigh pressed to mine.

"Everything's fine." I reach for my glass. Though we're flying home later—and I definitely need to be sober for that—I need the liquid courage right now. But it's not the wine that reassures me; it's the way he takes my hand, wrapping it in his and squeezing tightly. His skin is warm and rough, his palm large enough to encompass mine completely. "I was telling your mum what a tyrant you are at work."

He laughs. "Did you tell her about the coffee?"

"The coffee?" Margaret asks.

"I bought him a coffee on my second day at work, and he told me he didn't drink caffeine before nine. After that I had to go out at exactly 8:55 every morning just to satisfy his stupid drinking habits."

"You drink coffee before nine." Margaret glares at Callum. "I've made you enough mugs in my time to know you can't even function before you've had caffeine."

Callum smirks. I resist the urge to wipe it clean off his face.

"You drink coffee before nine?" I ask. "Seriously?"

Callum does a double take at my furious expression. "Hey, I was just trying to show you who was boss."

"But I was being nice," I protest. "I bought that cup of coffee as a peace offering."

"After calling me an elitist arsehole," he reminds me.

"If the cap fits," I goad. "It's not my fault you looked down on me because I didn't go to Oxbridge."

He puts a finger beneath my chin, tipping my head up so I'm looking straight at him. "Apart from the obvious physical aspect, I'd never look down on you, sweetheart. You've achieved so bloody much and all under your own steam. I'm in awe of you."

Oh, this man knows how to sweet talk. I'm so overcome by the vehemence of his words that I can't help but press my lips to his.

Then he's kissing me hard and fast, his hand cupping the back of my head. I wrap my arms around his neck, pulling him closer, needing to feel every part of him against me.

Margaret clears her throat, reminding us where we are. Though heat floods my cheeks, I'm relieved to see she's smiling, looking at us both with a fond expression.

"Sorry, Mum." Callum's grin is far from regretful. "I can't help it, she's always leading me astray."

Margaret shakes her head, "Callum Ferguson, it's one thing kissing a girl in front of your mother, another thing to be disrespectful about it. Now tell her you're sorry."

It's my turn to smirk. Callum frowns at my glee, rolling his eyes. "I'm very sorry for disrespecting you, Amy."

"I forgive you," I reply, my tone echoing his. "But I'm expecting a cup of coffee on my desk every single morning to make up for it."

"Babe, I'll buy you the bloody coffee shop if you like."

He gives me a quick kiss on the tip of my nose, then mouths "I love you."

I mouth it right back.

* * *

When we leave London City Airport and clamber into a black cab, a sense of sadness comes over me. The flight home was uneventful and sleepy, but as a consequence it passed way too quickly. As the weekend comes to a close, I can't help but think of work tomorrow.

I bury my head against Callum's chest, trying to block out the dark thoughts. But even his warm protection isn't enough to reassure me.

"I don't want this to end," I whisper into the wool of his sweater. His arms tighten around me, and I feel his lips press against the top of my head.

"It's not over," he says. "We're only just beginning, babe."

"But everything's so complicated. I'm going to have to walk past you in the corridor and pretend I don't want to wrap myself around you. I don't think I can do it."

There's a smile in his voice. "I'm confident you can restrain yourself. It's only a few months, then you'll finish your placement, get your degree and we can come out into the open."

He makes it sound so easy. Maybe it is to him, but all I can see ahead is darkness and difficulties. I can't even sit in a cab without wanting to hold him, how am I going to get through a day without touching or being touched? He's a drug and a comfort blanket combined, and I find myself craving his proximity.

"It's not me I'm worried about," I say in an attempt to lighten the situation. "I'm pretty sure you're the one who can't keep his hands to himself."

"Is that a fact?" He proves my point by pulling me closer, running his lips across my forehead, my eyelids, my cheeks. "You think I'll cave first?"

"I know you will." My heart flutters as his lips press at the corner of my mouth. "You haven't got an ounce of self-control."

"Not around you, sweetheart," he agrees readily. Then all words are silence as he kisses the hell out of me.

Twenty minutes later, we pull up outside my mum's house in Plaistow.

"Am I coming in?" he asks, putting my suitcase down on the pavement. His question isn't demanding or petulant, it's just a few words in a throwaway tone, but they still send me into a panic.

"Tonight?" I ask, wide-eyed. "Um, I don't know. Do you want to?"

"Don't panic," he whispers. "I won't come in if you're not ready. We've got all the time in the world." His lack of offense calms my anxiety.

"I want to introduce you to them," I tell him. "But not until I've prepared them all. I've only really told Lara—my sister-in-law—about you. I want them to treat you properly when you finally meet."

"Okay."

"Come over for lunch next Sunday, you can face the whole bunch. It will be like a swift sharp shock."

"You make them sound delightful."

"They're one of a kind. Noisy, opinionated, and they won't stop asking you questions. As long as you're prepared for that."

He cups my face with his hands, pressing a soft kiss to my mouth. "Babe, it'll be fine. I want to meet them."

"If you're sure?"

"I'm sure."

I'm still smiling when I put the key into the lock of the front door, waving as the cab pulls away. Though I can't see Callum through the tinted glass, I blow a kiss anyway. When it disappears around a corner, I walk into the hallway, and call out loudly.

"Hello?"

A scuffle comes from the living room, and a low, uttered 'shit." Half-intrigued, half-worried, I open the door, my eyes seeking out movement in the low, ambient light.

My mum is the first to sit up. She clutches a piece of fabric to cover her naked chest, and it takes me a moment to realise it's her blouse. Then Digger jumps up, pulling his jeans up hastily, and I realise I've walked in on something extremely embarrassing.

It's something no child should have to see.

"Oh my God!" I spin on my heels and run out of the room, wishing I could erase the image from my memory. She's done some stupid things before—had relationships with losers and married men—but I can't help but feel she's hit a new low.

My mum and my dad? The thought not only nauseates me, but it also sends me into a tailspin. If Alex ever finds out, he'll never forgive her, and I'm not sure if I can cope with that.

Leaving my suitcase in the hall, I clamber up the stairs, ignoring Mum as she calls my name. I don't want to talk to her, I don't even want to see her, and to make the point I slide the bolt through its cage.

Later, after I've climbed into bed, I hear the front door shut quietly, then the tap-tap of Mum walking up the stairs. She knocks softly on my door, and I bury my head under my pillow, not ready to talk to her about what happened down there.

When I fall asleep that night—after a text conversation with Callum that tells him everything—my mind is racing with thoughts of all that's happened, and I start to worry that Edinburgh was simply the calm before the storm.

As it turns out, I'm right.

25

Monday is taken up with a series of meetings, each one more tedious than the last. I'm not sure if it's boredom that makes me check my watch every five minutes, or the incessant need to see Callum that's nagging at my chest. I can't even message him on my phone—we have clients in and if they saw me tapping away at the screen it would look disrespectful.

It doesn't stop my fingers from itching to type, though.

By the time my final meeting ends at 6:45pm, I'm flagging. My stomach is rumbling from being ignored since breakfast, and my limbs ache as though I've been through five rounds with Floyd Mayweather. In short, I'm a mess.

That's exactly how I feel when I bump into Callum just outside the second floor bathrooms. He's wearing his suit jacket and carrying a satchel slung across his shoulder, and though I hate to admit it, he looks ten times better than I do.

"Hey." He stops in front of me, leaning his shoulder against the wall. I loosen my grip on the handle to the bathroom.

"Hi."

"Good day?" He raises an eyebrow and cocks his head to the side. A lock of hair falls across his brow, and I lift my hand up to brush it away before remembering where we are and just how inappropriate that would look.

"Busy. Long, tiring. But I think we slayed some dragons."

His other eyebrow lifts up, joining the first. "Dragons?"

"It's what Jonathan says to us before we meet with a client," I tell him. "'Let's ride in on our white horses and slay some fucking dragons'."

Callum laughs at my pitiful attempt to take on a posh accent. "Jonathan's full of shit." The fondness in his tone belies his words. "Sounds as though the pigs are sleeping in the beds. What happened to the girl who was railing at me about elitism and chauvinist crap?"

"Where did the pigs come from?"

"George Orwell. In *Animal Farm*, when the pigs start sleeping in the house..." He trails off when he notices my confused expression. "You didn't study it at school?"

This time I take on a London accent, over-egging it until I sound like Dick Van Dyke on speed. "Nah, guvnor. We didn't have them new-fangled fancy book things when I was at school."

His lips twitch, but somehow he manages to swallow down a smile. "Explains a lot."

"Like what?"

"Like why you're a stubborn, hot-headed, gorgeous siren of a woman," he says, pushing me against the wall. "And why every time I think I have you figured out, you end up surprising me."

He lowers his head, brushing his lips against mine. Though we're in the middle of the corridor, I find myself kissing him back, frantically bunching his shirt in my hands, needing to feel his skin against my fingertips.

Next to us, the bathroom door bangs and we jump apart. We both turn to look at the door. Callum tucks his shirt back in while I smooth down the hair he's messed up with his roving hands. Neither of us sees anybody there.

"Close call." Callum whistles, running his hands down his jacket to get rid of the wrinkles. "I'd have to tell HR it was all your fault for being so goddamn sexy." His voice lowers at the last bit, his accent turning gritty.

"Good to see all that chauvinistic crap hasn't gone completely." Though I'm joking, I still feel a bit shocked. Anybody could have walked down that corridor—*anybody*—and I can't believe we came so close to being caught. My mind skips back to that HR meeting we had a few months ago, after Charlie's spectacular fall from grace, and I realise how near I've just come to messing everything up.

Whatever happened to degree, job and getting the hell out of Plaistow?

I know exactly what happened. Callum happened. Callum and his soft, sexy voice and his hard, greedy hands. The man who can make me forget about every single bit of ambition I have with one toe-curling kiss.

"Are you ready to leave?" he asks. "I'll wait for you if you want to go in there." He gestures at the bathroom door. Somehow, in the mayhem of seeing Callum, the urge to use the bathroom has disappeared.

"Let's go," I say, trying to keep my voice light. "I just need to drop a couple of letters into the post room then I'm good to go."

"You want to come back to mine?"

The offer is enticing. So attractive, in fact, that I'm about to agree when I remember last night and that I'm supposed to be going to my brother's flat to discuss my situation. A sense of disappointment washes over me from head to toe.

"I can't, I have to go and see Alex and Lara. I need to tell them about Mum and Dad." That phrase sounds so stupid when it should be natural. *Mum and Dad.* It slips off the tongues of kids the world over, yet for me it's stilted and thick.

"Afterwards, then?" His voice holds a promise which makes me shiver.

"Afterwards."

* * *

A wall of noise hits me as soon as I step inside Alex's flat. Max is screaming loudly, while Lara is trying to calm him down and switch the oven off at the same time. Alex runs back into the kitchen to help, and I hang up my jacket, rolling my eyes at the scene unfolding before me.

It's all too familiar, and immediately transports me back to my school days. There was always somebody yelling—usually Alex or Mum—and the noise makes me feel almost wistful. Now that it's just the two of us in the house, things are so much quieter.

I wonder how much longer the relative silence will last, now that Mum has something going with Digger. Will she move him in with us? How will I feel about that? Am I even going to want to spend the night under the same roof as a man who once broke my bones?

I'm getting ahead of myself, as usual.

Ignoring my runaway thoughts, I walk into the kitchen. "Can I do anything to help?"

Before Lara can respond, I scoop Max out of her arms, leaving her free to sort out the oven. Alex is banging a wrench against the pipes under the sink, muttering away about something, so I decide to take Max into the living area to play with his toys.

"Car" He points at the luminous-yellow jeep that seems to take up half the floor space of the flat. "Wan car."

"You want the car?" I repeat. Lara prefers that we repeat his words back, but saying them like adults. Apparently it will lead to him having better vocabulary or something.

All I know is it makes me sound as if I'm going mad, talking normally to a kid who hasn't even reached the age of two.

Max stares at me, his face serious, as if he thinks I'm weird, too. Poor kid, he must get sick and tired of having everybody throw his own words back in his face. I start to imagine him turning around one day and telling everybody to stop bloody repeating him, and the picture that paints in my mind is enough to start me giggling, which only makes Max look even more appalled.

He must think his Auntie Amy is a nutcase. Maybe he's right.

"What's so funny?" Lara passes me a glass of white wine and lifts Max up in the same, smooth movement. Her ability to do more than one thing at once while surrounded by Cartwright men impresses me. Do they teach that at antenatal classes?

"Nothing," I shake my head, unable to suppress my grin. "I was just imagining what it's going to be like when Max can talk properly."

"I'm dreading the day," she whispers, conspiratorially. "Considering how much he looks like his dad, I'm pretty sure he'll have the same loud mouth."

"I heard that," Alex calls out from the kitchen. "You don't usually complain about my mouth, sweetheart."

I wait until Lara has taken Max into their glitzy bathroom before I say anything to Alex, mainly because I want to shield them from his reaction.

"So, um, I walked in on Mum with another bloke last night."

Alex wrinkles his nose, sending me a 'why-the-hell-are-you-telling-me-this' kind of look. "Again?"

I grimace, remembering all the other times we've found her 'entertaining' a man. Nothing too lurid, but when you're fourteen and coming home from a night with your mates, the last thing you want to see is your mum lip-locked with some strange guy.

"Again," I confirm. "Except this time I knew him."

Alex comes closer, as if I'm about to share a juicy morsel of gossip. For a moment, I wish that I could say it was someone other than my dad, and then we could have a good laugh. His wide-eyed, interested look is going to last approximately two seconds as soon as I tell him the truth.

"It-was-Digger," I blurt out, as if saying it quickly will somehow shield us both from the consequences. "I saw Mum kissing my dad."

Alex is silent. Long enough to make me shiver, because Alex without words is a dangerous thing. It means he's about to explode.

The fallout comes less than a minute later.

"What the hell? She kissed that douchebag? How could she? Doesn't she remember what he did to us, what he did to you? For fuck's sake, I've seen her sink bloody low, but this really takes the biscuit. I'm going to kill her."

He starts to pace the room. Walking back and forth, he tugs at his hair with his hands. Lara's head pops around the bathroom door, and she catches my gaze, her eyes wide. I try to send her a look that conveys I have this all under control, but I think it just ends up looking as though I'm eating a lemon.

"How long's it been going on?" He stops his pacing to look at me.

"I don't know. It could have just been a one-off, I didn't stay around to ask them about their relationship."

"Good girl." He squats in front of me, taking my shoulders in his hands. His grip is firm and reassuring. I've always felt safe in the arms of my big brother. "I don't want him anywhere near you, not after everything that's happened, and I can't believe Mum would either."

I say nothing because Mum's actions say it all. Even if I don't hate my dad in the way that Alex does, I'm still wary enough not to want him in my house. Again I start to wonder what her plans are, whether she's thought this through. What if they decide to give it another go?

It's going to tear our family apart.

Ten minutes later, Lara joins us, fresh-faced from Max's bath and bedtime routine. Though she's put Max in his cot, we can hear him softly singing to himself, and I'm half inclined to make a joke about him and Alex forming a band. Only this doesn't seem like the right time for jokes.

"Here's what we know," Lara says, pouring a fresh glass of wine. "He and your mum were kissing in your house, but you don't know if they'd just started, or if it was more than a friendly thing. It could be nothing."

I take a huge gulp of wine before speaking. "Um, she had no top on."

Lara coughs, spluttering Chardonnay everywhere. When she catches my eye, I feel my mouth twitch, and before I know it I'm collapsing in a heap of giggles. She joins in, laughing hard, and it takes a full minute before we can get ourselves under control. By the time I finish, my stomach is aching from the exertion.

"I can't believe you saw that," she says, trying to stifle her laughter. "Oh my God, it must have hurt your eyes."

"It wasn't the best thing I saw all weekend," I admit, my mind immediately turning to Callum. "But at least she had the good grace to cover herself up quickly."

"What about him?" Alex asks, markedly less amused than Lara and me. "Was he naked?"

"Ew!" I screw up my face. "I don't know, I didn't look. I just ran up the stairs as soon as I realised what was going on."

"You should have come here instead."

I shake my head. "As disgusting as it was, I don't think I'm in any danger. It's not as if he's going to march into my bedroom and snap my wrist, is it? Even if he did I would fight back."

Alex's eyes narrow. "You're not living there while she's seeing that arsehole. We're going to have a family meeting, and we're going to sort this out. In the meantime, you need to pack up your stuff and stay here with us."

It isn't the first time Alex has asked me to move in with them, and I don't expect it will be the last. His protectiveness is lovely, but it's stifling, too—a reminder that none of my family realise how much I've grown up.

I decide to take a calculated risk. "It's okay, I'll stay at my boyfriend's."

Lara and Alex turn to look at me, their mouths dropping open as if they are synchronised. Alex is the first to recover. "You're back with Luke?"

"No!" I shout. "My new boyfriend. Someone from work."

"Okay…" he says slowly. "I want to hear all about this. Especially why you think it's okay to spend the night with someone you've just started seeing."

With that, Mum's forgotten, at least for a moment, and the spotlight turns onto me. Although I usually hate it, the need to talk about Callum overrides everything else. By the time I leave the flat, Alex and Lara are in no doubt that I'm in love with a certain Scot from Richards and Morgan.

* * *

I leave Callum in no doubt, either, as soon as he opens the door to his house.

"Hey, how was…"

I silence his words with a kiss, pushing him inside until he hits the cool wall of his hallway. I move my lips against his, hard and demanding, needing his touch to erase the fatigue of the day. He doesn't try to talk again, just cradles my face with his large, warm hands, and I let the heat seep into my skin.

It radiates inward, soaking into my muscles. He drags his hands lower, feathering down my spine, cupping my bottom as he pulls me to him.

I thread my fingers into his hair, tugging hard, needing to have him closer still. I want to feel, to be felt, to forget about everything except just how good it is to be in his arms.

"What was that for?" Callum asks when we separate. He's as breathless as I am, his chest rising and falling rapidly. I place my hand in the centre, feeling his heartbeat, my fingers splayed out against his firm torso.

"I was just saying hello," I reply innocently.

"In that case, I can't wait to see how you say goodbye."

Smirking, I give him a wave of my hand and spin on my heels, heading toward the front door. "Bye!"

"Oh no you don't," he growls, grabbing my wrist and pulling me back. "You're staying here tonight."

I twirl, feeling light-hearted and giddy. This is what he does to me, every time.

"Oh, you want me to stay?" I bat my lashes at him.

"You're staying whether you like it or not."

"Ooh," I purse my lips. "Like a love slave."

"A willing love slave," he says, feathering his hands down my sides. "One who won't know what's hit her just as soon as I've thrown her onto my bed."

"Is that a threat?" I murmur, running a finger along his jaw. It's rough and dark from a day's growth of beard.

"It's a promise, sweetheart. There are some things you should know about me by now. I like my coffee bitter, my women sweet and I always keep my promises." With that, he lifts me up until my legs wrap around his waist, and carries me to his bedroom, throwing me on the mattress so hard that I bounce a couple of times. I only still when he lays on top of me.

"I can't promise to be sweet," I say, as his fingers impatiently tug at the buttons on my blouse. He pulls it open, until the white silk is covering only my arms, and my chest is exposed to the air. Sliding his fingers underneath the straps of my bra, he pushes them to the side until the cups fall down, and I'm almost naked from the waist up.

A shot of pure pleasure pulses through me when he pulls one of my nipples between his lips, his stubble scratching my skin as it skims my breast. My toes curl as he presses his palm to my stomach. His hand moves down, beneath my waistband and a soft sigh escapes my lips.

"So fucking sweet," he says, his words vibrating against me.

I'm too far gone to say anything, but I have to admit I agree wholeheartedly.

26

The next morning starts with a panic. I realise too late that I have no clean work clothes with me, and the thought of turning up to the office in yesterday's suit is too embarrassing. So I end up travelling halfway across London at some ungodly hour of the morning, taking a taxi-ride of shame.

Callum thinks it's hilarious. He goes as far as to offer me one of his shirts, which is tantamount to tattooing the details of our relationship across my forehead. When I tell him 'no', he shrugs, a grin still on his face, and I can hear his guffaws when I step out onto the street.

A few minutes later I receive a text. By that point I've already hailed a cab, hoping against hope that the morning rush hour hasn't started yet.

You're going to be late. You know that, right?

He's a smug bastard, but at least he's not as stupid as me. How difficult is it to remember that you actually need clean underwear and clothes if you're staying at somebody's house?

The taxi pulls up at some temporary traffic lights, and the cacophony of a road drill joins the growling of the engine to make my ears hurt. "Busy out there today," the driver remarks. "You going anywhere nice?"

I look down at my wrinkled skirt and blouse. "I need to pick something up."

Another message from Callum arrives after we get past the road works. It's already eight thirty, and I'm nowhere near home. This time it's a photograph—a large Styrofoam cup with steam rising up from the rim. From the background I can tell he's at his desk, and I try to ignore the jealous hunger that rumbles from the pit of my empty stomach.

I send him back a rolling-eyes emoji and switch my phone off, determined to have the last word. All thoughts of revenge are forgotten, as I squeeze my hour-long morning routine into thirty minutes. A perfunctory shower is followed by a spray of dry shampoo and a layer of makeup. By the time I finally walk into the office building I feel as though I've already done a full day's work.

Maybe that's why I don't notice the silence. Or the fact there's somebody sitting at my desk, until I'm practically sat on their lap.

"Oh, I didn't see you there." I jump back, my forehead crinkling with confusion. Diana Joseph from HR looks up at me with cool-blue eyes, and closes the top drawer of my desk.

Immediately I'm on edge. Why would she be going through my desk? It's not as if there's anything valuable in there—and nothing private—but the nonchalant invasion of my personal space seems so out of character.

"Amethyst," she says calmly, standing up and pushing the chair beneath the desk. "You need to come with me."

I glance at my watch. "I'm due in a meeting in twenty minutes."

"I've cancelled it. Just put your things down and we can go somewhere quiet."

Small beads of perspiration start to form on my upper lip. "What's this about?"

The smile she gives me is anything but friendly. "Not here, let's go to my office."

Five minutes later she's closing the door behind us and offering me a seat. Her office is much like her—well organised and pristine, with no stray pieces of paper or half-eaten chocolate bars marring the surface of her desk. To the left of her computer screen is a picture frame, showing a man who must be her husband, and her two perfectly-turned out children. It looks more like a Calvin Klein advert than a family photo.

"I need to talk to you about something serious," she says as soon as she's seated on her leather swivel chair. "This isn't a disciplinary hearing, although I do need to warn you that disciplinary action could follow. Anything we discuss today could be used as part of that action."

Her words sound eerily similar to the Miranda rights I'm used to hearing in American cop shows. There's no smile on her face now, no softness in her expression, just a piercing directness that tells me I'm in a lot of trouble.

My mind flies to all the things that have happened over the past months. The reprimands for drunken behaviour, the way Charlie and I spilled the cocaine on the pavement outside the pub. Then I wrack my brains to think of anything I've done wrong recently.

It comes up blank until I think of Callum. If anything had happened, he would have called me, wouldn't he? Warned me that we'd been discovered and I was about to walk into this.

Of course he would have called... and it would have gone straight to voicemail because I turned my phone off after his last message.

Shit.

A wave of nausea appears from nowhere, scratching at my throat, making my nose sting. I'm only half a breath away from throwing up when Diana opens a blue file in front of her.

"I had an interesting email this morning, making some accusations against you and a colleague. Is there anything you want to share with me?" She lifts a printed email from the folder.

"No."

"It would be better for you to come clean. Confess everything. I can explain to the disciplinary hearing that you cooperated."

I swallow hard, though my mouth and throat are so dry that it makes me cough. "I don't know what I'm supposed to have done wrong."

"Do you remember signing this when you joined us?" Diana pushes another sheet of paper towards me. I recognise it immediately; it's the Code of Conduct she had all us interns sign on our first day at Richards and Morgan.

I take it from her, skimming it quickly. My signature is at the bottom in loopy blue ink. "Yes, I remember." My voice is low, cautious.

"And you're aware that fraternisation is strictly forbidden?"

"Fraternisation?" I question.

"Office affairs." There's a sigh in her voice. "You're aware that office affairs are forbidden. You signed the paper after all."

"I said I did," I snap, then immediately want to change my tone. Any remaining bravado flows out with my words, leaving behind a mixture of shock and fear.

"Then I'm sorry to say you've been accused of contravening that policy."

This time she passes me a photograph. Though it's grainy—printed in black and white—there's no doubt that the two people in the picture are Callum and me, locked in an embrace next to the second-floor bathroom door.

"Is that you?" she asks.

For one moment I consider denying it. Telling her it must be someone else—another twenty-something with dark hair and a blunt fringe.

"I don't know." I can't even come out with a sensible retort. My mind is so full of conflicting thoughts that it can't process properly.

"I have a statement from another employee which confirms that the two people in this photograph are you and Mr Callum Ferguson. Your boss."

"He's not my boss," I say weakly. "Not any more."

Diana leans her head to the side, still staring at me. "This isn't a time to play semantics, Miss Cartwright. Do you understand how serious this is? You've been accused of contravening a Company policy. The consequences could be dismissal, which not only means you'll lose your job, but also your chance of getting your degree. Of course we will have to inform your university of the accusations, and I wouldn't be surprised if you're punished by them, too."

The tone of her voice is calm, but there's something else in it. An edge of relish, or maybe even self-importance. *She's enjoying this.* She actually wants to see me in trouble; maybe it's a big improvement to her normally-mundane Tuesdays.

I'm panicking, even while I'm trying to keep my exterior as calm as possible. I've worked hard for this degree, and the thought of it being snatched away makes me want to throw something at the wall. Tears sting beneath my eyelids, and I reach up, wiping them away, because I really don't want her to know how truly frightened I am.

"Aren't I supposed to have somebody with me in a meeting like this?" I ask. I'm not sure it's true or if I'm getting mixed up with those cop shows again. Maybe I should call a lawyer or something. But I don't have the money to pay for one, and Richards and Morgan could pay for dozens without blinking an eyelid. It's David against Goliath and I don't have a slingshot.

"This is simply part of the investigation," Diana says, snatching the Code of Conduct out of my hand. "I'm trying to find out all the details before I hand it over to the hearing."

I grip the arms of my chair tightly. My stomach feels as though I've been sitting on a rollercoaster. Tight and sickly.

"And if I say nothing?"

"This isn't a court, Amethyst. The more information we have, the better your chances are. If you show regret, and if you tell me everything you know, then maybe there's an opportunity to save your job." Her voice drops, as if she's suddenly become a conspirator, rather than an accuser. "I'm sure Mr Ferguson is telling his side of the story."

A memory flashes into my head. This morning when I lay in Callum's bed, watching him shaving through the crack in the bathroom door. He'd caught my stare and stopped, half his jaw still covered in foam, and given me a deliciously wicked smile. Then his eyes had softened and I'd felt a real and deep bond between us.

Did I imagine it? He wouldn't throw me to the wolves in an effort to keep his own job, would he? Was I being stupidly naive, believing that love would trump everything, and nothing else mattered except how we felt about each other?

Your degree matters, the voice in my head tells me. Your degree, your job and your future. Are you really going to give those up for a man? You're just like your mother, throwing everything away for a roll in the hay.

I start to heave, quickly covering my mouth with my sweaty palm. Diana stands up, her eyes wide, and pushes me towards the door. Somehow I make it into the bathroom, falling to my knees as I vomit up the contents of my stomach, spasms wracking my stomach.

When the sickness subsides, I splash my face with some water at the basin, though it does nothing to calm the redness of my eyes. I try to wipe away the mascara that has smudged beneath them, but all I manage to do is make myself look more haunted.

Diana is waiting for me outside the bathroom, as if I'm a naughty schoolchild needing to be escorted everywhere. She even takes my wrist, pulling me along, but I feel too weak to protest.

Outside her office a shadow falls over us. I look up, a flash of hope shooting through me that somehow Callum's come to save the day. When I realise it's Jonathan, my shoulders drop, and I have to close my eyes to prevent the tears from starting again.

"What's going on?" Jonathan asks. His lips are thin and tight.

"Nothing for you to be concerned about," Diana replies, a little too breezily, "Just something I need to discuss with Amy."

I notice that she uses my preferred name for the first time.

"I *am* concerned," Jonathan says. "I'm Amy's boss and she's supposed to be working on my project. There's a critical meeting this afternoon and I need her input." When he glances at me, his eyes widen. "Are you okay, you don't look very well?"

"I've been sick," I say. I want to tell him more, but I've no idea what Callum has said. I feel completely alone.

"Then you should go home," he replies firmly. "I'll call you a cab, we can charge it to the project."

"I'm afraid that's not possible," Diana folds her arms in front of her chest. It's as though the two of them are fighting over a toy. "I need to finish interviewing her before she leaves."

"She's clearly unwell," Jonathan says. "Let her go and you can finish your meeting when she's feeling better. I'm her boss, I'm responsible for her welfare."

Diana opens her mouth to protest, then closes it with a snap. Shaking her head, she shrugs and steps back, giving Jonathan enough space to step forward and put his arm across my shoulders. He leads me down the corridor as I try to swallow down the bile that's collecting in my throat.

"Make sure you keep your phone on," Diana shouts, before we turn the corner. "I'll call you later to rearrange the meeting."

I don't reply, because Jonathan is opening the door to his office and ushering me inside. He shakes his head when his PA starts to talk to him. Instead he sends her out for coffee, closing the door firmly behind her, and sits me down in the easy chair next to the window. Then he hands me a handkerchief and hunkers down in front of me, an expression of concern written across his face.

"I think you'd better tell me what's going on."

27

Talking to Jonathan is so much easier than being interrogated by Diana. He listens patiently as the words spill out with the tears, silently handing me his soft, linen handkerchief. The whole story comes out; from the first kiss to the declarations of love, and it feels as though a weight has lifted off my chest.

When I'm out of words, he hands me a glass of water and leans back against the desk. There's no look of shock on his face, no expression of surprise, and I find myself wondering how much of this he already knew.

"You don't seem too perturbed by a woman crying in front of you," I say, as much to break the silence as anything else. "Most guys would be running away screaming."

"I've got four sisters," he says, the corner of his lip quirking up. "I'm used to the waterworks and drama. They trained me well."

It's strange how you only see one side of people until the shit hits the fan. I'd never have put Jonathan—my ever-so-posh, very restrained boss—into the confidante category, yet he's playing the role very well.

"Callum texted me and asked me to get you away from here," he says.

"Where is he?" I lean forward. "Can you take me to him?"

Jonathan shakes his head. "I think the partners are grilling him while Diana grills you. I spent half an hour wandering the corridors looking for you."

I look up at him with a watery smile. "Thank you."

"So now I need to get you home. I'll get us a cab."

This time I shake my head. "You're too busy, there's that meeting at three. I can take my own taxi."

"I've postponed it until next week," Jonathan tells me. "You don't think I'd go in there without my project manager do you?"

He calls for a cab anyway, and I sit quietly next to him as we wind our way through the busy London streets. I lean my head against the door, my mind still racing as I wonder what the hell Callum is saying, and whether he's about to lose his job too.

We knew about the damn policy, we simply didn't think it applied to us. Apart from a couple of kisses, we conducted our relationship away from the office. But now I realise how obvious we must have been. Especially last night when we ended up making out in the corridor.

Eventually we pull up to my street. Any embarrassment I might have felt at Jonathan seeing the state of our road is blotted out by the sickness that is still tugging at my stomach. I mutter a goodbye and grab my bag, practically falling out of the cab and into the gutter.

Not a metaphor, I tell myself.

Before I close the door I look back at Jonathan. "If Callum calls you first, can you ask him to ring me?" I say. Jonathan nods his head and I slam the door shut, using my other hand to dig into my purse to turn my phone on.

There are missed calls and texts, from both Callum and Jonathan. I listen to Callum's more than once, just to hear his voice. At the end, there's a message from Charlie—who asks me what the hell is happening—and I realise the news is already spreading fast.

I try to call Callum while I sit on the front step, unwilling to enter the house right away. It goes directly to voicemail, and I leave a message, asking him to call me as soon as possible. After I hang up, I try Charlie. He answers after the second ring.

"Amy? Are you okay?" He's breathless, as if he's been running. "Is it true what they're saying?"

I squeeze my eyes shut, rubbing my forehead. My brain is starting to hurt. "What are they saying?"

"That you've been having a massive affair with Callum Ferguson. Someone said you were caught shagging in the toilets."

"We didn't have sex in the toilets."

"Caro said she saw you practically humping him outside the bathroom," he says, almost cheerfully. "Were you?"

"Caro Hawes?" I echo, recalling the bathroom door banging just as I was kissing Callum. Then I remember the grainy photo that Diana showed me, of the two of us in the corridor.

"Did she say anything else?" I ask.

"Like what?"

"Somebody reported us to HR and sent them a photo."

"And you think it was Caro?" he asks.

"If she saw us outside the bathroom then yes." Now I feel even worse. Not only were we caught, but the one person who hates my guts happened to be the person who spotted us.

"So you *are* having an affair?" he asks.

I sigh. Callum and I hadn't discussed what we were going to tell the office. It was as though we were in this little bubble, floating mindlessly above everybody else, oblivious to the fact our world was about to crash land.

"I'm in love with him," I whisper. A car comes speeding down the road—a souped-up Ford Focus—and the sound temporarily drowns out Charlie's response.

"What?" I ask as soon as the engine quietens.

"I said, 'oh fuck'."

"Well that's helpful," I reply.

"What are you going to do? Caro reckons you're going to lose your job. Do you think they'll sack you?"

"I don't know," I admit. "It's possible, I suppose." The tears start to flow again, but this time I don't try to blink them away. They weave a hot trail down my cheeks, dripping from my jaw and onto the step.

"Shit," he breathes. "Listen, if you need anything, anything at all, you call me. And in the meantime I'll put a hit out on Caro."

"I think you'll find that's illegal."

"I know," he says, grimly. "But I'll risk it anyway."

* * *

When I let myself into the house, Mum's sitting at the table in the kitchen, a cigarette balanced between her forefinger and thumb as she scrolls through her phone. She looks up and crushes her cigarette into the glass ashtray.

"You're home early," she says. I glance at the clock; it's just after 1:00 p.m. Early is an understatement.

"I got sent home," I tell her. "I was sick in the toilet."

Why don't I tell her the truth? Fear, maybe? An unwillingness to see the disappointment in her face?

"You poor thing." She stands up and puts a cool palm against my forehead. "Ooh, you do feel hot. Have you got a temperature?"

"I'll be fine." I pull back, wrinkling my nose at the smell of smoke wafting from her. It does nothing to stem my nausea. "I think I'll go to bed."

"Are you sure you'll be okay?" she asks. "I've got a shift in half an hour but I could call in sick."

"I'm just going to sleep it off anyway," I lie. "You go ahead."

She looks at me closely. "It's not about the other night is it? Because it was nothing, you know? Digger and I were having a few drinks and talking about old times and one thing led to another... it won't happen again. I promised your brother that."

"It's not about that, Mum, I'm just a bit sick." I grab a glass from the cupboard and fill it with icy cold water. "I'll see you later."

"If you're sure." She sounds almost disappointed. As much as I hate to admit it, she'd do almost anything to get out of work.

"I'm certain."

I spend the next couple of hours holding on to a phone that doesn't ring. I send Callum messages and leave more voicemails but get no reply. While I wait for him I Google employment rights and learn that I pretty much have none. If Richards and Morgan want to sack me tomorrow, they can do so without causing themselves any problems.

The thought depresses me enough to cry myself to sleep for half an hour. I'm disoriented when a shrill ring cuts through the afternoon air, making me sit straight up in bed. I grab my phone, scrambling to answer the call. It's hard to hide my disappointment when I see the name that flashes across the screen.

Diana Joseph.

For a minute I consider not answering, but the need to know what's going on outweighs any ostrich-like tendencies I might have.

"Hello?"

"Amethyst, how are you feeling?"

So we're back to that. "A little better. I've had a sleep."

"That's good to hear. We'd like to meet with you tomorrow morning. In the management conference room at ten o'clock." Her voice sounds different somehow. More conciliatory maybe? I wonder if Jonathan has worked his magic on her, or even better, maybe Callum has.

Where the hell is Callum anyway? I check my watch; it's almost four o'clock. There's no way they would have kept him for this long, so why hasn't he called?

"What's the meeting about?" I ask. The drugged, just-woken feeling is finally wearing off.

"It isn't a disciplinary hearing," Diana says quickly. "Really, it's nothing to worry about. We just want to talk to you about a few things."

"We?"

"Me and the partners on the Conduct Committee."

Clearing my throat makes me realise how parched I am. I reach for the water beside my bed, letting the lukewarm liquid moisten my lips. There are cracks forming in the corner of my mouth.

"But it's not a disciplinary?" I ask.

"No, not at all. Please don't worry about the outcome, we just need to talk it through with you, and ensure that everything is okay."

"What about Cal... Mr Ferguson? Is he going to be there?" I take another mouthful of water and swallow hard. The need to see him is pulsing through my veins. I'm desperate to talk to him, to check he's okay, to feel his arms around me. More than anything I want to hear his voice telling me that *I'm* going to be okay.

"Mr Ferguson has met with us separately." Her voice drops, as if she's confiding in me. I still can't interpret the weirdness of her change of tone. "You don't have to worry about him being there tomorrow."

I want to tell her I'm not worried about him being there. I *want* him to be there.

"Should I come into work as normal?" I ask, trying to work out whether I'm in as much trouble as I think.

"No need, just arrive at ten. We can talk about everything after that."

She ends the call with a brief goodbye, and I stare at the screen for a moment, watching as the red phone symbol fades into nothing.

* * *

By six o'clock that evening I'm starting to feel like a prisoner in my own bedroom. The shock of the day seems to have paralysed my mind and body, and my thoughts can only focus on one thing: the need to find Callum. I've been calling him non-stop but his phone doesn't connect. I'm guessing his voicemail is full of my messages.

I type out another futile text, and try to ignore the ache that's throbbing in my chest.

I love him.

I'm completely in love with Callum Ferguson. At twenty-three years old, that should be enough. It's not the nineteenth century, nobody should tell me who I can be in love with. What possible right do Richards and Morgan have to comment on our relationship? As long as it doesn't affect work, then it shouldn't be any of their business.

But it did affect work, the aggravating voice whispers again. You two were caught kissing in the corridor; you're telling me that wasn't their concern?

I try to forget about that kiss in his office, and all of the flirty, funny messages we sent each other across the network, but they lie in my mind like a list of misdemeanours. If Richards and Morgan want to get rid of me, all they have to do is call up the IT department.

But then they'd have to get rid of Callum, too.

The need to take action arrives from nowhere, but it's a welcome change to the paralysis. It pulls me up from my bed, forces me to check in the mirror and attempt to make myself look suitable for the outside world. I run down the stairs and grab my bag, making my way to Plaistow station. The rush-hour crowds are pouring out of the entrance, and I have to fight through them, like the one fish in the sea swimming against the tide. Arms brush against me, briefcases hit my legs and bruise my skin, but I ignore the pain, pressing my Oyster card against the reader before rushing through the barrier.

The westbound platform is relatively deserted. Nobody travels out of Plaistow in the evening, only back in. It's a place to sleep, not somewhere to commute to. A semi-suburban town full of people living part-time lives.

People like me.

The District Line train arrives five minutes later, and I grab a seat between two builders. Their ragged trousers are flecked with paint, their hair grey with plaster dust. They edge away from me as I sit, trying not to cover me with dirt. My phone is still firmly gripped in my right hand, and I occasionally touch the screen with my thumb, lighting it up, hoping that there'll be a message from Callum on there.

There's nothing. Only a photograph of Edinburgh on the wallpaper, and a grid of useless apps staring back at me. Once the train goes underground I stop checking, knowing the signal doesn't reach that far down. It's one of the few places in London resistant to 4G, and usually I like the silence it brings.

Getting off at Victoria, I walk the last mile to Callum's house, past the smart restaurants and fashionable wine bars. More than ever, I feel like I'm playing with the big boys, about to lose badly.

There's no sign of Callum's car in his road. Still, I head for his door and bang on it, my heart hammering from a mixture of adrenaline and desperation.

I knock again to no response, and the disappointment is enough to weaken the muscles in my legs. I sit down heavily on the stone step, resting my elbows on my thighs.

Where is he?

It's gone seven. The sun is free falling like a pebble into an ocean, leaving a trail of pink and red mist in the dark blue sky. As the shadows descend, so does the cold air, and I pull my thin cardigan closely around me to stave off the evening chill.

"Amy?" A voice makes me lift my head. Jonathan's standing at the end of Callum's path, holding a set of keys in his hand. He twirls them around with his fingers.

I stand. "Do you know where Callum is?"

He clears his throat noisily. "Um, I just took him to the airport."

I open my mouth but nothing comes out. Dizziness overcomes me, and I reach out for the wall of the house to steady myself, but instead of bracing me up, I collapse, my head knocking the corner of the brick.

"Amy, are you alright?" Jonathan leaps forward to catch me, dropping Callum's keys as he holds me up by my waist. I lean into him with all my body weight, and he staggers, before regaining his equilibrium.

"Amy?" he says again, this time placing a finger beneath my chin to bring my face up. I see concern in the depths of his eyes.

"He's at the airport?" I whisper. "Why?"

"He's on a plane to Edinburgh," Jonathan slides his gaze away. "It should be in the air by now."

"When's he coming back? Tomorrow? I could meet him at the airport." I calculate how long tomorrow's meeting will take. If it finishes in an hour I could easily get to Heathrow for the afternoon.

"Amy," Jonathan's voice is gentle. "He's not coming back."

The words don't sink in straight away. Instead they dance around confusingly.

"What?"

"He's been transferred to the Edinburgh office. There's a project that needs immediate help, so he had to leave straight away."

"But he didn't tell me."

"No, he didn't."

I take a step back and try to force some air into my lungs. "But why? Why's he gone? Why didn't he tell me?" My voice wobbles on the last bit. I'm five words away from tears.

"He wanted to," Jonathan says. "He wanted to call you, but he couldn't. He had to get up there right away, it was important." He shifts awkwardly, kicking the paving slab with the front of his polished shoe. "I can't really tell you any more than that."

"You can't or you won't?" A feeling of anger starts to build from the bottom of my stomach, joining the fear that's already resident in my chest. The cocktail makes me jittery, almost punchy.

"Amy." A look of pity washes over his face. "I can't…" He reaches out for me and I back away, putting my hands up in front of me.

"Don't," I say in a low voice. "Don't touch me. Just tell me where he is."

"In Edinburgh."

"At his apartment?"

Jonathan nods.

"Then I'll go there."

Jonathan grabs me by the top of my arms, his fingers digging into my skin. "Amy, he doesn't want you there."

28

Ellie pours the last of the wine into my glass, shaking the bottle until the final drops fall into the pool of red. She and Lara have been force-feeding me Merlot all night, telling me that for the next few hours I'm going to forget about the shit storm that's my life.

Of course, it doesn't work. Nothing does. All that happens is the wine makes the tears flow a little freer, and my wails a little louder. It also loosens my tongue, until I'm regaling them with the entire, sordid history of my relationship with Callum.

Girl sleeps with her boss and then he disappears, leaving her to mop up the mess he's left behind. While I'm due to meet with the Conduct Committee tomorrow, he's starting a new job in the Edinburgh office, far away from the knowing leers and sly looks I'll be getting.

It always ends up this way. The man gets off scot-free while the girl is the scapegoat. Where's the justice in that?

"You don't know what happened," Lara says gently, after another of my alcohol-fuelled tirades. "You need to talk to him, find out what's going on."

"Of course I bloody do," I snap. "But the bastard isn't answering his phone."

"There could be a good explanation for that," she says, "give him a chance."

Ellie coughs into her wine glass. "Yeah, a good explanation like he's saving his own arse."

Lara snaps. "That's not helping."

I put my glass on the coffee table, being careful not to smear the wooden surface. "He isn't answering and hasn't tried to contact me. I need to face the fact that he just isn't into me." Though I try to smile, the tears are pouring down my cheeks. "I'm on my own, as usual."

Lara hugs me, rubbing my back as I bury my face into her shoulder. She's warm and comforting, but it's a poor substitute for what I really want.

I'm in the wrong arms. It should be Callum consoling me. We should be discussing the situation, making plans, moaning about our terrible luck. Instead I'm confused, lonely and starting to resent the way he's making me feel. There's no excuse for this lack of communication.

I want to hate him, but I can't, and that thought alone makes me want to throw something against the wall.

"You should probably try to get some sleep," Lara suggests, still holding me tight. "You need to be at the meeting tomorrow, plus you have a bit of alcohol to burn off."

The prospect of a hangover doesn't even phase me. I couldn't care less if I walk into the meeting tomorrow with vomit spewing from my lips and mascara dripping from my red eyes, because he's not going to be there. Is there really any point in bothering at all?

It would be easier to hide in my bed and pretend I haven't messed everything up. My job, my degree, and most definitely my relationship. In a few short months I've gone from a woman who wanted to make something of herself, to someone proving that you can take the girl out of the East End, but you can't take the East End out of the girl.

I'm a walking cliché. I thought I was better than this, I believed Callum was better than this, but all that's happened is I've slept with my boss and been burned.

Stupid, stupid, Amy.

"I won't be able to sleep, anyway," I mutter. Nevertheless, I pick up our glasses and carry them out to the kitchen. Lara throws the empty wine bottle into the recycling bin, and goes to grab her coat. After another long hug, she and Ellie take a cab home, leaving me alone in the house that seems more of a prison than anything else.

Being me is a life sentence.

Like a glutton for punishment, I send him another text message before walking up the stairs. It's short, but surely he can't ignore the plaintive tone.

Call me. Please.

I don't expect a reply and I don't get one. Instead I ready myself for bed, brushing my teeth and scrubbing off my makeup while refusing to look in the mirror that hangs over the basin for fear of hating the person I see staring back. By the time I crawl into bed my skin feels red-raw from a combination of astringent cleanser and salty tears, and I'm completely wide-awake.

At some point in the night the tears disappear, leaving my eyes painfully dry. I stare into the darkness, seeing the shapes of the furniture form in the shadow of the gloom. The only light comes from the shafts of moonlight that fight their way through the gaps in the curtain.

The clock on my phone counts the hours until morning. When there's only two left to go, fatigue wins out, pushing me into a series of half-lucid dreams that all end up in the same way—I am alone. Callum leaves, Callum dies, I see him sailing away while I wail with my arms flung open. He's always out of reach.

I wake at seven with a start. There's a blissful moment of half-awareness before all the facts come crashing back into my consciousness.

By the time I make it into the office, I'm running on autopilot. I don't remember showering, or getting dressed, or whether I've put on any makeup. When I sit at the table in the directors' conference room, staring at a glass of water that has been placed in front of me, I don't care whether I have a job or not.

The door opens and Jonathan walks in. He takes one look at me and his expression softens. Breathing in deeply, he grabs the chair next to mine and sits down.

"How are you?" he whispers. When I shrug, he carries on. "I'm here to support you. If you want to stop at any time, or to ask any questions, just give me a nod. I'm not going to let them walk all over you."

I couldn't care less what they do, and my lack of response is probably all the answer he needs. He reaches out and squeezes my hand.

A minute later Diana Joseph walks in, followed by two men who I've seen before but never spoken to. They're senior partners with offices on the top floor; the ones with views across the river that turn the rest of us green with envy.

"Amy, this is Sam Haken and Dominic Shaw," Diana says, taking a chair on the opposite side of the table. "Sam, Dominic, this is Amethyst Cartwright, one of our interns."

For two men who are usually wining and dining, they look surprisingly chipper. Sam reaches across the table and shakes my hand, while Dominic flashes me a toothy smile. "Amy, it's good to meet you."

Still mute, all I can do is nod back.

Dominic continues, "We wanted to come and talk to you today to see how you are doing. Once we've had a chat, we'd like you to meet with Lucy Minor, the head of our legal department."

"What about?" Jonathan asks.

"Maybe we should start from the beginning," Sam says. "First of all, we'd like to offer you a sincere apology."

I do a double take, my eyes wide. "An apology?"

There's another squeeze from Jonathan, as though he's telling me to be cool.

Dominic clears his throat loudly, pushing up the sleeves of his jacket to reveal tanned arms. "We pride ourselves on our intern program, Amy. Not only do we believe that providing training to young people is important, but it also allows us to build our reputation in the City. We want to be the go-to company for graduate applications."

"That's why we were so concerned when we heard what happened to you," Sam says, a lock of his grey hair flopping over his forehead. "I was aghast to hear that any employee of Richards and Morgan could be subject to such treatment."

"What treatment…" My words are cut off by Jonathan. This time he grabs my thigh. It isn't a sexual move, nowhere near it, just the act of a man who clearly wants me to shut up.

Sam continues as if I haven't said anything at all. "We take harassment very seriously, Amy, especially sexual harassment."

I frown, turning to look at Jonathan. His expression is as bland as he can possibly make it, and when our eyes meet he gives absolutely nothing away. Deliberately, I lift his hand from my thigh and drop it away.

"I haven't harassed anybody," I say, my voice much stronger than I feel. "I don't understand."

"Of course you haven't," Dominic says, laughing lightly. "Mr Ferguson came to see us and admitted everything. He told us he's been harassing you for months."

My jaw drops, and it's as though everybody in the room disappears. Confusion turns my brain into cotton wool, my thoughts failing to penetrate the fuzziness.

I push my chair back and stand up. "*What?*"

Jonathan stands next to me, positioning himself slightly in front, as if to shield me. "Maybe we should stop it here, Miss Cartwright is clearly too upset to discuss this."

His voice is calm, reasonable, and his lack of shock makes me realise he knows more than he's letting on. Jonathan knew what Callum had told them, and he yet didn't even bother to warn me.

"I understand that this must be very stressful," Diana says. "But we want to try to make things right. Obviously we'll be dealing with Mr Ferguson separately, but in the meantime we'd like to offer you a financial settlement to compensate for the distress that he's caused."

My previous lethargy disappears, overcome by the adrenaline that starts racing through my veins. I push Jonathan to one side before placing my hands on the table, leaning forward.

"You want to pay me off?"

Diana laughs awkwardly. "It's not like that. We just want to show some goodwill. We know how upsetting this situation must have been. There's only three months until the end of your placement, and we'd like you to put this behind you and concentrate on that."

It's getting harder to breathe; the muscles in my chest lock. "I don't want your money," I whisper. "I want to know what you're going to do to Callum."

"He's being dealt with," Dominic says, "Don't you worry about that. As I said, we take this type of thing very seriously."

The injustice hits me like a sharp slap on the face. Callum's being 'dealt with'—disciplined I assume—while they're offering me money. Don't they know we both walked into this with our eyes open?

"No." I look down, unable to meet their gaze. "You can't do that."

"Amy," Jonathan grabs my hand again. "You need to be quiet now."

"Why?" I turn to him, my face creasing into a frown. I want to shout, to tell them how stupid they're being.

He didn't harass me. He loved me. Maybe he still does.

"Because Callum's told them what happened." Jonathan's voice is low. "And he's willing to accept the consequences."

Jonathan's stare doesn't waiver. He's trying to send me another message. Telling me to back the hell off, that Callum knows what he's doing, and I just have a part to play.

But I don't want to act the role. I want to see my boyfriend. I want to run into his arms, I want to hear him whisper my name as he holds me. The last thing I want is their blood money.

"It's not right." Finally, I turn to look at Dominic and Sam. When they glance at each other I can see genuine concern. Sexual harassment is serious; it could ruin their reputation.

"I'll sign your settlement agreement," I tell them, the words escaping almost as soon as the decision is made. "But I don't want your cash."

I grab my jacket and stalk out of the room, barely able to stop the tears from rolling down my face.

* * *

"What the hell was that about?" I ask, as soon as Jonathan finds me in the corner of the canteen. A cold mug of coffee is in front of me. The sheen forming on the surface is a testament to my lack of appetite.

"I'm sorry, I should have warned you." Jonathan slides into the chair opposite. "But to be honest, the element of surprise worked well."

The fury I managed to suppress in the meeting rises to the surface. "Is this a fucking game to you? We're talking about people's careers, about their lives. The element of surprise?"

Jonathan leans back. "It isn't like that. Do you think I wanted to sit there and hear all that? One of my best friends has just sacrificed his bloody career and I had to nod and agree with them."

I take a deep breath, but fail to find much equilibrium. "Why did he do it? What did he do? I need to know what's going on."

Jonathan's shoulders relax. "I'll tell you what I know. But you need to understand I made a promise to Callum that I'd do everything I could to protect you. I intend to keep that promise, even if it pisses you off."

"Tell me," I demand. "Tell me what he's done."

"The first thing I knew about this—the first time I heard you were in a relationship—was when he called me yesterday morning. I was in a teleconference and ignored the phone initially, but the fact he kept calling made me realise something was wrong."

He shifts in his seat. "Callum was about to go into a meeting with the partners. By that time he'd been told about the accusations, and realised that you were going to lose your job. They'd made no bones about that. So he came up with a plan to protect you. It was the only way."

My throat is so tight I can barely speak. "What plan?"

"He told them he'd been harassing you. That you'd turned him down a number of times but he couldn't help himself. He said he knew it had been an act of gross misconduct, and he was willing to pay the consequences."

Tears sting my eyes. "He sacrificed himself for me?"

"He said it was the only way. As his friend I tried to talk him out of it, but he wouldn't listen." His cheeks flush as he speaks. "He wouldn't let me go until I agreed to help him."

I pick at the napkin in front of me, fibres falling to the floor like feathers from a bird. "What did they do to him?" I ask. "Has he lost his job?"

Jonathan shakes his head. "He came close, and to be honest by that point I don't think he cared. But in the end they came to an agreement." He shifts again, clearing his throat. "He had to transfer to the Edinburgh office right away, and agree not to contact you again."

"What?" I try to catch my breath, but it isn't there. "What do you mean he can't contact me? I can still see him, can't I?"

"No, they made that very clear. Any contact between the two of you and he'll be dismissed. Clearly they think that you never want to hear from him again after what's happened, and we need to keep it that way."

A sob escapes my lips. "But I love him. They can't keep us apart, they can't." I drop the shredded napkin. "It's just a stupid job, it doesn't matter."

"Of course it matters," Jonathan says sharply. "Callum's job was the only thing that kept him going after Jane died. I know he cares about you, Amy, but this isn't some bloody romance novel, it's real life. There's no way he wants to be responsible for messing up your career, not to mention losing your degree. This is the only way."

"It can't be…" My voice trails off as I try to think of another solution. Of course I want my degree, but the need to see Callum is so much stronger than the need to succeed. For the first time I realise that I'd sacrifice it all to be with him.

Exactly when he's surrendering everything to be without me.

"You need to listen to me." Jonathan hunches forward, his voice urgent. "If you try to contact him, they'll find out, and it will be obvious he lied to protect you. You'll both end up losing your jobs and that can't happen."

"But I love him." The dam bursts as tears start to stream down my face. "And he loves me, he told me. This can't happen."

Even as I protest, I realise the truth. It *is* happening.

29

"Can I come in?"

The voice emanates from the other side of my closed door. Two days later and I'm still wallowing, shut up in my room where my only companions are a glass of water and the ballads streaming out of my stereo speakers. I'm curled up in a ball on top of my bedcovers, eyes red, nose streaming.

"Go away." My words are muffled by my pillow. The poor thing has been pummelled and cried on until it resembles a wet rag.

My voice is obviously too stifled, because the handle on the door turns, and the person I least expect to see pops his head around, eyes searching the room until he finds me.

"Amethyst?"

"It's Amy." I sit up and grab the last tissue from the cardboard box next to my bed. "And I want to be alone."

Digger walks in anyway, wringing his clasped hands as if he were drying washing. "I know, I just wanted to…" He swallows nervously, his eyes still darting around. "God, this room takes me back."

Since I left the meeting at Richards and Morgan—and Diana suggested I take the rest of the week off—a succession of friends and family have paraded through my bedroom as they attempt to find a way to cheer me up.

I get the feeling this is their last try. If I don't react to Digger then nothing will work.

"Can I sit down?" He gestures at the brown easy chair in the corner of my room. The same one my mum used to nurse all three of her children in, it has enough sentimental value for her to never throw it away. Right now it's covered in a pile of clothes, and I watch as Digger lifts them off. I can't even muster the energy to be embarrassed.

Seated, he looks as uneasy as he did when standing. Leaning his elbows on his long legs, he rests his chin on his hands, and stares at me with familiar blue eyes.

"Your mum says you've had a bit of trouble at work."

Hearing the mention of my job is enough to send a shiver down my spine.

"I'm fine." The monotone in my voice tells a different story, but I'm hoping that it might send Digger running out of the door. I don't want to talk to anybody.

That's a lie. There's one person I want to see.

Digger coughs, and it's loud enough to make me look at him. He doubles over with the paroxysms, his tattooed hand covering his mouth, and my brow furrows with concern.

Why on earth am I worried about him?

"Are you alright?" I ask. It's the first time I've voluntarily said something in two days.

He takes out a handkerchief and wipes his face. "English colds. Something I didn't miss while I was away."

"That's what killed off the aliens in *War of the Worlds*," I tell him, in an attempt to fill the silence. "A simple cold."

He smiles. "Your mum's right. You're a clever kid."

I open my mouth to tell him I'm not a kid, and then close it again, because right now that's exactly what I am. Curled up in a ball, wailing at the inequities of the world, I'm nothing but a child.

"I know you're hurting," he says, running a hand across his stubbled chin. "And believe me, I know what that feels like. But bottling everything up and refusing to talk is the worst thing you can do. I know that from experience, too." He swallows, his Adam's apple bobbing. "After I came back from the war, I was in a state. I'd seen things nobody should have to see, done things nobody should have to do. I thought I could forget about them or put them to the back of my mind. I really believed that if I threw myself into looking after you and your mum then I'd feel better."

His eyes are watery when they catch mine, the reflection of the sun making them glint. I don't know if he's tired, or if he's upset, but either way I stay silent.

What he says next shocks me.

"I'm so sorry I hurt you. Every day I think about what I did, how I broke your wrist. I hate myself when I look in the mirror."

This time, it's me who starts to cry. Fat, hot tears that trail down my cheeks, dripping onto my nightshirt and staining the pale fabric. "You didn't know what you were doing."

"What kind of man hurts his own kid?" he asks. "A baby at that. I wasn't a man, I was a fucking devil."

A lump forms in my throat. "It was a long time ago…"

His head snaps up. "Don't make excuses for me. I was the worst kind of father. I still am, I haven't been here, haven't made things up to you, and I'm so bloody regretful about it all."

"I thought you were dead, I didn't know any better."

Digger squeezes his eyes shut. "I can't tell you how many times I wished I *was* dead. Or how long I waited to come and find you, too scared to admit what I'd done."

He's crying openly. The tears stream down his face unwiped, making him look even younger.

"I'm not scarred by that," I whisper, somehow needing to reassure him. He might have hurt me when I was a kid, and he might have disappeared from my life, but at the end of the day he's a man who did something he regrets. "There are no lasting effects. Bones break and they heal again."

"So do hearts," he says pointedly. "Even if it doesn't feel like it at the time." His eyes shine even though the tears have stemmed.

"I don't think mine will." I let out a sob, covering my mouth with my hand. "I'm never going to be happy again."

I miss him, Christ how I miss him. His smile, his touch, the knowledge he feels the same way I do. It's hard to believe it's only been three days since I last saw him; three days since his lips last pressed against mine. A day without Callum seems dark as night.

"Oh, sweetheart." Digger covers the short distance between the chair and my bed in less than two seconds. Maybe I shouldn't let him scoop me into his arms and drop my head onto his shoulder as I cry hard, letting his t-shirt soak up the tears. But I do it anyway, and it actually makes me feel better, if only for a moment.

"I love him," I wail, holding onto him.

"I know."

"And he doesn't want me."

He strokes my hair softly. "Who wouldn't want you? You're beautiful, you're funny and you're clever as anything. I'm so proud to see how you've turned out."

His words begin to warm my ice-cold heart. "It's not enough," I say.

Digger wipes the tears from my cheeks with his thumbs, their roughness a contrast to the smooth skin of my face. "You are enough," he tells me. "You're more than enough, and nothing else matters. You might not realise it now, and it's going to take a while for you to get over this, but one day you'll look back and realise just how strong you are. And how proud you make me."

I look up, catching his gaze through slick eyelashes. "Thank you," I say. I mean it, too. It's not as though I'm throwing myself into his embrace like a long-lost daughter and begging him to become part of our Brady Bunch, but the fact he's put aside his discomfort—not to mention risked provoking Alex's ire—to come up and talk to me is enough right now. I might not want to call him 'Dad', and I certainly don't want to see him kissing my mum again, but part of me wants to give him another chance.

After everything that's happened, this might be the only positive chance I get.

* * *

"How are you?" Charlie slides onto the swivel chair next to mine, his legs splayed so his feet can pivot on the floor. "Feeling any better?"

I look up from my laptop. It's my first day back in the office and it's taking longer to boot up than usual. As if it's fed up with me for ignoring it for five days.

"I'm okay," I say, rubbing my eyes. They're tight and itchy from too many tears and not enough sleep, but a good covering of concealer has hidden most of the damage.

Charlie pushes himself along on the chair until he's close to me. The arm of his chair hits mine.

"Hey, we're not on the dodgems," I tell him.

He raises an eyebrow. "The whole point of dodgems, Amy, is to dodge 'em. You're thinking of bumper cars."

I glance at him warily. "I can guarantee that's not what I'm thinking." What I'm actually thinking—in the small amount of consciousness that's not aching for my laptop to load so that I can see if Callum is logged on—is that I want to be left alone. Preferably for the next two months.

Right up to graduation.

Charlie gets the message and backs away. "I bought you a Mars bar," he says, laying the black-wrapped chocolate bar on the desk in front of me. "I thought you might need the sugar rush."

I run my finger along the bar. "Thank you, I'll save it for later."

"You really aren't alright."

Doing my best to attempt a smile, I look over at him. "I'm fine."

"No, you're not. If you were fine you'd have shoved the whole of that bar into your greedy gob by now. If you were fine you'd be begging me to make you a cup of tea to go with it, or suggesting we head over to Starbucks for an early coffee."

The mention of coffee makes my chest hurt.

"Okay, so I will be fine. In time." It doesn't even convince me. As for Charlie, he wrinkles his nose and goes to grab the Mars bar. I snatch it back from him, pulling out my desk drawer and depositing it inside. I may not want it now, but it's chocolate after all.

"Oh, by the way, I gave Caro a talking to," Charlie says, standing up and pushing his chair back to where he found it. "Left her in no doubt what a bitch I think she is. I wanted to slap her, really, but I was too scared I'd get done for assault."

The corner of my lip twitches. "That's a shame."

"It is," he agrees, cheerily. "But there's nothing to stop you."

"Apart from my need to keep this job. And the small matter of my degree." My voice is dry. "But thanks for the suggestion."

"Any time." With that he leaves, and although the invisible band around my chest hasn't loosened much, it seems more bearable than it did before.

* * *

The next hour is spent reading my emails. I start to whip out replies, my fingers flying across the keyboard, before realising I'm late for a project meeting. I arrive ten minutes after it's started, all too aware of my dishevelled appearance, and find myself grilled on project costs and overruns.

When I get back to my desk, I click on instant messenger and type Callum's name into the box. The system finds him immediately, and the little green icon tells me everything I need to know.

He's online right now.

I reach out for my coffee mug, hoping the bitter liquid will give me the courage I'm sorely lacking. I want to message him— of course I do—but after days of being ignored, my ability to take rejection has hit an all-time low. Unanswered emails have filled up my 'sent' folder, and I don't know how much more I can subject myself to.

I type and delete over and over. 'Hi' seems too vacuous, 'Why won't you talk to me' too demanding. I try—and fail—to hit the right note, to sound breezy without being careless, and in the end I settle for an old favourite.

Cartwright, A: How are you?

I hit return and stare at the screen until the little tick appears, confirming it's been received.

The wait for a reply is excruciating. The program tells me that **Ferguson, C** is typing, and knowing he's going to communicate sends my heart into a tailspin.

I only realise I'm holding my breath when my chest starts to protest, a burning sensation causing me to blow the air out. I sit, stare, and wait for my laptop to ping, knowing that any minute he's going to respond.

But he doesn't. Instead the 'typing' icon disappears, followed quickly by the green icon next to his name. Within a minute he's offline, and it doesn't take a genius to realise he's deliberately turned off messenger.

The bastard's ignoring me again.

I pick up my coffee cup, wanting to throw it in anger, but then I think better of it. As much as I'd love to see the mug fly across the room and make a satisfying dent in the wall, the last thing I need is another chat with Diana Joseph. Instead I let out a furious shout, my yell cutting through the background noise, causing everybody to turn and stare at me.

My cheeks flush, and I gesture at my laptop, as if to tell them I'm having an IT problem. Curiosity sated, they turn back to their work, leaving me staring at the blank computer screen.

I'm completely and utterly enraged. If Callum was here now I'd happily smash my fist into his gorgeous face. How dare he just walk away and ignore me as if everything that happened meant nothing to him? My hands flex with the need to hit something, but there's nothing here to punch.

I do the next best thing—I write him an email. My fingers hit the keyboard with angry jabs, each word an attempt to hurt him as he's hurt me. I want him to know exactly how I feel and precisely what I think of him. I want him to understand the pain I'm going through.

From: Amy.Cartwright@richardsandmorgan.com
To: Callum.Ferguson@richardsandmorgan.com
Subject: Arsehole

You're a coward, do you know that? I've been calling you for five days, sending you messages and emails and still you haven't got the guts to answer. I don't care if you think 'it's better this way' or that you told Jonathan you're doing this for my own good, because if you'd bothered to ask me what I wanted, you'd know that I didn't want this.

Do you remember saying you loved me and you'd never let me go? Yet at the first sign of trouble you've run away to Scotland and left me facing everything on my own.

You can't go around playing with people's emotions like this. You can't simply decide what's best for me without consulting me first. You can't send me a message through your friend like a fourteen-year-old schoolboy and expect me to do what you say.

I LOVE YOU, you arsehole. I love you and I care for you and I want to be with you. I want to be with you more than I want this job. More than I want my degree. As far as I'm concerned, the whole of Richards and Morgan can go and take a running jump.

You told me that I made you breathe again. Well, I'm the one who's suffocating now. I'm scared and I'm alone and I can't believe you've left me without a word. What kind of man does that to the woman he's supposed to love? What sort of person ignores her when she calls him in tears?

The type of man I've fallen in love with, I suppose.

Before you say it, I know sending this through the IT network could put my job in danger, and maybe I'm hoping that it will. Because if I can't have you, I don't want this job either, so I hope IT read it and report me to every single director. Right now, I couldn't care less.

I know you're not going to reply, and I can promise that I'm not going to email you again. Somewhere deep inside me, I still have a shred of dignity left.

Did I tell you you're an arsehole?

Amy.

I hit send before I can persuade myself out of it, then lean heavily back in my chair, weariness overtaking my body. My anger slowly dissipates until I feel nothing but numb, not even regretful at the tone of my message.

Later that afternoon, when I come back from a meeting, I get a reply. It's short, sour and it's everything I need to know. It breaks my heart with seven letters.

Goodbye.

30

"Your lipstick's smudged." Ellie reaches out with a tissue, wiping red from the corner of my mouth. Chucking the balled-up paper into the bin, she reaches out to hug me, her yoga-toned arms wrapping around mine.

"What's that for?" I ask.

"Because you only went and bloody did it. You're about to graduate with a first class degree and I'm scared stupid that you're not going to want to be my best friend any more."

"Don't be silly." I squeeze her tight. "You'll always be my best friend. I won't forget everything you've done for me."

Her eyes glisten when she steps back. "I'm going to miss you so much."

"It's only for six months," I tell her. "Anyway, you're going to come and see me, right? Even if I have to buy your air ticket."

"An all-expenses paid trip to New York? Let me think about it…" Ellie scratches her chin with her forefinger. "Um, okay, if I have to."

The smile I give her is genuine, and warmth floods my chest when I look at her. If it wasn't for her support over these past two months I don't know if I'd have survived. "Your sacrifice won't go unnoticed," I tell her.

She's about to say something when a voice comes over the tannoy, announcing the start of the ceremony.

I shout a hasty goodbye and run back to my chair in the auditorium, my navy-blue graduation gown billowing behind me. As I sit down I tuck my hair into the matching mortarboard that we've hired for the day.

A good thing about having a surname near the beginning of the alphabet is that I'm one of the first to be called. Of course, everything is relative, and there are still hundreds of 'As' and 'Bs' before me, but in a fairly short time I find myself crossing the stage to be handed my degree.

I'm no longer a student, but a graduate. I have a degree that nobody can take away. And this qualification has led to an offer of six months in New York, working for Daniel Grant.

When I climb down the steps on the other side of the stage, I scan the audience for my family. Mum, Alex, Andie and Lara are clapping madly, and when my brother catches my eye, he waves, pride written all over his face.

I don't know how he managed to get a ticket, when the allocation was strictly two per graduate. A couple of weeks ago he called to tell me he had managed to secure another two, and that he and Lara would be accompanying Mum and Andie. I hate to think what he did to get them—knowing Alex it was probably highly immoral or costly—but I'm so glad he's here.

After all, it was their love and support that got me here.

With my rolled-up certificate firmly in my hand, I make my way back to my seat. In spite of the warm day outside, there's a chill breeze in the auditorium, and I can feel goose bumps break out across my skin. My mind wanders as I sit and shiver, barely noticing as names are called out, and friends and strangers alike walk across the stage.

Instead I wonder why I'm not feeling more victorious, and why this achievement doesn't taste as sweet as it should. After all, I've crossed off two steps in my plan; I've got my degree and I've secured a placement in New York, enough to get me the hell out of Plaistow.

It doesn't take long for my thoughts to turn to *him*. Like a compass, the needle always points north. To Edinburgh.

In the months since I last saw Callum, I've had no contact. Nothing at all. Every now and then, when I was feeling particularly masochistic, I looked his name up on the messaging system at Richards and Morgan. Seeing the online icon lit up next to his name always made my heart speed, the same way it did when he used to smile at me.

I don't know how I got through that first month. Each day was a struggle. Getting out of bed felt like wading through tar. The pain was physical as well as emotional. My chest ached, my stomach turned, and my muscles felt as though I'd been through ten rounds in the boxing ring. Sleep led me an elusive dance—always beyond my reach.

In the final few weeks of my placement, things were no better at Richards and Morgan. Half of the interns ostracized me—on Caro Hawes' instructions, I assumed—and the others just looked at me with pity. Gossip followed me around the office like vultures around a carcass, but whether their suppositions came close to the truth I never found out.

I simply didn't care.

The nights were the worst. In the daytime, even when I was at my lowest, I could be distracted by work, conversation and the lure of bitter coffee. But when I went to bed there was nothing but darkness and the twisting spirals of my depressive thoughts. Each memory would be like a hand crushing my heart, reminding me of all I had, and of everything I lost.

The second month was better. Though the pain remained, my placement coming to an end was a balm to my troubled soul. I'd loved my work but I hated the office, and I especially despised the memories that seemed pasted to the walls like paper. I couldn't wait to leave, working in the same company as him was stopping me from moving on. That's why I jumped at the offer of a job in New York. Leaving London was the only thing I had to look forward to.

"Amy?" I look up to see Alex standing in front of me. Before I can say anything he pulls me out of my chair and against his chest, his tattooed, muscled arms wrapping around my slight frame. "I'm so proud of you," he whispers into my hair. "The first Cartwright to get a degree."

Before I know it my family are surrounding me, and we're a tangled mess of hugs and tears. My mum sobs loudly, enough for people around us to stare, and Andie suggests we head to the pub. I say goodbye to the few friends I made on the course, and let my family lead me out of the hall. As always, everybody is talking at once.

We've hired the function room at a local pub; a small, wood-panelled room with high, vaulted ceilings and dusty windows that block out the sun. Alex and Andie clubbed together to pay for the buffet, and Mum has laid on the Prosecco. Shortly after we arrive, the room fills with family and friends. They hug me and ask me to model my mortarboard for them. In the end I cave in and let them take photos, all too aware that these embarrassing pictures will follow me around for the rest of my life.

Digger walks in about twenty minutes later, and comes over to congratulate me. He presses a card into my hand, his fingers rough from years of hard work, his eyes wary when Alex approaches us. Though neither of them says a word to each other, I count the lack of punches as a victory. Today is my day, and for now an armistice has been called.

A few of the interns and managers from Richards and Morgan—those who are still talking to me—pop in during their lunch breaks from work. Although they're still on Company time, it doesn't seem to phase them as they accept glasses of sparkling wine and stuff their mouths with sausage rolls. A few months ago I'd have been mortified for them to meet my family, but now I introduce them to Mum, Andie and Alex with pride.

"Pleased to meet you." Charlie reaches out to shake my brother's hand. He looks alarmed at all the tattoos and the muscles that define Alex's arms but he manages to keep his calm.

Jonathan runs in for ten minutes between meetings. I've already had my leaving presentation at work, when he said lovely things before gifting me a Mont Blanc pen and £300 worth of Amazon vouchers. He takes the time to introduce himself to my mum, making sure to tell her how well I've done, and how sad Richards and Morgan are to see me go.

For the first time in months I find myself feeling content. There are fifty people in this room, and the fact that they've come out on a sunny Friday afternoon to join in the celebration is heart warming. A shaft of sunlight breaks its way through the window; dust dancing in its spotlight. When it hits my face, spreading warmth across my skin, it makes me want to smile.

So I do.

Man, it feels good.

I look for Ellie, wanting to tell her about the weather in New York in September, hoping it will be enough to persuade her to visit. But when I glance across the room it isn't my friend I see.

Callum steps into the bar, his shirtsleeves rolled up, and everything turns blank. My muscles stiffen in shock and the champagne glass I was holding crashes onto the dark wooden floor.

31

The next few minutes are a blur. I'm in a stop-motion scene, standing still while everything around me is on speed. Somebody pushes me away from the broken glass while others fuss and sweep it up, and I think they're trying to talk to me, but I can't hear a word. The buzzing reaches a crescendo, and it's only later that I realise it's the rush of blood through my ears.

When Callum walks toward me he's the only thing I can focus on. I see him in high definition, noticing the dark hairs on his forearms, the light tan he's managed to get on his skin. His sleeves are crumpled where he's pushed them up, though the rest of his shirt is crisply ironed. A lump forms in my throat as I stare at his chest, remembering the way his body felt under my palms.

When my gaze reaches his face I feel my breath falter. He's as glorious as ever, his dark red hair curling over his forehead, his eyes bright and sparkling despite the dark smudges beneath them. If anything, he looks even more beautiful than I remember. A shadow of beard growth darkens his jawline, and all I can think of is dragging my lips across it.

I shake my head at my inappropriate thoughts, wishing they'd leave as quickly as they arrived. Then he's standing in front of me, and his presence is like a shot of heroin to my veins.

"What are you doing here?" I whisper, my breath still short from his proximity.

"I came to congratulate you."

Frowning, I take a step back. His closeness is too intoxicating. I need space to think, to get some clarity.

"A card would have done." I don't know if I'm joking or being petulant.

"Can we talk?" he asks, looking around warily. For the first time the crowd comes into focus, and I realise everyone is staring at us. Lara has an arm around Alex's waist, successfully stopping him from coming over, but I can tell it's only a matter of time.

"Here?"

Callum shakes his head. "It's a beautiful day outside, we could go for a walk, or find a café somewhere." He's still staring, and I can't decide if it's pissing me off or making me happy.

"Okay."

A few minutes later we're walking beside the river, our bodies dwarfed by the imposing warehouses that line the waterway. In spite of the blue skies and the warm sun, the shadows the buildings cast are enough to chill the air.

"Are you cold?" Callum asks. Not waiting for an answer, he drapes his suit jacket across my shoulders, his hands lingering for a moment before letting go. Even though there's thick fabric between his palms and my bare skin, it makes me shiver.

We're silent for a while, and the sounds of the river fill the emptiness. Distant engines hum, water crashes against the wooden piers, and the occasional shout of a river man cuts through the quiet. We're off the beaten track, in the less glamorous part of London, and besides the boatmen, the only people we see are workers having a crafty smoke outside their offices.

"How've you been?" Callum finally asks. His question is enough to bring me to a halt. He takes another step and then, realising I've stopped, whips around, his brow wrinkled.

"I've been shit," I say honestly. I'm not going to gild the lily; if he wants the truth I've got it in spades. "Somebody told me they loved me then two days later he disappeared off the face of the earth."

There's anger in my voice neither of us expected. Callum reaches out, trying to touch me, but I move back, dodging his hand.

"Don't touch me," I warn. He bites his bottom lip, his torso rising in a slow breath.

"I'm sorry," he says. "I know it's been shit. It really has."

"I tried to call you, I tried to message you, but you wouldn't answer." I don't mention the emails. The less said about those, the better.

"I couldn't," he whispers. "I wanted to talk to you, I wanted to see you, but I couldn't."

"Bullshit." The ache in my chest that's been my constant companion for months has disappeared. It's as if someone has unlocked my ribcage, letting all the emotions out. I want to shout at him, to scream how much he hurt me, to tell him what hell he unleashed when he ran away.

I want to tell him I still love him.

"It was the only way you could keep your job," he says. "Please let me explain, Amy."

"You think I cared about my job?" I laugh, but there's no amusement. "You really think I gave a shit about Richards and Morgan? If you'd have asked me to live with you in a hovel I'd have said yes. I didn't give a damn about my job, I just wanted you."

"That's what you say now," he replies, running a hand through his thick hair. "But after a while you'd have resented me. You'd have realised that you gave up a job and a degree for nothing."

"I would have had you," I tell him.

"I'm not enough."

The expression on his face is twisted, as if he's experiencing physical pain. For the first time I realise that he's being going through the same thing as me, and the aching void of our separation wasn't only mine to bear.

He's hurt as much as I am.

"What do you mean you're not enough?" I ask softly. "You were everything."

The corner of his lip twitches. "I couldn't ask you to sacrifice your dreams, not again…"

His voice trails off and suddenly I'm back at his house, comforting him after a bad nightmare. I'm remembering the way he asked his wife to move to Edinburgh, and how the move slowly tore them apart.

"I'm not Jane," I tell him.

"Don't you think I can see that?" he asks, his voice harsh. "But I also know how hard you've worked for all you've achieved. How you've fought your way through your degree, how you came to Richards and Morgan even though you knew there were people who'd look down on you. I couldn't let you give all that up."

I blink back tears. "Instead you gave up on me."

He shakes his head slowly. "I never gave up on you, not for a single minute. I've spent the last two months thinking of nothing but you. Calling Jonathan at all times of the day just to make sure you were okay. Asking Charlie to do stupid things like buy you a coffee to leave on your desk so you wouldn't feel so alone."

"That was Charlie?"

"Did you really believe I'd have left if I didn't care?"

There's a sweetness in his words that turns my insides to liquid. "So appearing on graduation day is all part of the plan?"

Callum smiles. "I meant to arrive for the actual ceremony, but my flight was delayed." He looks down at the pavement. "I've spent the last five hours asking every stranger I met—every air steward and pilot and taxi driver—to hurry the hell up."

I open my mouth but there are no words. I want to explain the conflict that's raging in my mind, that the need to touch him is as strong as the need to slap him. I want to hate him, but there's no room for hatred when I'm so full of love.

"What do you want from me?" I ask.

"I want whatever you're willing to give me. I want to be your friend. I want to be the best bloody friend you'll ever have."

My heart drops. *A friend?*

"Don't look like that," he cajoles, reaching to me. "You think I don't want more? I've dreamed about you for the last two months."

"Then why do you want to only be my friend?"

"Because I have no right to ask for more."

"You have no right *not* to." I stare at him defiantly. "What happened to the man who shoved me up against the wall, the one who stole my kisses as if they were his dying breath?"

"Amy," he warns. "Don't tempt me."

My smile is a challenge. He glances at my lips, his glorious eyes narrowing. When his mouth falls open, a shallow sigh escaping, I feel as though I've already won.

He pulls me toward him and presses my body to his. As he tips my head back, his jacket slides off my shoulders, falling onto the concrete ground.

A moment later his soft lips touch mine. His fingers twist into the hair on the back of my head as he starts to move his mouth. He whispers indecipherable words as he continues to kiss me. Except it doesn't feel like a kiss, it feels as if he's devouring me, trying to take every bit of love that exists inside. I'm a willing victim, looping my arms around his neck as I kiss him with needy lips. Desperate to taste, to feel, to love.

That's how we stay for the next ten minutes, holding each other as if we're too afraid to let go. My body melts into his, my skin singing as he strokes the nape of my neck, our breaths hot and fast as we part for long enough to gasp for air. Though it's clear that things aren't resolved, and I've no idea what's going to happen next, for once, I allow myself to savour the moment.

* * *

That evening we're sitting on a restaurant terrace by the South Bank, looking across the river to St. Paul's Cathedral as the evening sun descends below the skyline. This part of London has a continental feel in the summer, as if you could be in sunny Barcelona rather than grey old England, and the vibe is almost contagious. The waitress brings out our dishes—a collection of mezes that Callum chose—and when the aroma of food wafts up from the table I recognise how hungry I am.

Ravenous might be a better description. Callum watches as I shovel food into my mouth, an amused smile playing at his lips. He calls the waitress over and orders another three dishes.

"I'm sorry," I say, swallowing a mouthful of tabbouleh. "I haven't eaten all day."

Callum lifts his beer. "You look like you haven't eaten for a month."

I'm about to get offended when I realise he's talking about my weight, and to be honest he has a point. During those first few weeks after he left I wasn't able to stomach more than a slice of toast. The pounds fell off me.

"I'm making up for lost time." I snag the last falafel. "So sue me."

"Suing you is the last thing on my mind."

I raise an eyebrow. "That's very forward of you, Mr Ferguson. I'll have you know that I'm not that kind of girl."

He shakes his head slowly. "No, you're not. You're the kind of girl I take home to meet my mother. The sort of woman that I want to introduce to all my friends as the *one*. The only one."

The intensity of his words ignites me. The atmosphere between us turns serious, the light banter of a few moments ago forgotten. I take a sip of wine to moisten my dry mouth, and try to formulate a reply.

I'm still trying when the waiter leans across, taking my now-empty plate, stacking it on top of the others he's amassed. Callum's eyes are fixed on mine, strong and unwavering, and when I look into them all I can see is emotion.

Love.

It's the kind of passionate stare that you read about in novels. The type that's likely to pin a girl down. It's all Heathcliff and Darcy, dark and brooding, and it sends a shiver down to my toes.

"I'm moving to New York," I blurt out, instantly regretting it. "My flight's next week."

I sit back, waiting for him to get angry, but instead a smile flits across his lips.

"I know."

"You do?" I take another mouthful of wine. "Who told you?"

Callum places his hand over mine, barely missing my wine glass. Then he lifts my palm and kisses it, shocking me into silence.

"I've been keeping tabs on you," he tells me. "Jonathan is the obvious spy, of course, but Daniel Grant has been keeping me up to date with the project. I didn't stop thinking of you, babe, not even for a second." He reaches across to pour more wine. "Leaving you was the hardest thing I've ever done."

There's a significance to his words which resonates. He's been through hell; marriage, addiction, death. If leaving me was harder than all those things, it says a lot.

It says everything.

"I missed you, too." I look up at him. "Every day. I couldn't understand why you wouldn't contact me."

"I couldn't risk it. If the partners heard there was something more going on with us, you'd have lost everything."

"And now?" I ask, wondering why he's changed his mind.

"Now you have your degree. Richards and Morgan may have some influence, but they can't take that away from you."

"But they can fire you." I look over at him, alarmed. His expression gives nothing away. "Wait, they haven't fired you already have they?"

He laughs at my wide-eyed shock. "No. It's impossible to fire somebody who doesn't work for you."

I frown. "I don't get it."

"I handed in my notice this morning. They've put me on gardening leave for three months. Getting paid to do nothing has a certain ring to it."

"Why did you do that?" I demand. "You didn't know if I still wanted you, or if I'd already moved on."

"I know that, Amy, and though I'd do anything for you, this decision was for me. I don't want to work there anymore, not in a company that would rather see a young student fail her degree than show some kindness and leniency." This time, when he reaches for my hand, his fingers curl around mine. "Besides, I've already been offered another job."

"You have?" He's full of surprises. Not for the first time tonight, I feel confused. "Where?"

"Grant Industries."

When I try to pull my hand away, he simply holds on tighter. "And before you say it, I had no influence on your internship offer. The first I knew about it was when Daniel started talking about his new project manager during a telephone call yesterday."

My voice cracks. "Where is it based?"

"I haven't accepted it yet. If I do, I'll be travelling a lot, but my home office will be in New York." He says the last two words slowly, deliberately so, to maximise their impact. "You won't have to see me if you don't want to," he adds hurriedly. "Grant Industries is a big company, and I won't be in the office very much."

Our hands are still intertwined. I can feel his warmth leeching into my skin, and the tenderness of his thumb as he strokes it gently against my palm. Callum looks at me expectantly. It isn't the time for holding back my emotions.

"You hurt me," I tell him. "By making all these decisions without consulting me first."

"I know, and that's why I'll only accept the job if it's okay with you. Grant knows that."

A loud crash comes from the kitchen, and when I look around I see that the restaurant has emptied out. Apart from a group of students in the far corner, Callum and I are the only ones here. The lights have dimmed, leaving the flickering candle in the middle of the table to illuminate us both. He stares at me, face orange from the reflection, waiting for a reply.

"You broke my heart."

"Let me mend it," he says softly. "Let me rebuild you, piece by piece, the way you rebuilt me."

The sweetness of his words touches me. There's no doubting his sincerity, it's in the shine of his eyes and the curve of his smile. It's pouring out of his soul.

In spite of the tears rolling down my face, a huge grin spreads across my lips. I'm nodding and then he's standing and pulling me into his arms, pressing his mouth against mine. The next moment my arms are around his neck, and I'm kissing him just as hard, laughing as he starts to swing me around.

"New York, baby," he says, grinning, when he finally puts me down. "We're going to have a ball."

"We're going to *work*," I say pointedly, though the smile remains.

"You know what they say about all work and no play…"

"It pays the bills?"

"It'll certainly buy you a lot of coffee," he replies. "Which is a good thing, as I'll expect one on my desk every morning just before nine."

I shoot him a warning glance. "There's only one place I'll be shoving your coffee," I say. "And I don't think that's what Starbucks has in mind."

He leaves some money on the table, waving away my offer of going Dutch. "I'm tempted to say you've become mouthier since I first met you, but we both know that's not true." With his arm around me, he steers us out of the restaurant door and into the evening air. "You've been giving me hell since you walked into my office."

"I don't intend to stop."

He dips his head to kiss me, still smiling. "That's what I'm counting on."

EPILOGUE

We leave New York in the middle of a heat wave, arriving at Heathrow on a dismal July morning. As soon as we step out of the terminal I pull my woefully inadequate cotton jacket around me, shivering as a gust of wind lifts up my hair.

"Welcome to London," Callum says, throwing his arm around my shoulder and holding me close. "Is this what you've been missing?"

It's been months since I last stepped foot on British soil, and I've been hankering for a taste of home for a while. As much as I've loved living in New York, it's felt a bit like an extended holiday.

A black cab drives past, its wheels hitting a puddle. I jump back, narrowly avoiding getting splashed, then have to hide my smile when I realise Callum wasn't quite so fast.

"You've got a little something on your trousers," I tell him, gesturing at the inky black stains running the length of his jeans. He glances down, rolling his eyes, then reaches for me, trying to manoeuvre me into the puddle.

"Hey! Not fair!" When I try to move back his hold is too strong, but instead of dragging me into the dirty water, he pulls me close, looking down at me with a smile curling his lips.

"What?" I ask, trying to work out his expression.

"You're beautiful," he says, his voice low. "Extremely annoying, but beautiful."

"I'm not annoying." I pout. "It's not my fault you have the reflexes of an old man."

"I don't remember you calling me an old man last night when my face was between your thighs."

Reddening, I look around to see if anybody heard him. "Hush."

293

He presses his lips to my ear, his voice taking on a high tone as he attempts to mimic mine. "Oh Callum, right there, oh God," he whispers. "Don't stop, please don't stop."

"Shush!" I say it louder, my cheeks burning. "Somebody might hear."

"That's what I told you last night, babe, but it didn't seem to worry you then."

We climb into a cab, Callum loading our cases into the boot, and I lean forward, to give the driver Mum's address. We talked about booking a hotel instead—something impossibly expensive and boutique-like, knowing Callum—but in the end we decided to keep the peace by staying in Plaistow. The taxi pulls out, into the right hand lane, and we begin our slow journey across the city.

It's almost lunchtime when we arrive and I'm feeling sluggish and achy from the overnight journey. Without having to say anything, Callum tenderly massages my back, trying to loosen the stiffness that eight hours of travel has formed.

"You doing okay, babe?"

I give him an exhausted smile. "I'm fine."

"Let's just get you home and I'll take you straight to bed." He winks and I widen my eyes, trying to look affronted.

"Mum says we can't share a room because we're not married," I tell him. "You're in Alex's old room."

The look of horror on his face makes me giggle.

"What the hell? I'm not sleeping in a separate bloody room. We live together for God's sake, that's pretty much the same as being married."

I bite my lip, holding back a laugh. "Tell that to my mum."

She couldn't give a damn whether or not we share a bed, but I'm enjoying this too much to stop. "You won't get lonely, though, because the cats love Alex's bedroom." I grin, glancing at the driver to make sure he's not listening. "You'll be surrounded by pussies."

Callum chokes, and I can't hold the laughter in any more. I start to snigger even louder when the look of realisation washes over his face, and he frowns. "Amy," he warns. "Don't mess with me, you might not like the result."

On the contrary, I think. I love it when he gets all mad and alpha. Callum in a mood sends shivers down my spine.

"Try me," I whisper, and his eyes darken, before he leans forward and kisses me hard.

* * *

A little later we're perched on the sofa at Mum's house, being crawled over by three cats and my nephew. Mum's keeping up a constant stream of conversation while we drink our tea. She tells us about Andie's trip to Australia, surprising me when she says that my big sister finally has a boyfriend, then lowers her voice to inform us that Lara is pregnant again.

I've absolutely no idea why she's whispering; at his tender years I don't think Max understands a word. Still, it's fantastic news and I can't help but grin when I think about having another nephew or niece.

That's the reason we're here, really. When Alex called to tell us they'd brought forward their renewal of vows, I didn't bother to ask why, but now I'm guessing it's so Lara can walk up the aisle, rather than waddle. They've decided to go the whole hog, with stag and hen parties tonight, and the ceremony tomorrow.

"Have you heard from your dad?" Mum asks. Though her tone is airy, her interested expression gives her away. I suspect she'll always hold a little torch for him—and he for her—even though there's been no repeat of the lounge incident.

"He sent me an email last week," I tell her. "He's good."

Max trips over one of the cats, landing face first on the carpet, and immediately starts to cry. Callum reaches Max first, swinging him into his arms. Maxie buries his face in Callum's broad shoulder, muffling his sobs in his shirt.

For a moment, I get a tiny glimpse into the future. Callum holding one of our babies, his huge hands rubbing their backs. It's such a contrast, the big man and a tiny child, and I find myself longing for that day.

We haven't talked about children yet. We've barely mentioned marriage, but we both know our future is together.

"Give him here." Mum takes Max from Callum and carries him into the kitchen, whispering in his ear that he's going to be all right. By the time she's sat him on the counter his tears have stopped, replaced by a lisped request for a band-aid.

"I remember when a plaster solved everything," Callum smiles. "Especially if it had the Mr Men on it."

"Some things don't change." I step into his embrace. "You've always been a big baby."

"Don't think I didn't see you staring," he whispers, brushing his lips against the shell of my ear. "Did you like what you saw?"

I hide my smile in his chest. "I think you made my ovaries explode."

A laugh rumbles in his throat. "That sounds painful."

"Looking at you is always painful," I lie. "But I consider it my duty."

Leaning down, he presses his lips to mine. "In that case, consider this an obligation."

He kisses me softly, and I find myself being very obliging indeed.

* * *

It's almost midnight, and we end up in a nightclub near Soho, sitting in a cramped booth as the bass pumping out of the speakers makes the entire room vibrate. Beth is at the bar, getting a round in, while the rest of us are pinning condoms and party rings to the veil fixed on Lara's head.

"I don't get why I have to wear this," Lara whines. "It's not like I'm getting married. I've already done that."

Beth arrives, sliding a tray of shots onto the sticky table. "You know why. Because Alex wants it to be traditional this time. Hen nights and church services and the whole shebang."

Lara starts to reply, but her grumble is cut off as we make her do the first shot—a non-alcoholic one, of course. Holding her nose, she tips her head back, letting the syrupy green fluid flow into her mouth.

"That's disgusting." Screwing her nose up, she puts the glass back on the tray. "What the hell is that anyway?"

"Apple schnapps for us, and some disgusting non-alcoholic concoction for you," Beth replies, "On the house. Apparently hen nights are good for business."

I see what she means when I look around the dance floor. Men outnumber women by a good percentage, and from the predatory looks some of them are shooting, it's only a matter of time before they start offering to buy us drinks.

"Ugh," Sally, one of Lara's co-workers from the clinic, is the second to take a shot. "They'll be disappointed when they find out we're all taken."

"When has that ever stopped them?" Lara mutters. "I told Alex this was a bad idea."

While they start discussing the best way to fight off unwanted advances, I sneak a look at my phone. My heart races as soon as I see there's a message from Callum.

Remind me again why I'm not allowed to come and see you?

I quickly tap out a reply. **It's tradition. The stags and hens should never meet.**

Fuck tradition, I want to dance with my girl. Where are you?

I can almost hear the impatient brogue of his voice.

Not telling. ; p

Don't try and hide from me, babe, you know I'll always find you.

Smiling, I slide my phone back into my pocket and pick up one of the glasses to take a shot. I've hardly put it down before the first of many guys approaches the table, asking us what we're doing here. It's patently obvious that Lara has a wedding veil pinned with condoms on her head.

We're not exactly on a nun's night out.

By the time we've shaken our heads at the third hopeful guy, it's clear we're all feeling weary. We're about to call a taxi when another man offers us a drink. Lara stiffens, and she's about to launch into a diatribe when she realises who it is. Alex leans down and kisses her, before taking a condom off her veil and throwing it on the table.

"We won't be needing those," he says smugly.

"Why, are you shooting blanks now?" Niall, Beth's husband, asks. We all start laughing at Alex's horrified face, while he mutters something about having super sperm.

I stick my fingers in my ear. "La la la, I don't want to hear this. You're my brother, for heaven's sake."

When I look up, Callum is staring at me from the crowd of men. He's wearing a sexy, knowing grin that makes my whole body light up inside. We may have been living together for the last nine months, but one look from him still sends my heart racing.

"Hi," he mouths, his smile deepening.

"Hi," I mouth back.

The next instant he's walking over to where I'm sitting, pulling me out of the chair and onto my feet. "Why didn't you tell me where you were?" he whispers in my ear.

I turn my head until my lips reach the corner of his jaw, and murmur, "Where would be the fun in that?"

Before I know it, he's dragging me onto the dance floor, pulling my body tightly to his as he starts to move to the rhythm of the music. The bass is low and sultry, and Callum has enough skills for the both of us.

"You okay, babe?" he asks, his cheek pressed to mine.

"I am now."

He puts his hand just above the swell of my bottom, leaning me backward as my hair cascades down my shoulders. "I missed you," he says, dragging his lips down my neck.

"Missed you, too," I gasp. "Did you have a good time?"

"Not really. We spent most of the night talking about you lot, and wondering how many guys were hitting on you. Eventually we decided to call it quits."

"You were lucky, we were about to leave," I tell him. "How did you know where to find us, anyway?"

"Didn't I tell you? I've been tracking your phone by GPS."

"What the hell?" Why would he do that? The invasion of privacy riles me.

He shrugs. "It's just a precaution. I barely use it."

"You can't do that!" I start to yell, and he steps back, surprised. I'm considering whether to slap him or stomp away when he starts to laugh.

"Your face is a picture." He grins, making him more impossibly handsome than ever. "As if I'd track you. I'm not a stalker."

I punch him lightly on the shoulder. "No, you're an arsehole."

"It was payback for the trick you played on me earlier. The one about the bedrooms," he says. "Except this was so much better."

"Says you," I mutter, already planning my revenge. "And for that, you're definitely sleeping in Alex's room."

* * *

The following day we're standing in the churchyard, waiting for Alex and Lara to emerge onto the stairs. Though the rain has gone, the cotton wool clouds remain, stubbornly hiding the sun with a greyish lemon glow. Max is running around the graveyard while Allegra—Niall and Beth's adopted daughter—picks up her skirt and chases him, leading to loud giggles as he gives her the slip.

I turn to Callum, who's standing next to me, his hands stuffed awkwardly in the pockets of his suit trousers.

"Are you okay?"

It's as if he hasn't heard me. He stares at the church, a strange expression on his face, and I start to worry that I've done something wrong.

"Callum?"

This time he acknowledges my voice, but the frown on his face remains. I smooth the lines that have formed between his eyebrows, and he grabs my wrist and kisses it softly.

"You okay?" I ask again, this time quietly. He hesitates for a moment, still staring at me.

"I'm better than okay," he says, glancing at the church again. "Do you think they'll come out soon?"

I still don't understand his edginess, but I nod anyway. "They're just having a couple of photos taken. We won't have to wait long, I promise."

"I don't mind about that," he tells me. "There's just something I wanted to do."

Before I get to ask what, Alex and Lara emerge from the church, looking like rock and roll royalty as they walk down the stairs. My brother is wearing a tight-fitting grey suit with a skinny black tie, while Lara is resplendent in a cream lace dress.

The next twenty minutes are filled with more photographs. We're herded into a variety of formations, and I notice Callum getting increasingly agitated. He's not usually this nervous, and I'm starting to wonder if he dislikes my family.

My suspicions are only heightened when I see Alex catch Callum's eye, raising his eyebrows in a challenge. Callum shakes his head slowly, as if telling him to back off, causing the nagging worry in my gut to grow.

"Is everything alright with you and Alex?" I whisper as we get in line for the big family photo.

"Why wouldn't it be?" He sounds almost suspicious.

"I don't know," I reply. "He just looked at you strangely."

"Babe, there's nothing to fret about. He didn't look at me funny, he barely looked at me at all. He's too busy posing for photographs."

I say nothing, but stay on high alert, trying to catch them squaring up to each other again. The thought of the two men in my life not liking each other isn't something I've ever considered.

"What happened last night?" I whisper between photographs. My cheeks are starting to ache from too many fake smiles.

"What do you mean?"

"Between you and Alex. Did you have words?"

He cups my face with his hands, dragging his thumbs across my cheekbones. "Babe, there's absolutely nothing to worry about. I'm not looking at your brother weirdly; I've not had words with him. You're seeing something that's not there."

"If you say so," I huff, determined to corner them both later. I'll make them friends even if I have to force them to talk.

When the photographs are all taken, people start to head back to their cars, making their way to Hoxton Square where Alex has hired a bar for the afternoon celebration. Instead of calling a taxi, Callum grabs my hand, and pulls me over to a pretty corner of the churchyard where roses are growing against a dry stone wall.

My brows dip as I try to work out what's going on, and brace myself for his confession. Instead he smiles, and my almost-petrified heart starts to beat again.

"I did talk to your brother last night," he says. "But only to ask him a question."

"What question?"

"I know it's old fashioned, but I'm a traditional kind of guy. I wanted his blessing before I asked you to marry me."

Everything stops. My pulse seems to slow, the blood hardly moving in my veins. All I can hear is the rustling of the leaves as the light wind lifts them in her dance.

"What?" It's all I can say. I'm dumbstruck.

"I know you're still young, and we don't have to get married for a while. But I'd be the happiest man in the world if you'd agree to be my wife." He slides his hand into his pocket and pulls out a small, black box. When he lifts the lid, there's a gorgeous pear-cut solitaire nestled in a velvet cushion, the diamond catching a glint from the sun. "If you don't like it we can exchange it," he says. "That's if you agree to wear it at all."

I realise I haven't answered. The tears stinging at my eyes spill over, coursing down my cheeks, but the biggest grin forms on my lips. "Of course I'll wear it," I tell him. "It's beautiful."

"Like you," he whispers, sliding the ring onto my finger. "The most beautiful girl I've ever seen."

He drops down to one knee, bringing me with him until I'm sitting on his thigh, our faces inches apart. He wipes the tears from my cheeks, and then holds me closer, until our mouths are touching.

"Amy Ferguson," he whispers. "It sounds good."

"Callum Cartwright," I reply. "That's not so good."

"Ferguson-Cartwright?".

"Cartwright-Ferguson?" I retort. "It's classier."

He kisses me firmly, his warm lips moving against mine as his hands cup my neck, thumbs brushing my skin.

"I don't care what you call me," I say breathlessly, the moment we pull away. "As long as you keep doing that."

His smile is almost as broad as his accent. "Miss Cartwright, I think you've found the one thing we agree on."

The End

Letter from Carrie

Thank you so much for reading Canada Square. I hope you enjoyed following Amy and Callum's journey as much as I enjoyed writing it.

Scoliosis is a condition which I know a bit about, as my daughter was diagnosed with it at the age of 15. Unlike Amy, my daughter underwent spinal fusion surgery to straighten her back, and I'm pleased to say she is now doing very well. For more information on Scoliosis, The Scoliosis Association and the National Scoliosis Foundation are good places to start.

If you enjoyed this book, I'd be so grateful if you could write a review. These are lifelines for independent authors, and can help readers find the right book for them.

Until the next time!

Carrie xx

About the Author

Carrie Elks lives near London, England and writes contemporary romance with a dash of intrigue. At the age of twenty-one she left college with a political degree, a healthy overdraft and a soon-to-be husband. She loves to travel and meet new people, and has lived in the USA and Switzerland as well as the UK. When she isn't reading or writing, she can usually be found baking, drinking wine or working out how to combine the two.

www.CarrieElks.com
www.facebook.com/CarrieElksAuthor
www.twitter.com/carrieelks
carrie.elks@mail.com

Acknowledgements

Thank you to Lucia, Meire, Kate and Claire for pre-reading this book. Your feedback is always invaluable, I hope you know how much I appreciate you.

Ash, thank you for your time, patience and encouragement.
All my love to my friends both online and offline—writers, readers, bloggers. I love the romance community, and the way we all support each other. I love seeing you all whether it be on twitter, Facebook, or in real life at signings, and hope to meet so many more of you soon.

Finally, lots of love to my family; you guys are my rock. I couldn't do this without you. I wouldn't want to.

Printed by Amazon Italia Logistica S.r.l.
Torrazza Piemonte (TO), Italy

13331904R00182